Freshman Fourteen

Beth Rodgers

Published by Clear Stone Press, 2014

Copyright © 2014 Beth Rodgers

Published by Clear Stone Press

ISBN: 069231444X
ISBN-13: 978-0692314449

DEDICATION

To Evan – I wish for all your dreams to be fulfilled, even if they sometimes seem unreachable.

And to David and the rest of my family and friends – thank you for standing by me as I worked to achieve my dream of being an author. You have helped me in more ways than you know.

ACKNOWLEDGMENTS

A thank you goes out to the young adult authors I love to read and can only hope to one day be named in the company of: Sonya Sones, who writes the most spectacular novels-in-verse, as well as Carolyn Mackler, the incomparable J.K. Rowling, and a slew of others are among my favorites to read, and I would not have pressed on without their words to keep me focused, energized, and inspired throughout my journey to write this novel.

Thank you also to the writers of television shows and movies such as *Gilmore Girls* (Amy Sherman-Palladino, et al.), *24* (Howard Gordon, et al.), and *Rocky* (Sylvester Stallone). You all make writing seem effortless and thrilling, and I am in your debt for making me feel as though my writing is worth all my persistence.

ONE

"Come on! Let's get out of here!" an eighth grader yelled over the ruckus that was overtaking the hallway. "School's out!" Dozens of students pushed and shoved to break free. Summer was on the other side of the double doors. Fresh air was mingling with a bright sun, and the students were not hesitating to spend each and every glorious minute of summer vacation outside of the confines of their school.

Another year had come to an end, and there couldn't be a time that the eighth graders had been happier. The summer had finally arrived, and with it the promise of a fresh start – high school was only two and a half months away.

Margot fumbled through her locker, picking up tiny scraps of paper that littered the floor. She hated the process of cleaning out her belongings every year. She was always given a different locker, and each one was always dirtier than the last. Next to the gum wads at the bottom of this one, Margot saw the vaguely legible word "Kodak." The picture looked tattered and worn as Margot picked it up. Some water must have spilled on it much earlier in the year, and it looked much worse for the wear. Two wide-eyed girls smiled warmly at the camera. They had their cheeks pressed up against each other and were holding each other in a tight bear hug.

Margot remembered the day this picture had been taken. Almost three years ago, at the start of the sixth grade, Ashley Burnham had made a pledge with Margot that they would be friends forever. Nothing could break them up. "Inseparable, unbreakable, indivisible…with liberty and justice for all," read their pledge that they both had signed, dated, and laminated. Ashley just had to add that plug to the pledge of allegiance; she considered herself to be a true American, as she had traveled the countryside far and wide with her

1

parents. She was always bringing back fancy souvenirs for Margot from exotic places like Kokomo. At least it sounded exotic when Margot heard the Beach Boys sing about it. That was until she found out that Kokomo, Indiana was nothing like Aruba or Jamaica.

A tear welled up in Margot's left eye and slid down her cheek until she tasted the saltiness on her top lip. If Ashley and her parents loved America so much, why were they moving to London, Ontario? Canada was just so far away from Franklin, Texas, a quiet suburb of San Antonio. Visiting Ashley would be so much harder, especially since Margot would have to go and get a passport from the post office in order to pass through customs. Ashley promised that they would talk every day, chat on IM, and e-mail each other constantly. Margot wanted to believe all of this would really happen, but the fact that she was losing her best friend was just too much for her to bear. Ashley said time and time again that it was just a job opportunity that her dad couldn't pass up. Margot knew that it was Ashley's parents who were drilling that into her head, and they obviously had every right to take their 14-year-old daughter with them when they moved, but Margot knew that Ashley was just putting up a front. She couldn't possibly want to move and leave the only home she'd ever known.

As if sent to awaken her from her daze, Walter Gribble suddenly appeared next to Margot's locker. "Hey Margot, want to come to my end of school party tonight?" He had always been friendly to Margot, and she did like him – really, truly – but was he really the kind of guy she wanted to be friends with – taped-up glasses and all?

"Sure Walter. What time should I be there?" Margot knew she had to go. Her parents would definitely find out about it from Mr. and Mrs. Gribble and ask her why she would rather stay home than go and have some fun at a party.

"Wow, you're great Margot! Thanks a bunch. Can't wait to see you... you'll really make the party a blast, I just know it... tonight at eight, alright?" Walter sounded overzealous, excited, too enthusiastic.

"No problem Walter. Just go home and before you know it I'll be there." Walter took this suggestion too literally, as he waved a quick goodbye and rushed out the doors at the end of the ghost town of a hallway.

Margot smiled to herself. At least she had made someone's day. Walter was happy because she was coming. It made Margot happy as well – a feeling she was a bit too unfamiliar with lately. She needed a pick-me-up, something special and invigorating to happen to her, to spice up her non-existent social life. Just then, what she needed the least seemed to find her.

"Hey *Margie*," called a friendless voice. "I see you've been talking to Walter *Dribble*." Ever since Walter had fallen asleep that one time in study hall, Max Poler had teased him mercilessly about the drool that piled up next to his mouth and attached itself dryly to his cheek. He had to go to the bathroom to take some water and wipe it off. Walter had been horrified, and Max had never let up with his teasing.

"What do you want, Max?" Margot asked reluctantly.

"Just to let you know how much high school is going to suck for you. If you thought you were unpopular in middle school, times are only going to get tougher. There are will be so many more kids to share your stories of doom and gloom with. I can't wait till next year. I'll be at the top of my game again, and you'll be...well...you. Too bad, isn't it? Some people just don't have what it takes to be popular. Enjoy the summer, because life is going to be another living nightmare when school starts again." Another tear showed up in Margot's eye, but not one that resembled anything like nostalgia.

"Gotta get back to Cassie now. She's waiting outside in her dad's new red Thunderbird. They're waiting to take me home. See ya, MM. Wow, just realized what great initials those are for you... you're round and well, that's it...you're round. Try to lose some weight this summer, huh *MM?*"

Margot's self-esteem was already shot. Her best friend was moving away. This other blow to her system wasn't one she had expected. She thought she was rid of Max Poler and his buddies. She thought having girlfriends had made them less immature and thoughtless. Boy, was she wrong. High school was shaping up to be all she hadn't hoped for and more.

TWO

It was a feeling of complete and utter bewilderment. The hallways were filled with people, doors opened and closed, and people filed in and out of rooms. Books lined the shelves, posters covered the walls, cafeteria smells wafted through the corridors, and papers rustled. The copy machine spat out copies, people greeted one another as they passed, and announcements were made after everyone was seated and accounted for. It was official. School was back in session.

Freshman year at Kipperton High School was looking promising. The incoming class was lively and had a great track record for being involved with extracurricular activities. Their academic record wasn't too bad, either. This class had the best overall grade point average that Kipperton High had seen in at least ten years.

Margot Maples was the embodiment of timidity. She had a zeal for theater, but was only involved in past plays because she let off that youthful essence that caused her to be typecast as one of the children, or she was put in charge of the programs, or some other semi-integral part of the play-going experience.

She had auburn wisps of hair that formed curls about her face, and she meandered up the hall on her way to and from class. She had a way of presenting herself that not even Margot herself noticed. She was quite pretty, aside from the features that every girl haunts herself with from day to day and wishes were different. Margot didn't like the way her glasses took over the top half of her face. Even though she had picked out the cutest frame she could to make her first day of school in them semi-bearable, she found them unbecoming, and was sure that all the boys did too. She had slender hips, as she had slimmed down quite a bit over the summer, but felt as though none of her jeans fit well enough to shape her body. These "flaws" to her appearance, as well as her never-ending fear of being the last girl on earth who would ever be kissed, pestered Margot to no end, and she often found herself sick with self-pity.

She especially didn't like the way her cheeks blushed a rosy pink when Peter Mulvaney entered a room. His dark brown hair was parted perfectly, and his hazel eyes shone with a dreamy quality that Margot found extremely attractive. His smile showed off his newly polished teeth, as it had only been the day before that Margot had guessed he must have been to the orthodontist to get his braces off -- he hadn't smiled so widely in the past two years. Even with braces, she thought he was the be-all and end-all of Kipperton High, and Perry Middle School before that.

She had talked to him a few times before. He was quite nice, and until the year before, she hadn't even known that he knew her name. One day in Mr. Morello's gym class the previous year, she had been about to serve the volleyball, and from the front row of her side, where he was standing, he said, in what Margot considered the friendliest tone, "You can do it Margot! Do it for the team!" Despite her serving the volleyball a mere two feet in front of her, and the other team laughing at her expense, Margot had never felt better in her life.

"Mr. Mulvaney. Please take a seat. The class cannot wait for stragglers."

Ms. Curren had been the eighth grade vocal music teacher, and had moved to Kipperton to teach the freshmen choir. She was quite familiar with all of the students, and as Peter entered, she let it be known that she was still an in-charge and take-charge kind of teacher.

"Yes, Ms. Curren. Sorry. It won't happen again."

Even though his smile was as wide as possible, he limped into class.

"I tripped on the way to class. I was rushing to get here, and my locker is on the other side of the school."

"Just don't let it happen again," said Ms. Curren. "Okay class, let's begin."

As Ms. Curren started class, Lisa Quinn and Carolyn Dippet hiccupped together behind Peter.

Carolyn said, "Hey, nerd-boy, just because you got your braces off doesn't mean you're cool now."

"Yeah, so don't hang around us like we know you want to," said Lisa.

A sullen expression formed on Peter's face that Margot could see from the other side of the half-circle the class had formed. Obviously Margot tried to ignore it, but she knew how it was. Peter was the antithesis of cool. That is, he was to the cool kids.

Nonetheless, Peter was the sharpest student. He was always raising his hand to give the appropriate answers to teachers' questions, shrugging off other students' responses that he deemed to be pathetic. The dizzying expression on Peter's face when Max Poler responded to Mrs. Rigby's question in the seventh grade about which galaxy the Earth was located in was saddening. He couldn't comprehend why some students just didn't take school seriously. When Max said, "The 100 Grand. No, no, wait. The Baby Ruth. Uh, wait... I know it. The Three Musketeers Galaxy." Before Max had a chance to continue his rambling, Mrs. Rigby silenced the snickering that was flitting about the classroom and called on Peter. "The correct answer is the Milky Way Galaxy, Mrs. Rigby," said Peter with a hushed note to his voice, as if he didn't want to be the one to ruin the joke, but didn't want to continue the stupidity either. Max Poler had always been nice to him as a kid, especially at Merton Elementary, where they used to play tag on the playground at recess and hang out after school. But ever since he had chanced a glance at Cassie Shearer, and she had returned his fleeting look, nothing had ever been the same. At least that's what Peter thought. He had never gotten a straight answer out of Max as to why Max had it out for him, and why their friendship had ended so abruptly. Max and Cassie had been the winners of "cutest couple" in mock elections in eighth grade, and they were on the road to becoming the new power couple of the freshmen class at Kipperton.

When choir class finished and Ms. Curren had finished giving them their first piece to start learning for homework, the students filed out, many headed to Ms. Pelham's English class. Peter was excited to be in honors English. He had heard that Ms. Pelham was a fun teacher who gave interesting, thought-provoking assignments – not one of those drab teachers who speaks in a monotone voice and never goes off on tangents to release the pressure of paying attention for the entire hour.

While Peter pondered the interesting assignments he was sure to get for the year, Cassie glided past the teacher's desk, with Carolyn and Lisa in tow, her hair highlighted by the sunlight that peeked in through the slits in the drapes. She plopped herself into her seat, pulled out her cosmetic compact, and moved her face up and down, back and forth, checking to be sure no spot was left untouched by her pretty pink blush and subtle blue eye shadow. She was trying to achieve that all-natural look that can only be accomplished when you've put in all possible effort. As the bell rang, and a few stragglers fumbled into class, almost running over each other, she slipped her compact back into her bag, and fumbled around for the novel she had been assigned for summer reading. A crumpled, beat-up copy of *The Great Gatsby* emerged. As she struggled with the zipper on her backpack to get it closed again, Margot entered the classroom, and tripped over Nathan Fromidge's bag.

The class, which had been silenced when Ms. Pelham started to take attendance, laughed under their breath. Margot even saw Peter chance a smile, but it looked friendlier and more understanding than those of the other kids. She took a seat in the far corner of the room and eagerly anticipated the start of the day's lesson so the focus would be taken off of her.

THREE

The backseat of Mr. Maples' car was a shambles. There were crumbs lining the edges of the seats, dog hair on the floor from when he had last taken their German Shepherd to the veterinarian (only a mere two months ago), and crumpled up papers that he had read, though in his haste to discard them he had accumulated such a pile that the space behind the passenger's seat had no room to place your feet. Margot plowed through all the clutter and situated herself between her oversized backpack and the vast heap of dry cleaning that her father had just picked up.

"So, Margot honey, how was your day?" Mr. Maples asked reluctantly, as he saw the depressed expression on his daughter's face.

"The usual," said Margot, as her face contorted to show her displeasure with the way it had gone. Mr. Maples knew this expression all too well. It was the same one that Margot had worn since coming home from her first day at Perry Middle School. For some reason, she just didn't fit in, and Mr. Maples couldn't for the life of him figure out why not. She was pretty and sweet, smart and charming.

"Make any new friends?" Mr. Maples offered as a means of getting his daughter to talk.

"Sure, Dad, I made a bunch of kids laugh today."

"Great honey, that's really great."

Margot didn't have the heart to tell him that she was the butt of the joke that had made them laugh when she tripped over that bag in Ms. Pelham's class. She knew all too well the outpouring of pity he would give to her if he knew the truth. She just didn't feel like giving her father any reason to consider her a disappointment, even though she knew very well that he could never think of her that way.

"Mom will be home around six from work, and then we thought we might go out for a nice dinner to Benino's. We know you just love the pizza there, and since it's your first week of high school and all, we thought a treat might be in order. Sound good?"

Margot thought about this. Benino's was the new hangout spot from what she had heard today at school. Some of the kids were saying that they were going to go there tonight, since the arcade was next door, and the pizza was the best in town. She was in high school now. Did she really want to be seen with her parents at Benino's, of all places?

"No!" Margot said insistently. "We can't go there. I mean, can't we go somewhere else? It'll probably be so busy tonight anyway."

"No busier than any other night. Plus, your mom and I have been planning this. Is there some reason you don't want to go?" Mr. Maples asked incredulously. He had never known his daughter to turn down Benino's pizza, or any pizza for that matter.

Margot thought for a moment. She weighed her options. She could either go to Benino's with her parents and be typecast the first week of high school as the goody-goody klutz who eats out with her parents and trips over people's bags, or she could find another place to eat with them that would have less of a coolness quotient, and therefore less chance of her being placed in the "nerd" category so soon.

"So, Margot, what'll it be?" her father asked. She could make out the look on his face and knew he really wanted to go there because he knew she liked it so much.

"If it makes you happy Dad, let's go. I guess it should be okay."

"Okay? Okay? Are you kidding? It'll be great. I hear they have three new pizza toppings on the menu. They should be fun to test out!"

Mr. Maples always got over-excited about the most uninteresting things. But his liveliness made her happy, so she couldn't turn him down. That night, they would go to Benino's, and she would summon up all the courage she had to get through the night in one piece, without losing what little of a favorable reputation she might possibly have at Kipperton.

FOUR

Margot positioned herself in front of her closet, determined to pick the perfect outfit. She had more clothes than she knew what to do with, but for the life of her she couldn't choose what to wear. If she had to go to Benino's with her parents, she wanted to look just right. The outfit had to be youthful enough to appease her parents, but also had to be similar to what the other kids at school were wearing. After staring at four tops and three pairs of pants for what seemed like an infinite amount of time, she settled on a loose knit, short-sleeved, deep red blouse. Then she pulled a faded pair of jeans out of the pile of clothes she had accumulated on her bed and wriggled into them.

Looking at herself in the mirror, Margot contemplated all the different scenarios that could occur while she was out that night. One went quite like she expected it to: she would get to Benino's with her parents, only to be seen by Cassie, Max, and their unimaginative friends who wouldn't know a creative insult if it hit them in the head, but were nonetheless the most popular kids in school. They would snicker and point at her while Margot's parents asked whether or not she knew those kids and why she didn't want to invite them over to the table. Then she wondered whether or not Peter would be there, and that brought on a whole new level of worry. This caused Margot to become flustered, thinking she might not look just right, and she might do something to embarrass herself, like tripping over the leg of someone's chair, and flying face-first into someone's pepperoni pizza. It was one of her worst nightmares. Who was to say it wouldn't come true? The third scenario, and one which Margot seriously hoped wouldn't happen (but secretly hoped would) in order to waylay her date with disaster, was that Benino's would have a small fire or some other non-fatal disaster, causing the restaurant to close, and the Maples family to have to go home, without having tried the new pizza toppings, and without any more impediments to Margot's reputation to deal with. Having one extra night to escape her retreat into geekdom would definitely help her formulate a plan for how to avoid being labeled a misfit once again in her young life. Middle school was hard enough. High school was going to be different. Margot had set her mind to it, and when Margot set her mind to something, she tried really, really hard to make it happen. *Tried* being the key word.

FIVE

I don't even have words for what happened tonight. I am so completely embarrassed that I just know I can never show my face at Kipperton again. Uggghhh!!! Why me? Honestly, what have I done to deserve this adolescent angst that so many kids never have to deal with? I mean, I'm sure that Cassie Shearer has NEVER had this happen to her. I can't even begin to believe that Carolyn or Lisa would ever be caught dead in that situation. But me, of course I have to get stuck with the short end of the stick. I HATE HIGH SCHOOL! I just want to be popular. Like that's ever gonna happen.

Margot bit her bottom lip, struggling for more angry words to put down on paper. She needed to vent her frustration, and her multicolored diary looked like just the place to do it.

If only I could be popular. I would never have to deal with this kind of ridicule, rejection, and suckiness. Those girls can just twirl their hair and look so wonderful and fantastic. When I twirl my hair, my finger gets it caught in a knot, and I look like an idiot trying to get it out. Hmmpph! Yeah, you heard me. I just can't take it anymore. I just want to scream at the top of my lungs and wake up a new person. Maybe someone more like Cassie, Lisa, or even the dippy Carolyn Dippet. I've always believed that names say it all. In her case, I just KNOW I'm right.

I guess the only upside about tonight was seeing Peter. It was only once he saw me that things really started to go downhill. If he had only turned away at that moment, I wouldn't be so upset and aggravated. It just had to happen that way, didn't it? It always does. Right at that moment when the boy you like most is looking your way, something incredibly awful and heinous happens to you. The only weird thing is that I think that all of these awful and terrible situations I'm describing – yeah, you know the ones I

12

mean – they always happen to ME. That's right. Me. I'm not saying that I don't believe other teenage girls don't go through the same types of troubles that I do. It's just that this instance – this one time that everything was destined to go wrong – it did. So much for trying to make the best of things. Maybe I should just join a convent and give up on ever having the possibility of going out on a date. After tonight, I don't think I'll be missing out on any offers anyway. If only there weren't four more years of high school to contend with. I thought things would change. I thought this year would be different. How could I have been so naïve and stupid? I bet if I wore a paper bag over my head for the rest of high school, people would laugh at me just as much as they did tonight. People want to live these years over again, huh? They can take my years. I would trade lives with anybody for the chance to be out of this nightmare. Isn't that what all teenagers are supposed to want? To be someone else? Well, what about girls like Cassie? There's no way she wants to be somebody else.

Margot clenched her pencil tight at this point, readying herself for the ending to her long and drawn-out rant.

If only I could be like Cassie. My problems would all go away.

SIX

THREE HOURS EARLIER: APPROXIMATELY 6:10 PM

"Mom, do we really have to go to Benino's tonight?" Margot asked after changing her clothes for the dozenth time.

"Honey, you love it there. What's the problem?"

Margot really didn't want to get into the day she had with her mother. She had already spared her father the gory details, and for the life of her, she didn't want to upset her mother either. She had two of the most understanding parents ever. A little too understanding, if you were to ask Margot to be candid about it. She wanted them to sometimes give her a little grief and ask her where she was going when she went out (usually the mall to people watch by herself), whom she was hanging out with (only Bob, the mall security guard, who usually shared his chips with her), and why she never had any friends over (she was the most unpopular girl who ever lived). Maybe then she could finally tell them the truth. She was a nobody. And she would never become a somebody as long as she went to school with those stuck-up snobbish annoyances like she had been doing since kindergarten. If she told them that, it might just bring on the breakdown that Margot needed in order to get her parents to realize that she was not happy in her present surroundings. However, Margot didn't necessarily feel that a change of scenery was what she needed. At least here she knew some people. She had Peter to think about and get her through the day. At a new school, she would have to try to fit in all over again. That was the last thing that she needed at the tender age of fourteen. To be rejected by a whole new crowd of wannabe populars.

"Nothing Mom. It's fine. Let's just go. The sooner the better. I'm really starving."

Margot wanted to get in and out of dinner as quickly as possible. She figured that if they got to Benino's by 6:30 or a quarter to seven, they could easily be out of there by 7:30 at the latest, which was when the teen scene would likely start to show up. Margot was determined to get her parents in, out, and still make them feel like she had had a good time, but was anxious to get home since she had so much first-day homework to complete. It was a foolproof plan.

Margot and her parents got into the car. Her dad was behind the wheel, a huge smile on his face as he buckled up and looked glowingly back at Margot.

"Dad, stop staring at me, okay?"

"You never seemed to mind before when I looked at you, honey."

"Dad, I'm in high school now. You can't look at me like that anymore. I'm growing up. I'm not a little kid anymore."

Mr. Maples was taken aback. This was a first. Margot usually loved when he showered her with attention. He loved doing it. The last thing he wanted was for this to change. He didn't understand what had gotten into her.

"Alright hon. Let's go," Mr. Maples declared with a hushed note of sadness in his voice as he switched into driving gear. Mrs. Maples patted him on the shoulder lovingly, and Margot sat in the back seat, her head rolled back, and her emotions going haywire. She wanted things to stay the same with her parents. Really, truly. But if she was going to change into the chic high school freshman, she needed to speed up the change. Her home life was the first step. If she could distance herself from her parents just a little, maybe they would realize that she was reaching out for some individual freedom. Then she could change her attitude at school and make people notice her more. Not the kind of noticing that causes people to snicker and sneer at her, but the kind that would cause her to be labeled as someone on the rise – someone who was destined to be a somebody at Kipperton, rather than the nobody that she already was.

SEVEN

TWO AND A HALF HOURS EARLIER: APPROXIMATELY 6:40 PM

The parking lot at Benino's was jam-packed with cars. Mr. Maples parked next to a Dodge Neon that had left its lights on, and a tall, angry looking man was yelling across the parking lot from the car to a woman who was continually shrugging her shoulders and making a "what-do-you-expect-me-to-do" face.

"My frikkin' keys are stuck in your car, Marie! The battery's gonna run out any minute now, and you're just *standing* there! Why aren't you helping?" He continued his ranting and raving well past when Margot got out of the car and started making her way across the strip mall's oversized parking lot. Benino's was at the far end of the mall from where Margot and her parents had parked. Why on earth were so many people out tonight? Margot looked at her watch. It was only about a quarter to seven. It usually wasn't nearly this busy so early. This didn't phase Margot any more, though. She dawdled past Cummins Books and stared in the window at the fudge shop, but besides the slight twinkle in her eye at the sight of the double chocolate peanut butter fudge, she remained completely without expression.

Upon entering Benino's, the aroma of pepperoni mingled with the crackling of crisp toasted bread was intoxicating. When it settled near Margot's nose, she immediately was taken in by the scent. She knew exactly what her father had meant when he said they were only trying to make her happy by taking her somewhere she loved to eat. This moment of sudden insight was cut short when she noticed her parents beckoning her to the booth with the little "reserved" tag proudly standing near the edge of it.

The mystique of the restaurant and its coolness were easy to see. From one corner to the other, kids were lining each and every spot of the establishment. Some of the tables had chairs that sat up high, while others sat lower, but all were taken. Waiters hustled and bustled around, each one smiling and waving to their friends, since this was the new hot spot to not only see and be seen, but to *work* and be seen. People had a much higher probability of seeing you if you were working there day in and day out and not just showing up at random times hoping to stand out in the in-crowd.

"Sally! Clark! So great to see you! Who knew you'd be here too?! Celebrating Margot's start to high school, are we?"

Kelly Gribble was one of the most outspoken people anyone will ever have the displeasure of being introduced to. Her husband, Larry, was always along for the ride, usually unopinionated, but generally passionate about his wife's outbursts. It wasn't that she was mean or offensive – just that she was annoying, and once she spotted you, you were basically done-for. There was no way out of it. Who knew that this lively, boisterous person, and her partner-in-crime husband, could ever have raised the geekiest, weirdest, goofiest son?

"Oh, hello Kelly. Larry. Why yes, we thought a night out was in order. We just sat down. Why don't you join us?"

"Oh, heavens no. We wouldn't dare intrude," gushed Kelly. "Larry and I are just so happy to see you is all. Walter is always saying such nice things about your Margot here. She really has blossomed into a beautiful young lady, hasn't she?"

"Well, thank you, Kelly," Mr. Maples gushed back, in mock imitation of Mrs. Gribble. She didn't notice his laughter at her expense, and continued on, looking to her husband for more thoughts to share. She seemed to have more to say, but couldn't find the words to express whatever it was.

"Walter is just over there, Margot, if you want to see him," Mrs Gribble announced proudly.

"And we know he's just dying to see you. He says he hasn't laid eyes on you since you started school. Those halls are just too big and wide for their own good!" Mr. Gribble said determinedly.

Margot looked over to the arcade on the other side of the restaurant and noticed Walter getting pushed around by a couple of junior boys who wanted to use the pinball machine. His glasses – the perpetual broken ones that his parents never seemed to fix for him – were hanging from the cord around his neck to protect them from falling any more than they already had. They must have been knocked off while he tried to score on the pinball machine. He waved a quick hello to Margot's vicinity when his parents yelled his name before being sloshed back around by the juniors.

"Isn't our Walter just super?" Mr. Gribble inquired. He's so sweet and gentlemanly, giving those boys the opportunity to play even though he's been waiting there for his turn. We sure raised him right, didn't we Kelly?"

In the next instant, Margot overheard an angry, bitter voice at the hostess stand. She knew it sounded familiar, but couldn't place it until she turned around. It was that angry man from the parking lot and a woman whom Margot could only venture to guess was Marie.

"I told you a hundred times! Keeping an extra set of keys in the glove compartment of the car is stupid! Just plain stupid! Who in their right mind keeps the extra set of keys in the car? How are we supposed to get them if the car is LOCKED?! You boggle my mind. I can't begin to understand you, yet you completely understand your own logic. I just can't even..."

"Sir? Sir? We have your table ready now; you can follow me this way. Ma'am. This way please." The hostess was at a loss for what else to say. She had repeated this same phrase over and over, progressively louder and louder, until finally the irate man had ceased his over-dramatized yelling and opened his ears long enough to hear her.

"This way, please," she repeated as calmly as she could. It seemed his tone was contagious. She couldn't help but want to yell at him, as she seemed to feel it was the only attitude he might begin to understand.

The man walked toward the booth and seemed to relax himself, even if only for a few moments, to look over the menu. Margot watched the man in disbelief, as he snuggled up close to his wife and asked her what she wanted. Marie just pointed at the menu, kissed him on the cheek, and plopped a pill out on the table, gesturing for him to pick it up and sip the water that their waiter had just placed on the table. Margot could only figure that it was an anti-anxiety medication, or some other such suppressant. Within moments, he had calmed himself down. It was incredible how easily the change had come about.

"Margot? Margot? Honey?" Mrs. Maples asked, ushering Margot out of what seemed to be a daze. "Margot, honey, move over. The Gribbles have decided to join us. You need to scoot over so Walter can sit next to you."

"But Mom," Margot whispered hesitantly. "Please don't make us squish together like this. Tell them you want to eat with just the three of us. That'll be better. Please..."

Mr. and Mrs. Gribble were trying to appear disinterested, but were obviously far from it. They were leaning ever so slightly to hear what Margot was whispering to her mother.

"Just move over, honey. They've already told the waiter to move their drinks over here. Come on, now. Scooch." Margot's mother obviously didn't realize the awfulness of this situation. So, Margot, her father, and her mother all squeezed together on one side of the four-person, half-circle booth, while the Gribbles squeezed themselves firmly into place on the other side. Walter was plastered right next to Margot. Their shoulders could barely move; they were fit in so tightly.

"So, Margot, Walter here has joined the chess club at school. Have you thought of joining the club, too? I remember how good you were at chess from those board game nights in elementary school." Mrs. Gribble just couldn't keep herself quiet. She didn't know how to close her mouth and keep it that way. Margot didn't really want to answer, but with a swift nudge to her side from her mother, she knew she better speak up or face the fate of a terribly bruised ribcage.

"Why no, Mrs. Gribble. You see, high school has taken up so much of my free time that I don't have time to do activities like that," Margot said with a sarcastic edge to her voice. Mrs. Gribble didn't pick up on it. Apparently, neither did Mr. Gribble, as he continued on with the conversation, changing the subject to the school play.

Still two months away, the freshman play was going to be amazing. Margot just knew it. They were going to be revealing which one they would all be lucky enough to audition for the following week. All that was known to those who wanted to audition was that they were to prepare a monologue in preparation for the audition process.

"Walter's planning to audition," said Mr. Gribble in a jovial tone, as Walter stared down at his piece of pizza, nervously awaiting the end of this conversation.

"Really, Walter, that's wonderful," Mrs. Maples interjected, eyeing Walter with a look of mingled excitement and pity at the fact that Walter would probably never get a great part in the play, owing to his nerdy demeanor and overly shy disposition. Walter mumbled a bit under his breath about his parents desperately wanting him to try out, and Mrs. Maples nudged Margot again, giving her that all-too-motherly look that she should say something nice to Walter.

"I'm auditioning too," Margot stated politely, and Walter looked up anxiously.

"Really? Well, maybe we can practice our monologues on each other – if you don't mind."

Margot instantaneously regretted chiming in, and secretly longed for that bruised ribcage again. Walter was definitely not her idea of a great practice partner, and she was set on getting a role in the first play of her high school career.

"Sure, maybe, we'll see." Margot couldn't think of enough tentative answers to fulfill her desire to make him realize she just wasn't all that interested. Walter, ever the apple who had not fallen far from the tree, couldn't have been more anticipatory than he was at that moment, and Mr. and Mrs. Gribble followed suit.

"Wonderful, just wonderful," Mrs. Gribble announced across the table to Margot's parents. "I see these two are going to be hard to separate now that audition season is in our midst. We'll have to make plans to get together and watch them practice."

Now you might think that all of this was enough to adequately humiliate me. But there's more. In the next few moments after we finished talking about the play, the most awful thing happened that I'm sure will forever be indelibly marked in people's memories. To put it in terms that people of all ages can understand, it was just the most incredibly unfair, unbelievable, embarrassing, and controversial thing that has ever happened to me. You're anxious to know what it was, aren't you? My feelings about recalling this memory more often than I have to aside, I will recount the hideousness that was this evening...

EIGHT

"Margot, would you be a dear and pass the salt shaker, please?" Mrs. Gribble said in a sing-song voice. "These fries are just in need of a sprinkling of flavor."

"Sure, Mrs. Gribble," Margot whispered under her breath, eager to shrink into oblivion and disappear from view. Benino's was getting busier and busier, and she had the impression that people were beginning to point and stare at the ludicrous spectacle of six people packed into a four-person booth.

The problem, however, was at this very instant, Walter, who had obviously missed the memo that his mother had asked Margot, turned his body ever so slightly and stretched his left hand a bit of a ways across the table to reach the salt shaker.

As Margot was turning her own body, she noticed Peter out of the corner of her eye, and saw that he was looking her way. In an effort to make herself look a bit better than she knew she did (especially sitting next to the Gribble family), she fixed her posture, smiled, and turned her head ever so slightly closer to the direction in which Peter was standing. And then, as if the gods hadn't rained down enough on Margot's life, it happened. Margot's lips touched Walter's – and they stayed there for not one, not two, but three whole seconds. It was unthinkable, really. Margot couldn't believe it was happening. She closed her eyes in a desperate attempt to make it all disappear. When she opened her eyes, she saw the dazzled, wide-eyed expression on Walter's face.

Before anyone had a chance to let the dust settle, Mrs. Gribble was astir with giddiness. "Oh, oh, I knew it. I knew that my Walter would find a nice girl. I knew you liked her, honey. I was hoping she liked you back. You two are such darling children. You will make the *perfect* couple. Smile!" And with that, Mrs. Gribble pulled out her digital camera, and snapped two faster-than-the-speed-of-light shots of her son and his new "best girl," a term that she had coined and already used at least three times in the course of her picture taking.

Margot was aghast. The look on her face couldn't have been one of happiness, she was sure. Mrs. Gribble was just too ecstatic for her own good, and Mr. Gribble was beginning to hold his wife back a bit, as she was continually fixing Walter's hair and telling him to sit up straight to be all that much more impressive for his new "best girl."

In as quiet a tone as she could muster, Margot turned to her mother, knowing her face must be the brightest shade of pink imaginable, and asked if she could be let out to go to the bathroom. Mr. Maples sat expressionless next to Mrs. Maples, visions of his only daughter as a quiet, non-kissing six-year-old running through his mind, until Mrs. Maples inched him out of the booth, allowing Margot passage to the bathroom.

Walter stuck his hand up in the air to wave when Margot turned around as her means of "pinching herself" to see if what had happened was real, and she turned around faster than ever at the realization that it had. She rushed to the bathroom, maneuvering past the overflowing pack of teenagers that was lining the insides of the pizza parlor. She looked around hurriedly and determinedly, checking to see whether anyone was watching her, or snickering, or laughing, or contemplating how next to ruin her evening, or worse yet, her life.

That's when she noticed Max. She didn't think he had seen anything. He seemed engaged in conversation with Lisa and Carolyn. Not knowing or truly caring at the moment where his "best girl" Cassie must be, she quickly pushed the door to the girls' bathroom open and veered off into the nearest stall. She immediately started to cry.

My first kiss. My first kiss. She couldn't help but keep repeating herself. It was all too much for her to take in at that very moment. She had waited so long for what she had hoped to be the most meaningful moment in her life.

Walter Gribble. Walter Gribble. Maybe if she said his name enough it might sound better to her. She could change it around in her mind and make it into something good, couldn't she? No, it wasn't possible. Walter Gribble was Walter Gribble, and no amount of wishing or hoping was going to change that. He was a nice, sweet guy, but not one she wanted anything to do with romantically.

Over Margot's sobbing, a voice from the next stall could be heard ever so slightly.

"Are you okay?" a young, sweet voice questioned.

Margot didn't know who was there or how to answer, so she went under the assumption that it was better to say nothing at all then risk the deplorable fate that could be brought on by discussing her situation with a stranger, and whimpered a few more seconds before she became quiet. The voice continued on, however, and Margot, being split between fortitude that someone actually cared enough to ask how she was, and fear that the story would reach the ears of her schoolmates, calmly listened, weighing her option to respond.

"Do you want to tell me what happened? I'm a really good listener. My friends all tell me so. You know, sometimes I listen so well, I think they don't hear my problems, my wishes, my needs. It's kind of annoying, really. Oh, oh, I'm sorry. Now I'm beginning to do the same thing to you. What's the problem? I'm sure something similar has happened to me, too."

"I'm really sure it probably hasn't," Margot said without thinking.

"Good, you're talking. That's a good start. Why don't you tell me what it was, and I promise not to talk again until you've finished. Go ahead, I'm ready."

Margot turned toward the right stall wall, grasping at straws about just who was on the other side. She was not about to reveal her most embarrassing, irritating woe to a stranger in the next stall. But the girl sounded so pleasant and kind.

"Why don't I tell you something about me so you feel a bit more comfortable telling me why you're crying," the girl offered. "You see, my parents are here tonight. I didn't come with them, you know. I'm in high school now. I love them and all, there's no question about that. I need some space, though. Some time to be myself, find myself, get to know more about life in my own way."

Margot couldn't believe what she was hearing. This girl knew her pain, her exasperation at the hard fact that her parents weren't ready to let her grow up just yet.

"My dad has a bit of a temper sometimes. It was so embarrassing when he and my mom walked in and he wouldn't stop yelling at her tonight. Apparently he had locked the keys in the car by mistake, and she didn't know how to help. I try to calm him down sometimes. And don't get me wrong. He loves us. And he never would hurt us. He just yells sometimes because he can't help himself. My mom gives him a little pill and he's back to normal in no time. It's just that when he yells, it makes me feel guilty for wanting my own life. Like he needs me to always be around or something to prevent his attacks, you know?"

Margot straightened herself up in her stall and quietly said, "I'm not as brave as you. I'm not sure I can tell my story to a stranger."

"Well, let's not be strangers then. My name's..."

Her voice stopped in its tracks as both girls, through their stall doors, heard the bathroom door creak open and the sounds of two annoyingly familiar voices could be heard in Margot's ears.

"Cassie! Cassie, you in here? Cass!"

"Hey, girls." The voice came from the stall next door as she exited and joined the girls by the bathroom sinks.

"Hey Cass, I can't believe you missed it. This is so good. I can't believe we saw it. Max couldn't get enough of it. We're going to have something to ride her about all year long, maybe longer. And *Walter Gribble*! That's just the icing on the cake."

"What about Walter Gribble? And who are you riding all year long about what? Come on, give." The voice still sounded pleasant and kind, but with an undertone of a love for gossip and a bit of sneakiness too.

"Margot Maples. You know her?" Carolyn asked with a tone of incredulity that Cassie would ever be caught dead in a situation that had her in close proximity to Margot.

"Sure, I know who she is. I think she's in our English class, isn't she?"

25

"Who cares what class she's in? The funniest, greatest, most incredible thing happened to her tonight. And Max is overly excited. He's always tried to make her life a bit more miserable. She gave him the perfect opportunity."

"Lisa, if Carolyn's not going to tell me what happened, would you do it already?"

"Sure, Cass." And with an obligatory whisper, in case someone might overhear and begin to use the information for their own good, Lisa said, "Margot Maples kissed Walter Gribble. Who knew that two geeks could find love, huh? This is too good, just too good!" The smiles on Carolyn and Lisa's faces were so wide that you would think coat hangers were holding them open.

"That is good. So good. Let's go talk to Max." Cassie gestured for the two girls to go ahead so she could wash up. "I'll be right behind you, okay?"

Margot was worried. Cassie Shearer had heard her cry. She must have known by now that Margot was the one whimpering and sighing in the stall next to where Cassie had been. This was too much. The perfect end to the perfect evening. How much more could go wrong before the heavens ever smiled again on poor, defenseless Margot?

"Margot, is that you? Come on, answer me."

Margot did not want to answer. If she gave in now and told Cassie it was her, she just knew she would leave the bathroom and go and tell Max, Lisa, and Carolyn, who would come in and do who knows what to Margot. Maybe even give her a swirlie in the toilet. Now *that* would be the imperfect end to an imperfect evening if there ever was one.

"Fine, don't answer. But don't worry. I'm not going to tell them you're in here. I'll try to get them off of talking about you. You've gotta understand, though. It's not going to be easy. When they set their minds on something, well, you know how it is. See you around, all right? Bye."

With that, the bathroom door creaked open and closed, and Margot was left all alone, to ponder her indescribable situation that landed her smack dab in the middle of an imperfect love triangle (imperfect because Peter was not yet in it, and Walter was unwanted), and a horrifyingly brutal situation in which Max, Lisa, and Carolyn were going to do all that was in their power to make her life a living hell.

Maybe freshmen year was shaping up to be more than she expected it to be. Way too much more, if Margot had anything to say about it. The popular kids were noticing her, after all – for all the wrong reasons. A boy liked her – the wrong one, of course. Cassie Shearer might just be okay – too good to be true. There's a catch to everything, as Margot so rightly understood.

NINE

TWO HOURS EARLIER: APPROXIMATELY 7:10 PM

"Billy! Get over here!"

Peter could barely be heard over the dozens of people surrounding him at Benino's. He was trying to clear a path to see his brother and be heard over the sounds of ordering meals and idle chit-chat that were happening nearby.

"Ya want pizza or not? Okay, okay, what kind then?" It was noticeable that Peter was more than a tad annoyed with how the evening had turned out. Ushering his little brother Billy around town was not his idea of a good time, despite having told his mother he wouldn't mind. He would have much rather been at home watching one of his many pre-taped game shows.

"I want a pepperoni pizza with anchovies, pineapple, and, well, I don't know Peter, you choose one." Peter's annoyance must have registered on his face quite quickly over Billy's hesitation, but Billy continued on, without notice. ". . . or maybe, well, nah, that's no good. Okay, okay, a pepperoni pizza with breadsticks and that dipping sauce they serve that's so good. Oh, oh, and a couple of those cheesesticks too. And..."

"Billy," Peter interjected with an overly critical tone to his voice, "just choose already. We already spent almost half an hour at the diner just to learn that you aren't in the mood for anything there, and now we're about to go through the same thing again. Get a clue already and choose something. Mom only left me twenty bucks. And that's for food *and* games."

"Okay, Peter," Billy whined. "One pepperoni pizza with two cheesesticks and that dipping sauce. That'll be good, won't it Peter?" Despite Billy's compulsion to drive Peter crazy with his uncertainty about anything and everything, Billy desperately desired Peter's attention and secretly loved being anywhere with his big brother. He looked up to him. Where else was he going to learn about girls but his big brother who was now a big-time high school guy?

Billy was in the sixth grade, and not nearly as sharp as Peter. He had some smarts, but his attention was consistently lacking. He always had his mind somewhere else, even when he seemed to be involved in a conversation with someone. Peter found this increasingly bothersome, and pestered his mother to no end to figure out a way to change this about Billy.

"Billy's special, honey. He's listening to you; you know that. You just have to be patient with him. You can do that, can't you? I know you can. Now, let's go eat." That was how their conversations almost always went, with Peter complaining, and his mother replying with something more or less similar to this, with the ending changed from eating to sleeping, or leaving to go somewhere, or some other such escape from the topic at hand. Peter felt that his mother was doing this to be even more of a nuisance to him. She knew that Billy's habitual inattention annoyed Peter, but she was doing basically the same thing by brushing off his attempt to fix his brother's issue. He couldn't stand it, yet he had to deal with it. Nothing was changing. He wasn't getting what he wanted, and he felt he never would. Giving up seemed like the only option.

Peter ordered the pepperoni pizza, cheesesticks, and sauce, and noticed by the time he was done that Billy was waiting in line at the pinball machine, as two older boys were finally giving up their possession of it. Peter had watched earlier as Walter Gribble was accosted by these same boys, and, despite his ever-increasing annoyance with Billy, he didn't want to see his little sixth grade brother being battered by two overly hyper high school juniors eager to make their mark as school bullies. To Peter's relief, the boys merely walked away and Billy took his post as the newly glorified pinball player.

It was at that moment that Peter realized he was standing alarmingly close to his old best friend and apparent nemesis, Max Poler. Peter still was flabbergasted about how they had lost their friendship. He didn't know what he had done, or how Max had made up his mind to give up something good in his life, but it still hurt him. Peter knew he wasn't the coolest, and that

Max had stepped into the in-crowd when he and Cassie had started to date, but they had stopped being friends before that, and Max's hanging around with those immature flakes Carolyn and Lisa instead of Peter was too much for him to comprehend. The saddest part was that Max seemed to really enjoy being with them, despite their aggravatingly poor understanding of what it takes to be a nice person.

That's when he started to look around and avoid glancing in Max's general direction. He didn't want to be called out as a wannabe or a geek in front of the hordes of people in and around Benino's restaurant. He just wanted to let Billy play a couple more games, eat the pizza they had ordered, and go home. His parents were coming to pick them up in another forty-five minutes. In his haste to continue looking around, his eyes rested upon the most beautiful sight. She was perfect, in Peter's mind. He knew he liked her, but didn't know how to talk to her. She was surrounded by people, which didn't help matters much. When she stood up, his eyes followed her as she made her way to the bathroom. Billy came back a few minutes later, after their pizza had been delivered to their table, and they began eating.

That's when she came out. Billy noticed her, too. She looked a bit sullen, but perked up when her mom made her way over to her. Peter reckoned her mother was telling her they had to go, because the very next moment she and her parents were out the door. Max, Lisa, and Carolyn looked pensive, but didn't even realize she had left.

"You like her, huh?" Billy calmly questioned. Peter didn't answer. He just stuffed his mouth with the remainder of his cheesestick and handed Billy a few bucks to exchange for quarters over at the arcade.

"I'll meet you there in a few, okay?"

"Don't worry, bro. I won't say anything," Billy volunteered. "It's our secret." Even though Peter pretended he didn't care about much of anything that Billy said or did, he acknowledged this with a slight nod in Billy's direction, and a pat on his left shoulder. "What's her name, anyway?"

"Cassie. Cassie Shearer," Peter said under his breath, half for fear that their conversation might be overheard and half to shut his brother up.

Max and Lisa looked up quickly when Carolyn mentioned that the bathroom door had reopened. Margot exited, flustered about just how to re-approach the table where Walter eagerly awaited her return.

TEN

If you want to hear about the rest of my night, I'll just tell you. It did not go as planned. Not that I really had anything planned, but I surely didn't count on any of what happened to me actually happening. It was all such a nightmare, I couldn't wait to be rid of Benino's, the crowded booth, or most especially the nauseatingly ridiculous Mrs. Gribble, her husband, and Walter. You wouldn't believe it if I told you, but he still had that ludicrously happy look on his face when I got back from the bathroom. He kind of looked up at me as I was coming, and looked down at the inch or two that was actually available next to him in the booth, and then back up, and down, and up, and down, until he saw that I had asked my mother to scooch over closer to him so that I could sit on the outside of the booth. If I needed to throw up or any such thing, I needed to be close to the bathroom, and I didn't feel quite able to stomach much at that moment. Between Walter's overly enthusiastic grinning, and Mrs. Gribble's non-stop enjoyment of the entire situation ("It's just so unbelievable. I knew that time would tell and you would be lucky, Walter. Just knew it!"), I desperately wanted to find the nearest exit and fling one after the other of them out of it.

I slumped myself over the side of the booth, and tried to implore my parents to take me out of this pizza place turned nuthouse by sighing louder and louder. This only served to aggravate my mother, who, never the one to be rude, was engaged in conversation – or what looked more like attentive listening to a monologue – with Mrs. Gribble (I'll let you guess who was the one going on and on about how wonderful everything was).

My father finally got my drift, and catching my eye, nudged my mother slightly to let her know that we had to go. He kind of glanced down at his watch and told her that it seemed to be getting a bit later than he had anticipated staying there, and one of his favorite shows was coming on and he just couldn't miss it. Before Mrs. Gribble even had a chance to say anything more, mom took her cue (heaven knew she wanted out of there, too, but just didn't have the nerve to cut short her never-ending listening to the ramblings of Walter's mom). She politely excused herself from the table. We (my mom, dad, and I) all backed out of the booth, leaving the three Gribbles with a look of despair over what they would do next. Mrs. Gribble anxiously wanted to continue planning the rest of mine and Walter's life with my mom, while Walter was stuck in a daze that he was seemingly never going to come out of, and Mr. Gribble was just sitting beside his wife, all happy-looking and content to listen to her for however long it might last. Now that's dedication. I have to say that he must be quite a man to put up with Kelly Gribble day in and day out.

We left the restaurant, but in the parking lot I was subjected to even more torture when my parents said they would go bring the car around, and I was left to wait at the front door. Why they had to do that was beyond me, but I can't go back in time and change it, can I? I've learned that the hard way. Enough bad stuff has happened to me that I know I can't change it. I only wish I could. When Max Poler opened the restaurant door behind me, and I turned around to see who it was (out of utter curiosity, as most people would do), I knew – just knew at that moment – that I could sink no lower than that for the night. When he passed me, I thought I had gotten lucky and would miss whatever awful thing he had to say to me, but he turned around right then, opened his mouth, and said something. The only thing was that I didn't hear exactly what it was. A car passed between us at that very moment, and gunned its engine as it sped out of the lot. Then my parents pulled up, and I got in the car, unable to hear Max's seemingly torturous words.

ELEVEN

The next day at school Margot tried at all costs to avoid anyone and everyone who had anything to do with the previous night. Things didn't work out, however. As she made her way past the lovey-dovey couple swapping "I love you's" before first period, and a pair of friends who were clumsily trying to pick up the books that had fallen out of their lockers, she noticed him. Walter Gribble was standing at her locker, looking confident as ever.

Margot tried to avoid eye contact at all costs, but Walter was trying to be too slick for his own good, and was maneuvering himself in all different directions to make sure his eyes locked on hers. Margot fumbled with her lock and wheedled out the combination. When she opened up the locker, she looked longingly for something terribly interesting to catch her eye and grant her a reprieve from Walter's tireless attempts to say something smooth. He kept trying to whisper sweet nothings in her ear, but they kept coming off as just plain bothersome.

"Oh, Margot," Walter said with a sweet caress to his voice, "your eyes are as beautiful as the color of the mixture Mr. Carlysle made in science yesterday." Or, "If you want to see beauty, look in the mirror." Despite Walter's attempts at being charming, Margot couldn't help but think that someone was listening and overhearing the cheerful words that he was saying, only to cause her anguish and stress later on. What was she to do? She needed to get him off her back, but how?

The phrase "saved by the bell" finally took on new meaning when the first bell rang, signaling the two minutes that remained before first hour officially began. Walter, ever the one to have to be in class on time or risk losing his perfect attendance glory, looked befuddled as to what to do next. It was glaringly apparent that he wanted to continue gushing over Margot, but his pride in maintaining his classroom status took precedence, and he uttered a hasty, yet adoring goodbye before rushing off in the opposite direction. Margot's first hour was right across the hall, so, unspeakably happy to be free of Walter's pestering, she shut her locker, clasped the lock, and squeezed through the groups of kids still lining the hallway.

For one hour, Margot was granted a reprieve. She listened intently and happily to Ms. Meloni speak about variable equations. Math was by no means Margot's favorite subject, but the thought of anything but her supremely inadequate life was more than enough to take her stress level down a couple of notches.

When first hour ended, Margot quickly rushed across the hallway to her locker, returned her algebra book to it, and grabbed her copy of *The Great Gatsby*. She was just in time to head for choir before having to rush through the theater wing and three other hallways to reach Ms. Pelham's English class. It was only one class away. Peter would be there, and Cassie, Carolyn, and Lisa too. *This should be interesting*, Margot thought to herself while she did her best to get past the slews of girls walking down the hallway. They seemed to always be right in the way of where she wanted to go, no matter which angle she tried to get past them. It was unnerving, really, and she couldn't understand how people could be so oblivious to the other people around them, people who actually gave a care about being where they needed to be on time. *At least I won't have to deal with Max*, she reminded herself, as she repeatedly tried to justify why she was even going to class when she knew how she was bound to be treated.

As she was entering her English classroom hallway an hour later, she spotted Walter several yards in front of her, shooting his hand up into the air, propelling himself up on his tiptoes, and craning his head back and forth to get her attention. Margot's eyes shot around frantically for a place to hide, but her classroom suddenly appeared, and she veered to her right, just missing Walter. She saw him peering through the glass panel next to the doorway, but seconds later, the two-minute bell sounded, and Walter jetted away.

She took her seat unobtrusively, and saw Carolyn and Lisa out of the corner of her eye, exchanging sneaky looks and glancing over at her, before immaturely reverting to their giggling, half-brained selves. How they ever made honors English, she didn't know, but rather than focus on that, she peered around the room, noting that there were many desks still empty. Peter wasn't there yet, either. Margot sighed, and to her chagrin, Carolyn and Lisa giggled louder and pointed in her direction.

That's when Cassie and Peter showed up at the classroom door. Peter looked a bit out of sorts. He seemed puzzled as to whether he should be gentlemanly and allow Cassie to enter first, or if he should walk in quickly and try to maintain a level of anonymity that he had worked hard to foster during all that time that he had braces. He thought his indecisiveness was over now. He thought that times had changed and that things would be different with his braces off. No such luck, really.

Margot perked up as she saw him enter the room behind Cassie, and smiled at him as he made his way to his desk. She had noticed Cassie murmur "thank you" under her breath to him, but doubted he had heard her, since he didn't acknowledge her thanks. He didn't dare speak to her. He knew the only words that would come out of his mouth were monosyllabic attempts at small talk that would sound embarrassing and childish. He made his way to a row a couple over from Margot and kept his head in his bookbag until Ms. Pelham instructed the class to listen to the daily announcements.

"Now, now, please listen closely. You're sure to miss something important if you don't stop all the chitter chatter." Besides a few whispers here and there, all ears began to listen to Dr. Perkins, Kipperton High's principal.

"There is one change in the schedule I have to announce," Dr. Perkins added hastily at the end of the announcements. "The freshman play auditions have been moved back a week, due to Mr. Richardson's schedule. Please have your monologues ready to present next Tuesday, instead of tomorrow afternoon. Mr. Richardson appreciates your interest and your dedication to preparing monologues over your summer break, and he looks forward to seeing you next week." With a crackling of the loudspeaker, Dr. Perkins signed off, not without first remembering to say the obligatory "have a great day, Kipperton" phrase in his most outlandish voice, because according to him, if he wasn't excited about school, why should the students be? He obviously had not been informed that students would rather be anywhere else than within the confines of a classroom.

Margot felt a bit of aggravation at the fact that the auditions had been moved back a week. She had been preparing her monologue for two weeks now, and she knew she was ready. An extra week would only serve to rattle her nerves, and the stress would weigh on her until she cracked under the pressure come audition day. She tried to relax herself, even though it was almost as hard to do that as to keep her German Shepherd from barking at the mailman when he stuffed the mail through the slot in their door. Ms. Pelham continued on with the lesson, while Margot did her best to focus her attention. Before she knew it, she was being gestured to the front of the room by Ms. Pelham.

"Margot, would you mind reading a couple of pages from *The Great Gatsby*? There are a couple of phrases I want to point out, and you look quite engaged already." Margot sensed the irritation in Ms. Pelham's voice. She obviously had appeared disinterested, her mind considering the monologue she had so anxiously prepared and been ready to recite. Ms. Pelham wanted to teach Margot a lesson, and this was her way of going about it.

As Margot stood up and walked toward the whiteboard, she could feel all eyes on her. She looked from left to right. Lisa and Carolyn were the first people she noticed. They were following her with their eyes, on the edges of their seats, waiting for her to be the klutz they knew her to be so they could have yet one more criticism to ambush her with next time they felt so obliged. On the other side of the room, Peter looked bored, off in another world, which made Margot all that much more flustered. She was the one the class was watching, and she wanted to make a good impression, but as she was passing the front row of desks, she tripped and fell, hitting her face flat on the floor. It was in this moment that she realized that bad thoughts definitely bring about bad karma.

Giggles broke out around the room, while a few other people stood up and leaned forward to get a better look at what had happened. Only Ms. Pelham rushed to Margot's aid, not without first yelling at the culprit.

"Nathan Fromidge! How many times have I told you to keep your backpack in your locker! I know that I have tripped over your bag myself, and now one of my students is hurt because of you and your carelessness! Margot? Margot, are you okay? Stand up, dear, and we'll have a look."

Margot stood up slowly and reluctantly, doing her utmost to stay facing the front of the room so that the rest of the class wouldn't see her tears. It had hurt more than she could bear to think. Ms. Pelham, though trying to make her feel better, did quite the opposite when she asked the class if someone would be kind enough to take her to the nurse. When Nathan Fromidge raised his hand as a sign of remorse, Ms. Pelham shot him down, citing his undeniable ability to make a bad situation worse. Having taught a class at Perry Middle School the previous year, she had encountered Nathan's lack of orderliness much too often. She did send him to his locker to stash his backpack away, and told him that she never, ever wished to see it in the vicinity of her classroom again.

When no one else volunteered, Ms. Pelham did her own volunteering. "Peter? Would you be so kind as to take Margot to the nurse's station? You know where that is, don't you? Right next to the counseling center. You'll see it. You can't miss it."

Peter shrugged his shoulders apathetically and stood up. Lisa and Carolyn had a sheer lack of sensitivity for Margot's plight. Again Margot wondered if anything like this had ever happened to girls like that, and then remembered that fateful night in the bathroom when she had learned that Cassie had been the one telling her about her father and his temper.

Margot couldn't decide which emotion she wanted to feel. She was more than halfway embarrassed about the fact that her nose probably looked like an even more lopsided version of the Leaning Tower of Pisa, but utterly mortified at the fact that Ms. Pelham had asked Peter to take her to the nurse. There was no way around it, of course. She couldn't say she didn't want him to take her, because Ms. Pelham would then question her in front of the whole class and wonder why a girl in Margot's condition would question someone doing her the not-so-small favor of getting her safely to the nurse's station. As she and Peter walked through the halls, she purposefully turned her head to face the wall away from him. At first she thought he wouldn't notice, since he didn't seem interested in her while she was on her way up to the front of the class anyway, but all of a sudden he started up a conversation.

"Sorry about your nose," he said as he gestured to it. "I don't know what Ms. Pelham thinks the nurse can do about it. Maybe give you some ice or something. If it was me, I'd want to go home."

"Thanks for the advice," Margot whispered back. "You know you didn't really need to come with me. Ms. Pelham shouldn't have made you."

"Whatever. I hate to say it, but I'm glad to be out of her class. *The Great Gatsby* is okay and all, but I just don't understand what a bunch of fictional people in a book by a guy who is no longer living has to do with me and what's happening in my life. Don't get me wrong. I like reading, but I prefer nonfiction. I watch *Jeopardy* and those types of shows. They make me think harder. They're real."

Before Margot knew it, she was defending Jay Gatsby and the whole of East Egg and West Egg. "But the storylines in that book *are* real." As Margot continued, she realized she was speaking from experience. She didn't realize just how true her words rang for Peter as well. "It's like a soap opera if you think about it. I know those aren't real, and you probably don't like them or anything either, but just think about it for a sec. Gatsby likes Daisy, but thinks his love is not returned. I don't know how it'll turn out yet or anything, but whether or not she likes him back, he obviously is whiling away his time focusing on her when she's married to another guy."

Peter thought about this as Margot continued on. There was no way he was ever going to steal away Cassie Shearer from his ex-best friend. His love was unrequited and always would be. Plus, they had never had a relationship before, and Gatsby and Daisy had. The differences were there, but the similarities were a bit too familiar.

". . . And you've got to consider that Myrtle is in the same kind of situation as Gatsby. She loves a man who is married to another woman. Who knows how that'll end up."

With that, Margot trailed off, wondering how she had gotten so involved in the episodic lives of the characters in the novel. She had never spoken so much to a boy before, let alone a boy she liked. No one her age, besides Ashley, had ever really taken the time to get to know her, or ask her opinion, or just plain want to talk.

"I guess I see what you're saying. Maybe it'll get more interesting, but for the time being, I'm sticking to *Jeopardy*. Maybe you can help me study for the test on *Gatsby* since it looks like you understand it much better than I ever will. Think about it, okay?"

There really was nothing for Margot to think about. She wanted to burst out of her skin right then and there, screaming with glee over Peter Mulvaney asking her out. But he hadn't – not really. He had just said they could get together to study. He liked the way she thought about things. It was a start, though. Her heart continued its rapid pitter-patter, and she and Peter turned the corner into the nurse's office.

TWELVE

The nurse had sent Peter back to class with a pass, and had then given Margot an ice pack and told her to call home. Margot picked up the phone reluctantly, not eager to be given sympathy from her oversensitive parents who didn't know how to handle their only daughter getting hurt. One time when she was in the fifth grade, she was riding her bicycle a couple blocks down from their house. She hit a small pothole in the street and fainted in front of a woman's house. Luckily, the woman who lived in the house was outside gardening at the time and called Margot's parents, whom she knew from their walks around the neighborhood with Margot's German Shepherd, Roxie. When Margot came to, her parents were standing over her, tears strewn across their faces, rendering themselves almost speechless as they hugged her so tight she was afraid she would faint again from lack of air. Who knew how they would react to a possibly broken nose?

She dialed her dad's number at work, and politely asked for him when the receptionist picked up. He came on the phone, frantic and nervous sounding, wondering why in heaven's name she was calling him.

"Something's wrong. What is it? Honey. Tell me. You're sick? Or hurt? Or something else? Is everything okay? When the receptionist transferred the call over here and I saw Kipperton High School on the caller ID I just knew something had to be..."

"Dad," Margot interjected. "Listen to me, okay. Everything's fine. I'm fine. I just need you to come and pick me up. The nurse thinks..."

"The nurse?!" Margot's dad was now in full-on parental worry mode. His nervousness before was nothing compared to what was to come. Margot regretted saying "nurse" as soon as she had uttered it. There was no turning back now. "What do you mean, the nurse? Just sit tight and I'll be there in a jiffy! I'll call your mother and tell her I'm coming to get you. The nurse, for heaven's sake! Why didn't you say something like that right away, honey? You shouldn't wait to tell me something like that, or else I get a bit crazy... You know that. See you in a few minutes."

Mr. Maples only worked about ten minutes away, and being the head accountant of his firm allowed him to leave whenever he deemed it necessary. This was a good thing, especially because there was no one who could hold him back when it came to his little girl. Besides his wife, Margot was all he had, and he was proud to be her father, however overprotective and overbearing he may come off to others.

"My dad will be here in a few minutes," Margot said to the nurse as she hung up the phone and watched a red light on the console disappear with the end of her call. The nurse motioned for Margot to sit in one of the plush chairs on the other side of the room, and resumed her duties, bandaging up a boy who had come in during the time Margot was on the phone. He had apparently slipped and fallen in chemistry, and hurt his arm on some of the broken shards of glass that had resulted from his loss of a firm grip on a beaker. As the nurse dabbed some rubbing alcohol on the boy's lower arm, he made a face that resembled nothing less than excruciating pain, but kept his emotions relatively calm, not wanting to be that boy who cried over the sting he surely felt.

Before she knew it, Margot heard her dad's voice echoing down the hallway. "I know it's here. They said this hallway. Oh god, where is it already?" As Margot listened to him rant and rave to himself about the lack of concrete directions that he had been given to find the nurse's station, Margot watched him walk at a quick pace past his destination. His head was bobbing back and forth, looking on each side of the hallway for where he knew his daughter must be.

"Dad, I'm right here," Margot said quietly, as he turned around, looking grief-stricken and overly concerned for her plight.

"Oh dear, oh my. Honey, are you okay? Well, of course you're not okay. Your nose. Oh my, your nose. We'll go to a doctor right away and get this straightened out. Oh dear, no pun intended, of course. I'm not trying to say that your nose isn't straight or anything. It looks fine, just fine."
Margot's dad was anything but subtle when it came to him trying to comfort

her. She knew she must look just awful, and despite his trying to cheer her up and let her know that everything would be okay, she knew she must look like a complete and total mess. "We'll stop by your classroom and pick up your things. Let me just talk to the nurse and check you out of school for the remainder of the day, okay? I'll just step over there and you wait here." Mr. Maples couldn't seem to stop talking. It seemed that he felt that if he kept talking, he would save her the despair of discussing what had happened. This was why she didn't tell him things, like the time she tripped over Nathan Fromidge's bag the first time and the whole class laughed at her.

"Oh, honey, what happened? Tell your daddy what happened."

"Daaaaad," Margot whispered through clenched teeth, with an annoyed 'what have I gotten myself into' expression on her face. "Don't say daddy. I'm in high school. We're here in my high school together right now. You can't say those things. Okay?" Margot refused to stop sounding aggravated with her father as they walked along the hallway. There were times that he just didn't get the point, and she could not let him get away with calling himself 'daddy' in front of the students of Kipperton High – especially the ones on the other side of her classroom door. "Here's my classroom."

"Oh, I'll go in for you, honey," Mr. Maples said, obviously not phased by Margot's indelicate anger at his use of words.

"No, Dad, that's okay. Let's just knock so Ms. Pelham can come to the door and hand the bag to you." Before Margot knew it, though, Ms. Pelham was opening the door to her classroom. She was in the midst of telling the rest of the students in the room that she would leave it open as long as their voices stayed down, when she noticed Margot and Mr. Maples standing there.

"Margot, you're okay. Wonderful. I was so worried. Nathan can't seem to concentrate since it happened. He got rid of that bookbag at least, but he keeps asking why I wouldn't let him take you to the nurse. Anyway, who is this with you? Is this your father?"

"Yes, Ms. Pelham. This is my dad. We just came to get my stuff. Do you think you can go in and get it for us?"

"Oh, Margot, why don't you just come in and get it? Everybody is so concerned about you, wanting to know how you are and all. Come in so they can see you're not as badly hurt as we suspected you might be."

This was the last thing Margot wanted to do. She knew that Peter had seen her already, but all she needed was for the rest of the class to see her in what she knew must look like the most hideous of ways her face could possibly look. She tried to stop Ms. Pelham, but the over-zealous teacher was already ushering Margot into the classroom, and insisted that Mr. Maples follow to see the room too.

"It's important that parents see where their children go to school, especially while school is actually in session. That's my philosophy, but the administration always does events at night. That doesn't give a real view of the classroom, now does it? This is the perfect opportunity for you to share in Margot's education, Mr. Maples." Ms. Pelham sounded quite happy about this, and Margot couldn't help thinking how awful yet another day had turned out to be, despite what had happened with Peter on the way to the nurse. Mr. Maples couldn't have been more excited. Ms. Pelham was his kind of teacher. Just another over-excited person to fulfill his wishes to make everything seemingly more important than it truly was.

"Class, Margot's back to get her things. Please excuse her as she walks down the aisle to pick up her stuff." Margot noticed that every area of the floor was free of books and bookbags. Ms. Pelham had instructed every single student to place everything either on their desks or in the holder underneath their desks. After today, they were to bring nothing to class except the necessary pens and pencils, books and journals. If there was anything else for them to bring, she would tell them in advance.

"Hey Margot, you don't look like you're feeling any better," sniped Carolyn. Her comment, inconsiderate as it was, prompted a slew of other students to comment as well. Some sounded sincere, while others sounded merely like a polite attempt to make Ms. Pelham happy. She seemed to be staring at her students with a bit of contempt since not too many people were speaking up to begin with, and she had already explained to them that in a similar situation, they would all want others to care, so they better show a bit of compassion.

"I'm sure Walter can make it all better," Margot heard Lisa say rather quietly. "He seems to be pretty good at making Margot blush lately." Luckily, the rest of the class was feverishly attempting to do Ms. Pelham proud, and Margot was pretty sure she was the only one who had overheard

Lisa's snide comment. Margot could only thank the heavens above that Walter had not been in her class when all of this had happened. The exasperating behavior of Lisa and Carolyn was enough, and Walter would have surely taken it over the top, trying to get a better look at what was wrong, and insisting that Ms. Pelham allow him the oh-so-dutiful task of taking her to the nurse. "I'm on it, Ms. Pelham," Margot could hear Walter saying in such a scenario.

Margot finally spotted her backpack and books amidst the array of students leaning in to see her nose. She walked down the aisle (slowly, as she didn't want any more accidents), picked them up, and walked toward the classroom door. Mr. Maples was stuck in the center of what had become a whirlwind of questions.

"So, you're Margot's dad?" Carolyn and Lisa asked together in a faux-sweet sounding tone.

"Why yes, I am."

"What do you think is going to happen to Margot?" Nathan Fromidge questioned in a deeply disturbed voice. "She didn't seem upset with me, did she?"

"I don't know. We'll take her to the doctor and see what's what. She's not upset. I didn't gather that she blames anyone, if that's what you mean."

The questions kept coming, one after another, about what kind of cast Margot might have to get on her nose, when she would be back in school, and, one especially meaningful comment kept getting thrown at Ms. Pelham. The students, obviously devastated by this sad turn of events that had occurred in their classroom, felt it necessary to push back the reading of *The Great Gatsby* until Margot was back and able to read the passage that Ms. Pelham had called her to the front to read before anything had occurred. It was only fair, in the students' minds, that Margot take a day or two off of school to recuperate, or all the time she needed, and they would wait patiently for her, doing something else other than reading F. Scott Fitzgerald's most famous novel. Ms. Pelham shot her students down, reminding them that time stops for no man, and Margot would have plenty of time to read at home, if she should find the need to stay there for an extended period. Ms. Pelham had seemingly forgotten about Margot's lapse in thought that had prompted her to be sent to the front of the room to read the book, and fell back on the idea that Margot was both smart and conscientious enough to do well on her own. This idea was obviously true, but brought Margot to the sudden realization that the monologues were still due in a week, and now that her face looked like an Italian landmark, she was even more nervous than ever to present hers.

Margot finally pulled her dad from the persistent questioning, and Ms. Pelham settled the class down. Margot and Mr. Maples walked out of the room, overwhelmed as ever.

"That was certainly interesting," Mr. Maples said. "Your friends are so kind and caring about you. You are a lucky young lady."

Margot didn't take the time to apprise her dad of the difference in definitions between friends and classmates. The majority of those people were certainly not her friends, and never would be. If she ever caught herself calling Lisa Quinn or Carolyn Dippet a friend, she knew that life as she knew it would never be the same, and she was not prepared to learn what it would be like. It was something she never wished on herself, let alone anyone else.

As Margot and her dad walked out of the school, she couldn't help but notice the smile on his face. He thought that his daughter was popular. It was making him so happy. In a sense she was popular, just not the kind she wished to be. She was well-known for being the goody-goody klutz she so didn't wish to be, but had fallen into the trap of being nonetheless. Plus, what had happened with Walter had only served to seal the deal to her never-ending aggravation. Margot wanted out of her daily life, and the play was her only chance to make her mark.

THIRTEEN

Margot was back in school two days later, despite numerous attempts to make the amount of time she stayed home longer. By the time she was seen by the doctor the day she had tripped and fallen, it was 5 pm, and he said that the X-ray specialist had already gone home for the day. He didn't find her to be in any real danger, so he asked if it would be okay for her come back the next day at 11 am for her X-ray. This allowed Margot one day off of school. One day didn't seem enough, especially with all the humiliation she knew was waiting for her through Kipperton's doors, but she knew her parents would never afford her yet another day off in her very first week of high school. They had already told her that she needed to call a classmate and get the schoolwork to complete on Wednesday night from both her missed classes on Tuesday and all of Wednesday. She agreed to this, without first realizing that the only classmate she knew a phone number for was Walter Gribble. He did have all of the same classes as her, only at different hours of the day.

The night Margot got home from the doctor's office there were three messages on the machine. They were all from Walter Gribble.

"Margot? Oh, it's a message. Mom! It's a message. Okay, okay, I'll leave one. I do want to talk to her though. I hate leaving messages. She's bound not to get it or something. You think I should? I want her to know I called. I mean, well, she's really..." The beep cut him off, and Margot debated whether she should continue on to the next message, assuring herself that it had to be no one other than Walter again. She was right.

"Oh, hi Margot. Your machine cut me off. It's Walter if you didn't know. I just wanted to check in and see how you are. I wish I had been there with you today. I would have taken you to the nurse and everything. You know that. Anyway, call me back. My mom wants to ask your mom something and I'm really worried about you. Promise to call me back, okay?" The next beep came, and with it, Margot's conscious effort not to drop dead at the idea of what Walter's mom could possibly want to ask Margot's mom. Margot also couldn't comprehend if Walter totally understood the idea of an answering machine not being a real person. How could she promise to call him back if she wasn't really talking to him and couldn't make a promise without having heard the message? This baffled her, but she listened to the third message anyway, figuring it was the doctor's office confirming her X-ray the next day. To her dismay, it was Walter yet again.

"Margot? Oh, Margot, you're really worrying me. I don't know where you are or how you are. I need to talk to you. I can't believe you haven't called yet. Please call as soon as you get this. I heard that Peter Mulvaney took you down to the nurse's office today. I made sure to talk to him and tell him what's what between us and all. He said he was just doing you and Ms. Pelham a favor, but I know better. Oh, wait, here's my mom." Margot cringed a little as she heard Walter's mom take the receiver and throw in her own two cents during the last few seconds of the message.

"And how is Walter's best girl? Please do call us back as soon as you get this. We're ever so concerned about you. Make sure your mother knows to talk to me as well. I have something important I must ask her. Buh-bye now." Margot was in shock. This was terrible. Not only had Walter called three times *and* put his mom on the phone, but he had talked to Peter about her. Desperate to know what he had told Peter, but absolutely horrified at the prospect of returning his call, Margot turned to her parents for support.

"Did you hear that?" Margot asked her mother in an exasperated tone after relating the contents of the messages. "Can you *believe* that?" Margot worked hard to put special emphasis on the word 'believe,' as she was truly amazed at what she had just heard. "Would you just call Mrs. Gribble back and tell her to tell Walter I'm sleeping or something. I can't talk to him. I just can't."

"Honey, I do admit that Walter's calls are a bit over the top, but he really is just worried about you. Can't you see that?"

"I guess," Margot hesitantly offered. "But could you please just do that for me, this one time?" Margot had a gut feeling that there were many more times such as this to come in the future now that they had the Gribbles to contend with, but she didn't want her mother to feel overwhelmed, so she stuck to what she had already said and repeated, ". . .this one time?"

"Fine," Mrs. Maples said, and indicated the stairway with her eyes. "But if I'm the one calling, and you're supposed to be sleeping, you better get on up to bed, because I'm not in the habit of lying."

Margot kissed her mother on the cheek, whispered her thanks, and watched as her mother dialed the final digit of the Gribbles' phone number. "Just be sure to come and tell me what she says, okay?" Mrs. Maples shooed her away at that comment, and Margot made her way to her bedroom before her mother yelled at her for not following a direct instruction.

Five minutes passed. Then ten. Before Margot knew it, it was almost thirty minutes after she had gone up to bed. Her eyes were wide open. There wasn't a hint of tiredness in her. She was waiting rather impatiently for her mother to come and tell her what had happened. Thirty-two minutes after Margot had plopped herself onto her bed, she heard footsteps coming up the stairs and down the hallway. There was a knock at her door, and Mrs. Maples peeked her head in.

"Margot, dinner will be ready in five minutes, okay? It's had just enough time to simmer on the stove while I was talking to Mrs. Gribble. Come on down soon, okay?" With that, Mrs. Maples attempted to do a disappearing act, but Margot was not having it.

"So, what did Mrs. Gribble have to say? You were talking to her long enough, weren't you?"

"Well, actually, she was the one doing most of the talking," Mrs. Maples began. "You don't really want to know, so it's okay."

"I *do* want to know. You've got to tell me. I can't take the suspense. Between Walter and his mom, it's like a bad car accident that I'm stuck dead in the middle of, and I can't help but look around and see all the wreckage. It's driving me crazy. Please, just tell me."

"I mean it though, Margot. You really don't want to know. It's not that I think you don't care. It's that you won't be too happy, so I'd really rather not tell you."

"Oh god, mom, what did you do? Tell me you didn't do anything that makes me have to see Walter again out of school, did you? You didn't. You wouldn't. You love me too much, right?"

"I *do* love you. There's no question there." Mrs. Maples' voice was becoming sullen and Margot was getting a bit scared of what was to come.

"Okay, mom, I can take it. Please just tell me what happened."

"Well, Walter answered the phone, and I told him it was me, and he sounded so concerned and sweet on you that I felt just horrible telling him you were asleep. He so wanted to talk to you and even asked how long you'd been sleeping so he knew how soon you'd be up. I told him you had just gone to bed and that by the time you got up it would probably be too late to talk to him. He sounded so depressed at that, but was glad to hear you were okay. Then he put Kelly on the phone – you know, I mean Mrs. Gribble. She was almost more concerned than he was, asking if she could do anything, and telling me how Walter had come home worried and sick over the fact that he hadn't been able to do anything for you at school. Then she asked if we wanted to come over to dinner on Friday, because they wanted to see that you're okay, and she had been meaning to have us over for so long that now just seemed like the right time. 'After all,' she said, 'our kids really do make the cutest couple, don't you think?' I told her we'd have to think about dinner, and she said she didn't know what there was to think about and that she would see us on Friday rain or shine. So, Friday dinner it is, I guess."

"You're kidding, right, mom? This is a long, elaborate joke to make me laugh, right?" Margot's mom made a face that proved to fully back her story.

"I'm sorry, Margot, but there is no way to say no to that woman. I couldn't do it. We'll just have to go."

"No. We won't. Maybe you and dad will go, but I'm staying here. I can't deal with this. You don't understand. It's not funny or fair or good in any way. Walter may seem like a cute, innocent type, but he is trying to be lovey-dovey and cutesy, and it's grossing me out. I don't like him that way, and I never will. It's bad enough what happened the other day at Benino's, but now you're subjecting me to going to their house for dinner? You've got to be losing it. I'm sorry, but it's true. I'm not going. I'm just not. And there's nothing you can do about it."

49

"Margot Maples. How dare you speak to me like that. You *will* do as I say, and what I say is that we are going to the Gribbles' for dinner on Friday night. That's that. You will be nice to Walter, and to Mr. and Mrs. Gribble. I am the first one to admit that they are not my favorite people in the world by any stretch of the imagination, but since there's no way out of this, we're going. Your father thought it was a fine idea, getting together with them. He thinks they're always good for a laugh, and you know how your father loves to laugh."

"Maybe they're good to laugh *at*, but not with. This is awful. Do you know what this first week of school has been like for me? You can't possibly imagine. This is just the stale icing on the burned cake that is my life."

"Okay, young lady, you have to get out of this funk. You are the only one causing yourself to be this way, and you know it."

"But, Mom..."

"No, you listen to me. You are making your life worse by continually thinking about how bad it all is. You've got to think positively. Come on. I know you can do it."

"Mom, listen to me, okay. I was thinking positively today. This boy that I like actually noticed me and asked if I wanted to study with him, and you wouldn't believe what Walter did. He said something to this boy. Something about my relationship with Walter. As if there was one to tell about. Now this boy I like must think I'm taken. By Walter Gribble. It's really unimaginable, don't you think? You can't possibly see an upside to this. There just isn't one."

"Even if there isn't one, you have to look for something positive. I'm not going to allow my daughter to talk *so* pessimistically about life when she has just started high school and is auditioning for the school play. You are a talented actress, Margot, and I'm sure you'll make the play, and then you'll feel all better. Don't you think you're overreacting a bit to things?"

The play stirred up emotions in Margot that she would rather not have felt. She really wanted to be in the play, but was too scared to audition now. Anyone who wanted to attend and watch the audition process was welcome, and she couldn't stand up there in front of her classmates and recite the monologue she had prepared. It was too late to start memorizing a new one, though. She couldn't turn back now. She knew it was her ticket into the play.

The embarrassment she would feel if she did it would be all her own doing, but she had to do it. It was so perfect and made her think of Peter. If only the world of bad had not happened to her over the course of this week. Then, she wouldn't be so nervous.

"Fine, mom, maybe the audition will make me feel better. But I can't help how I feel. You can't possibly imagine what it's like to be fourteen, anyway."

FOURTEEN

That night, after waking up from her nap and eating dinner, and after replaying Walter's messages over and over in her mind, Margot drummed up all the nerve she could muster and called Walter Gribble. She needed her schoolwork, and she knew that he could bring it by the next day on his way home from school.

"Hi Walter, it's me, Margot. I'm calling because I just needed the..."

"Margot?! Really? How are you? Oh, I'm so happy you called. I've been trying to get a hold of you since I got home from school. You got my messages, right? Well, how are you? I mean, how do you feel? What do you need? I can come over if you want. I'm not that far away, you know."

Margot knew all too well that Walter's house was only about a half mile from hers. He used to ride his bike by her house and wave at her, trying to show off his bicycling skills. The problem was that he didn't really have any. Every time he waved, he somehow seemed to lose his balance, and teetered on his bicycle for a few feet after his wave until he fell sideways off his ten-speeder. He would always get up, brush himself off, and smile and wave at Margot. He did this in such a way that his head was always tilted halfway down, his eyes looking up at Margot like a lost puppy, and his smile wider than ever. It was like he was invincible, even though Margot could see the scrapes on his legs from the pavement. The funny thing was that he never got the point and stopped waving while he was biking. It was something that was ingrained in him to keep doing day in and day out. Margot should have been smarter and realized he liked her as more than a friend, but she had never been a quick study in the art of flirtation. She just thought it was goofy old Walter trying to be friendly. Now she regretted ever smiling and waving back. What a lead-on that must have been.

"That's okay, Walter, really," Margot continued. "I don't need you to come over."

"But I can. I want to, really," Walter interjected quickly.

"Really, that's not what I'm calling about. I just need..."

"Margot, hold on just a sec, you've got to hear this. I've been dying to tell you. You weren't in school today during or after lunch, so you didn't hear."

"What is it, Walter?" asked Margot, sounding as pained and disturbed as possible to be putting up with listening to him any longer than she had to.

"It's just so cool. You see, the chess club met today, and they elected me President. Bobby Bishop is going to be Vice-President, and Jessica Monroe is the treasurer." Margot contemplated just what the chess club could possibly need money for, besides a couple of new chess sets for the five or so people in their group. "But here's the best part. Really, I know you're going to love this. I got them to elect you secretary! There was no one who wanted the position, and I said that you're really good at the game, and you would love to do it. Isn't that great? Now we can be in chess club together. The next meeting is a week from Thursday. We'll probably have one that Friday too, because there's a meet that Saturday. I can't wait. This'll be great. The team was so excited to know you were going to join!"

Margot didn't know how to hold back her outright anger at the idea that Walter had been so forward as to make her an officer of a club she had no desire to be in. It wasn't that she didn't like chess, but how did she expect to win any type of coolness factor if she was walking around with Walter, Bobby, and Jessica, debating whether it would have been a better idea to move her rook or Queen in the last round of their match. Then Bobby would undoubtedly make some kind of pun about his last name and how she should have moved her bishop piece, since that's always what served him the most luck. It was too much.

Her mother had always told her that if you can't say something nice, you shouldn't say anything at all, but Margot couldn't help in this instance wanting to break that dreaded rule that had been fed to her for as long as she could remember.

"Walter," Margot began, sounding miffed as ever, and continuing through clenched teeth, "I'm just calling to ask if you could get my schoolwork for me tomorrow. My parents can't pick it up, and yours was the only number I had."

"Sure thing, Margot," Walter said, completely missing the comment about him being her only contact. "And when I come by I can go over it with you and be sure you understand just what you need to do. We can talk about the chess club, too. And dinner Friday night. I'm so glad you and your parents can come."

After listening to three more rounds of Walter's excitement about coming over the next day and eating yet another sure-to-be-doomed dinner together, Margot bypassed any more pleasantries on Walter's part and told him that she had to go to get more ice for her nose. He offered to stay on the line and wait for her to return so they could talk some more, but she told him it was about time for her to take a shower so she could get back to bed soon. He finally relented, and told her she'd see him immediately after school tomorrow. When she hung up the phone, the scream that came out of her mouth was loud enough to wake the neighbors. Before she knew it, her father was bounding into the room, scared for his daughter's safety.

"Honey, what is it? Something terrible happened! What is it? Did you hurt yourself? The pain must be excruciating!"

"No Dad, don't worry. I'm not in pain, okay. I'm just..."

Without listening to a word Margot said, her dad quickly added, "I'll be right back. I'm getting you another ice pack. I can't stand to hear or see you in so much pain. Wait here, just wait here..." Margot felt that her dad's exclamations on her behalf were sweet and all, but before she could tell him it really wasn't how she was feeling physically, he had sprinted into the hallway, down the stairs, and was no longer within earshot. Within the minute, he was back in the room, a fresh bag of ice in tow.

"Thanks Dad, but it's not my nose. It's about something else. I'd rather not talk about it, though. Can I just be alone?"

"Honey, whatever it is, you can tell me. I'm always here for you. Unless it's one of those feminine things. Then I have to defer to your mother. She knows more about that stuff, you know. If I could help, you know I would, but I just don't have the stomach for it. Is that it, then? Want me to go get mom?"

"No, Dad. I really don't want to talk to Mom about this. She's already lectured me about it. You see, she just doesn't understand..." With a bit of hesitation, she quietly added, "...and I'm sure you wouldn't either. So, let's drop it, okay."

"I'm not one to push, Margot, but in this case, I feel it's necessary. You just screamed a scream loud enough to wake Uncle Gary, and he lives two towns away. I want to know what's wrong, and I'm not allowing you to tell me that neither your mom nor I would understand. We've all been through our ups and downs, and even if we've never faced yours exactly, we can figure something out. Now tell me what it is."

"Fine. If you really want to know, it's about Walter. Dad, he's driving me crazy. Today I wasn't even in school, and I became the secretary of the chess club. You know how? Walter joined me up and added me in to his presidential fold."

"Walter Gribble's the president of the chess club? How wonderful for him!" Mr. Maples added in a most interested tone. He just wasn't grasping the horror of what had happened.

"Dad, you're not getting it. You're just not getting it. You see, I told you. Can't we stop? Just go and I'll talk to you later. I've got to go to sleep anyway."

"Oh, honey, I'm sorry. Go on, okay, go on."

Margot sighed internally, then continued, "Well, he made me secretary of a club I don't want to be in. He told another boy that I actually like that something is going on between the two of us, and..."

"Well, isn't there?" The look of shock and revulsion on Margot's face made her father quieter than ever.

"What do you mean, isn't there? You thought so? I can't *believe* this!"

"Well, Margot, you did kiss him, after all."

"Oh...my...god!" Margot punctuated each syllable with the utmost stress and felt her mouth contort in as angry a way as she felt was possible. "I didn't kiss him. It was a mistake. A mistake! Why is everyone making so much of this?! Mom is telling me to be nice to him, you're telling me that you think we're a couple, and I'm stuck in this nuthouse of a life! Nothing is going on between me and Walter! Nothing!"

"Calm down, Margot, calm down. If you say nothing is going on, then nothing is going on. I'm sorry I hit such a sore spot. You'll get this all straightened out, now, you'll see."

"How, Dad? How do you propose I straighten this all out when everyone and their brother thinks Walter and I are together? What in the world can *possibly* be done to end this?"

"Well, I don't exactly know," Mr. Maples said softly, trying to calm his daughter's nerves, "but you're so smart, I'm sure you'll figure it out. Just don't forget that we're going there on Friday for dinner, and you are to be on your best behavior." It seemed as if everything Margot had just said had flown in one ear and out the other. Her father still expected her to go to Walter's house on Friday. Knowing that her father cared despite his witless attitude, she told him she was tired, and then added that she felt better. She just wanted him to leave so she could relive the painful memories of the day that would certainly keep her up through many more nights, only to be renewed once again with Walter's arrival at three o'clock the next day.

FIFTEEN

The whole next day, through her X-ray and even after coming home
and watching some of her favorite daytime shows as a consolation for what
she deemed the most horrific looking bandage, Margot wished that time
would stop and three o'clock would never come. She was loathing the idea
of seeing Walter, trying to figure out what to say to him to get him to realize
she was just not interested. There really was no foolproof way, in Margot's
mind, to do this, as he wasn't too perceptive.

Before Margot knew it, the clock changed from 2:59 to 3:00, and
almost as if he could see the digits turning, Walter rang the doorbell. Margot
was home alone with the dog, both of her parents at work for a couple more
hours. Margot opened the door slightly, peering out with half of her body
still on the other side of the door.

"Oh, Margot, it's so great to see you! Can I come in and show you the
homework I brought so you know what to do? It's all pretty self-explanatory,
but sometimes it just helps when someone who was there explains it. I have
new chess club info to share with you, too!" Walter's smile was growing
larger with each word he said. He was just too happy to be there with her,
and she knew she had to put an end to it.

"Walter, I'd invite you in, but Roxie threw up all over the carpet in the
living room, and I have to clean it up before my parents get home. I really
need to get back to that. Just give me the homework and I'll look through it
later. If I have any questions, I'm sure they can wait until tomorrow when
I'm back in school. I'm not too worried about it."

Always the one to hear only what he wanted to hear, Walter only
acknowledged Roxie, saying in no uncertain terms that he would be happy to
come in and help clean the mess up. He added that he was used to his

schnauzer running all over the house and tracking mud everywhere, so he could be of what he called "expert service."

"Tell you what. I'll go home and get my mom's carpet cleaner. I'll be back in no time. We can clean the mess together, and then you'll have time for me to go over stuff with you."

"Walter, I would hate if she threw up on you, too. So I have to say no. Please just go home." With that, Margot stuck her hand out the door, reaching for the homework packet Walter held. It slipped out of his hands and into hers, allowing her the right to try to get rid of him all that much more quickly.

"Well, okay then, I guess. Just don't forget about the chess club meeting next week, and the play tryouts too. I guess we'll have more time to talk on Friday when you come over! Can't wait for that. My mom said that she and your mom are becoming the best of friends. Wouldn't it be great if we could hang out every weekend together? That'd be so..."

"Okay, Walter. See you later. Gotta run before Roxie adds to her mess. Bye!" With a rushed and indignant tone to her voice, Margot shut the door quickly, while Walter continued talking on the other side of the screen.

"Well, bye, Margot. So happy you'll be back in school tomorrow. I've missed you!" Margot cringed at the idea of Walter missing her, and worse yet, the idea of him telling people how he missed her, or telling them that something was going on between them. The scenarios were too awful to consider, so Margot tried to postpone contemplating them and went to the kitchen table to begin rifling through her pile of missed work.

The bus ride to school the next day was uneventful, allowing Margot to bask in the silence and sweetness of no Walter, no Max, no Carolyn, and no Lisa. When she arrived at school, the dreaded posse was standing at the ready, seemingly attempting to engage her in battle. Max stood on the front line, watching her exit the bus. He made a comment under his breath to Cassie, who chortled a bit with laughter, but looked at Margot with kinder eyes than Margot would have thought possible with Max, Lisa, and Carolyn around. Max walked closer to Margot, eyeing her with a look that belied a sneer, and started snickering in her direction.

"Hey, *Margie*." Oh, how Margot hated the sound of her name when it crossed Max's lips. It sounded friendless, immature, and degrading.

"Something's waiting by your locker for you. That night at Benino's was really too much. You make it too easy, you know?" Margot started to walk away, realizing that she didn't have to stand and take anything that Max said to her. She was old enough and smart enough to not let him get to her. The trouble was that despite being old enough and smart enough, she wasn't strong enough. She walked away quickly, through the doors that led to the hallway in which her locker was located. Before she even heard the outside door shut behind her, she noticed Walter, standing by her locker with a goofy grin spread across his face. He noticed her and straightened himself up, much like Margot suspected his mother had told him to do whenever his "best girl" happened to be around. The thought of this made her mentally shudder.

"Bye, Mrs. *Dribble*." The words spouted out of Max like nothing Margot had ever heard. She turned around slightly and noticed Max and his lackeys eyeing her curiously, eager to see just what she would do next. Since Margot had her books with her already, she didn't allow them the benefit of seeing her approach Walter, but turned down the side hallway before her locker just as the two-minute bell rang. Max looked flabbergasted that his plan hadn't worked out the way he would have liked, but shrugged it off and went on his way to class with his friends in tow. Walter merely stood at Margot's locker for a few seconds after he noticed she had turned the corner, hoping she might return, looked a bit confused, and wandered the remainder of the way to class lest he be late and lose his no-tardies record.

When Ms. Pelham's class came around, everyone still had their bookbags and other materials shoved under their desks and out of the aisles. Margot maneuvered past Nathan Fromidge's desk as he continually professed how truly sorry he was for what had happened. He told her she didn't look too bad, and that he was sure the bandage on her nose would be off in no time. This served to make Margot feel even more insecure than she already had, since no one had yet taken the time to take notice of the bandage – not even Max, which made her suspect he was saving up his insults. The doctor had said it wasn't broken, but she needed to keep the bandage on for three days to allow it proper time to heal and no chance to move around in a way that would hinder its ability to be fixed in a normal amount of time. This had made Margot a bit relieved, as she had gotten it on

Wednesday, meaning she could have it off by Saturday. The monologue presentations for the play were the following Tuesday, so she'd be free of it in adequate time for her audition. This was the best news she had gotten since school had started just a few days prior.

"Class. Now, class, be quiet for the announcements, okay? Dr. Perkins needs our undivided attention." Dr. Perkins had already been through the first few announcements by the time Ms. Pelham calmed them down. They all finally got quiet and listened to the remaining few that followed. Nothing too important was mentioned, and Dr. Perkins was about to sign off of the loudspeaker when he said that one more announcement had been received a bit late, so he just noticed it in his pile of information.

"Now, staff and students," he began, "let's all express our congratulations to the newly elected members of the Chess Club." Margot looked at the speaker, overwhelmed by what was clearly about to happen, knowing her luck.

"The new president is Walter Gribble. Vice-President Bobby Bishop. Treasurer Jessica Monroe, and Secretary Marge Mables. Oh, I'm sorry, that's Margot Maples. Yes, I see the error. Someone made the "p" with a bit too much of a line on the top, making it look like a "b." Well, anyway, it's Secretary Margot Maples. Congratulations to our new Chess Club officers."

Margot didn't even have a chance to process what had just happened before Ms. Pelham was congratulating Margot and leading the class in a round of applause for this seemingly great accomplishment. Margot hastened to add that she didn't want the position and didn't ask for it; it was forced on her and she was determined to get out of it, but no one heard over Ms. Pelham's happy thoughts and well wishes for Margot's success.

Another day down the tubes, Margot made her way home. The next day was sure to be just as unpleasant, she thought, as she mulled over the indescribable agony she was sure to go through at the hands of Mrs. Gribble.

***

School on Friday was at least a bit bearable, as there was an assembly at the end of the day for the freshman class. Dr. Perkins was discussing various school policies that he wanted the students reacquainted with, as some of the upperclassmen were beginning to test the limits, and he didn't wish to see the effects trickle down to the "impressionable underclassmen," as he called them a multitude of times. He continued to say how every freshmen class was the same, and he wanted to ensure that the foolishness of the older students did not rub off on the younger class.

"You must realize the consequences that errors in judgment lead to," he inserted at the end of his drawn-out speech. Even though it was long and boring, Margot knew it was better than going to gym class and being the last one chosen for every sport. When he was finished speaking, Margot saw Walter standing on the other side of the seating area, trying to make his way toward her. She tried getting around some of her classmates, but there was no luck to be had. Everyone was milling around, talking to one another as the bell was about to ring, and they weren't allowed to be released from the auditorium until the final bell of the day sounded.

"Margot, I'll see you tonight, right?" Walter asked, gleefully. The fact that Margot had gotten through the rest of the day unscathed by insults or injury was for naught. It was at that instant that Max Poler appeared as if from nowhere. He walked up to Walter, stuck his hand around his shoulder, and smiled devilishly. Walter looked flabbergasted at the fact that Max was not only near him, but touching him, yet happy that he had been noticed by someone so outwardly cool.

"So, you two are getting together tonight?" Max asked Walter curiously.

"Hey Max, what are you doing here anyway? This isn't any of your business," Margot offered.

Walter side-stepped her annoyance with Max's surprise arrival and, seemingly forgetting about the new last name Max had penned for him since that day he had fallen asleep in class and drooled all over his desk, he said, "Yeah, Margot's coming over tonight for dinner. Her parents too." Max looked positively delighted by this revelation on Walter's part. He was about to add his two cents when Margot worked up her nerve and began to tell Max off – except it came out as if she was looking forward to the evening.

"Why don't you just get out of here? What we do together is our business anyway, Max. Walter didn't do anything to you, so leave him alone."

Max just looked at her and walked nearer. He got close to her ear, and whispered in it, "You don't know what you're up against, Margie. You see, your misery makes me happy. But the fact that you're actually happy to hang out with Dribble over here is too good for me to ignore." Margot regretted her words to Max. She knew they sounded like she was sweet on Walter, or at least like she enjoyed being around him. It was just the opposite. Not that she cared if Max knew that or not, but she didn't want the whole school thinking she was a Walter-lover. How would that look for her? She couldn't even contemplate the scenario.

As Max walked away snickering, Walter looked happy as a clam that Max had noticed him. "I can't believe this, Margot. First I get you, and now Max Poler is being friendly to me. I guess I've been doing something right lately, huh? What do you think it is? Is it my hair? I've been fixing it up a little differently. Or maybe it's my clothes. My mom just bought me these new pants at the Gap. This is great. I'm getting to be cool. I've got to tell my mom. She'll be so pleased." Noticing Margot looked a bit like she wanted to get going, he hastily added, "You know, I don't tell her everything. There's *some things* that I keep secret. You know what I mean." Then he winked at Margot, sending her into a frenzy to get past the crowd that was riddled with talk of how lame Dr. Perkins' speech to them was, and how the upperclassmen were just rebelling against the aggravation the administration was causing with all these rules thrown their way.

She pushed past the throngs of people, causing many to look at her with disgust and resentment that she would dare run into them while they were having a conversation. Walter rushed after her, but he got lost in the sea of people still remaining in the auditorium. She made it to her locker, grabbed her things, and was rushing out the front door of the school when she heard Walter yell behind her, "See you tonight, Margot! Sorry we got separated in there! Can't wait till later!"

The night hadn't even begun yet, and Margot already wished it was over.

SIXTEEN

"Honey, pass Mrs. Gribble the salt," Margot's mother requested. "She asked you for it three times already." Margot reached her hand over to grab the salt shaker, and immediately woke up, searching around frantically for any sign of Walter. He was nowhere in sight, Margot happily realized, as she reset her alarm for another ten minute power nap.

She couldn't shake the feeling that something was going to happen again tonight at the Gribbles'. She was bound to be in some situation that would be appalling, yet the Gribbles would find fantastic for their dear son, Walter. Another situation making her any more the apple of Walter's eye was so far from what she needed that Margot held out hope that something would keep them from heading over for dinner that night. However, at 5:50, the Maples family was piling into her mom's car. Margot did her ceremonial whine about doing something that she had no interest in, and got the same retort from her mother about being nice to Walter and his parents despite her annoyance with them.

As they approached the Gribbles' house, Walter was standing outside, presumably waiting for them, all done up in a suit jacket and tie. No one had told the Maples' that it was going to be dressy, but Mrs. Maples had worn a pair of nice slacks and a blouse, and Mr. Maples was still dressed from work, in his normal suit attire. Margot was still wearing her school clothes, as she had refused her mother's insistence on changing for the evening. No one had told them it was fancy, and she wasn't about to dress up to impress Walter Gribble.

As they got out of the car, Walter rushed over to Margot, telling her how wonderful she looked in as many ways as he could think to say.

"Oh, Margot, you look good in anything you wear. I can't remember the last time you wore something so wonderful. You have such great taste. Do you shop at the Gap?" Margot was about to interject and say that she had bought these clothes months ago and had no recollection where they were from, when Walter continued, "My mom takes me there because she thinks they have the most stylish stuff. I guess she's right, because you look just great." Margot decided it wasn't worth the bother of telling Walter she had put no care into her clothing for the evening, and kept walking toward the front door of the house, while Walter stayed completely in step.

He ushered them into the front hallway, and Mr. and Mrs. Gribble were just as complimentary to Margot as Walter had been. They didn't seem phased by the fact that she hadn't changed since school, or that she didn't seem at all interested in being there with them. Mrs. Maples kept looking over at her with angry eyes, imploring her to say something nice instead of continually looking the part of a party pooper.

Margot would have brought up the fact that the auditions for the school play were coming up, but she didn't want Mrs. Gribble to once again bring up the idea that she and Walter should practice their audition pieces together, so she racked her brain for what to discuss. As her mind mulled over various thoughts – from her injury earlier in the week, to Walter's making her secretary of the chess club, to his discussion with Peter that ended who knows how – she could only think of negative items to get angry with Walter about. The injury wasn't really his fault, but what had happened at Benino's had made the entire experience much more horrendous to deal with, and Margot didn't know how her freshman year had come to this awful state of being in such a short amount of time.

She was about to compliment Mrs. Gribble on what truly did smell like a delicious dinner, hoping to pawn off the conversation on someone else so she could sit back quietly and hope for a quicker end to the evening, when she saw it. Staring down at her from the mantel was a framed shot of Margot and Walter in all their infamous awfulness. The picture showed Margot looking completely befuddled, with a look of incoherence on her face as her head was tilted bleakly toward the camera. Walter was shown just as wide-eyed and smiley as Margot remembered. Why in heaven's name was this framed for all to see? Anyone who walked in the house was going to see it. It was the most proudly displayed frame, even over Walter's baby pictures and Mr. and Mrs. Gribbles' reprint of the Mona Lisa. That had always been their talking piece from what Margot remembered when she and her parents had visited the Gribbles when she was younger. They prized that reprint above all else, or at least they had, until this new photo had taken the spotlight.

Walter noticed Margot looking at the shot. "It's great, isn't it?" he asked with a twinkle in his eye. "Mom just put it up today."

"Yes, Margot, we have one for you, too. I've placed it by your mother's purse so you won't forget it when you leave. It's all framed and everything. I didn't want to put you to the trouble of getting one yourself, and the inscription that was on the frame when I bought it seemed just perfect. I couldn't pass it up." Margot walked closer to the frame, noting the giddy expressions on all three of the Gribbles' faces from the corner of her eye. Her parents seemed to be just as caught by surprise as she was, and sat expressionless except for a few sweet smiles by her mother in Mrs. Gribble's direction, as Kelly couldn't stop gushing about how perfect the wording was.

"Go on, Margot, read it out loud. You'll see what I mean," Mrs. Gribble insisted.

"Our own unique love story," Margot read. It gave her chills to read it out loud. It really was unique what had happened to her, she inwardly admitted. Nothing like this must have ever happened to any normal teenager in the history of the world.

"Our own unique love story," Mrs. Gribble repeated as if in a daze. "Beautiful, isn't it? I knew it. Just knew that Walter would find that special girl. This dinner is in honor of you two. We're having all of your favorites. I did ask your mother what your favorite meal is, Margot. She told me you really like cashew chicken, so I put that together for you."

Margot tried to stifle a smile. She didn't want to seem happy about anything while being in the Gribbles' house, but she knew she had smelled something wonderful earlier. It must have been the cashew chicken. "We're also having fresh fruit salad, and Walter's favorite side dish, mashed potatoes and gravy. I hope that sounds good?" Mrs. Gribble asked, gazing at Margot for what she hoped would be a positive affirmation of her cooking choices. Margot nodded pleasantly, not wanting to relay any sign of enjoyment. The only thing she was happy about was the meal, but if she smiled in the slightest, Walter would most definitely construe it as affection for him, and that wasn't at all what Margot wanted conveyed. Mrs. Maples glanced at Margot knowingly, and gave her an "I told you so" kind of look.

While dinner was going on, the majority of the conversation took place amongst the parents, but Walter, who had taken the seat next to Margot, was nudging her once in a while to see how she liked the meal.

"It's good, isn't it? I helped my Mom make it. I threw the cashews in there when it was going into the oven."

"I'll be sure to think of you when I see a nut from now on," Margot said, thinking of just how nutty the Gribble family truly was. Walter looked so happy that she was even saying she would think of him, that he smiled widely and continued to eat while looking at Margot out of the corner of his eye every few seconds to continually widen the grin on his face. When he tried to talk to her again, she just nodded in response to his questions, and pointed back at her food with her fork to show that she wanted to get back to eating. Walter was so happy that she was enjoying the meal, he didn't mind at all that she didn't continue to talk or respond to him with words.

"This cashew chicken is delicious, Kelly," Mr. Maples said happily. "You must give us the recipe. We always just go out for this type of meal to Wei's Garden. It would be wonderful to have another meal on the docket at home, wouldn't it, dear?" Mrs. Maples looked a bit disgusted with him for saying that she didn't make this herself, but, remaining as unflustered as she could, looked at Mrs. Gribble and said how lovely it would be if she could get that recipe. Margot thought it was funny how Mrs. Maples was having to follow her own advice for a change, when she looked as though she wanted to do absolutely anything else but ask Mrs. Gribble for cooking recipes or anything else that might be interpreted as a need for help. Mrs. Maples was an independent woman, and she knew that, like Walter had done to Margot, Mrs. Gribble would latch on tightly to her and not let go. Mr. Maples, unaware as always, just kept smiling and pointing at his food, proving his truthfulness at how tasty he thought it was.

"The school play auditions are finally going to be here on Tuesday," Walter warbled, crumbs lining the corners of his mouth. "Are you ready, Margot? I know you're just going to be great. Just great."

"Yes, honey, that is Tuesday, isn't it? I still don't understand why they had to push it back, but I guess it just gave you more time to prepare now, didn't it?" Mrs. Maples swiftly added to the conversation, addressing Margot.

"I guess so," Margot mumbled, keen to make it look like she was still engrossed in her meal. She was taking her time eating, but not letting it look like she was moving too slowly, as she wanted to have something to divert her attention from the incessant rambling of Mrs. Gribble and her doting son. "I've been ready for a while now."

As she said this, Margot glanced around at the others to make an attempt at eye contact so no one would accuse her of being completely devoid of manners. It was then that she noticed a look of recognition on Mrs. Gribble's face. She had, unknowingly of course, just given Mrs. Gribble an idea. Despite Margot's belief that it was the worst possible idea ever, Mrs. Gribble came out with it anyway.

"I know what would be the perfect way to continue this already delightful evening. Margot and Walter will perform their monologues. It's perfect, just perfect! Come on, Walter, you go first. Make Margot feel comfortable and all. You're a natural dear, a natural!"

"Yes, son, I've been hearing you in your room for days now, just going over line after line after line. You have to be prepared. After all, you are a Gribble. We Gribble men are quick to learn and even faster to impress. Come on son, give us your all!"

Margot tried to hold back a snicker at Mr. Gribble's comments. Walter was by no means an impressive young man. He also was not overly perceptive, at least in the case of Margot's romantic disinterest in him.

"Mooooom. Daaaaad." Walter said their names with a note of desperation in his voice that Margot found all too familiar since she used it often with her own parents. They were putting him on the spot, and even though Margot could tell he was eager to show off his ability to impress her, he was nervous.

"That's okay, Mr. and Mrs. Gribble. Our monologues should be a surprise on Tuesday," Margot chimed in, trying for a reason unbeknownst to her to help the struggling Walter.

"Nonsense, dear," Mrs. Gribble feverishly responded. "Walter has been practicing, and you two are going to perform your monologues. I've been eager to hear them for days now, and Walter's bringing up the play made me remember just that."

Walter smiled at Margot, then maneuvered his way into the middle of the living room. Everyone turned their chairs to be sure they were facing him, giving their full attention.

"Okay everyone. It's from *Romeo and Juliet* by William Shakespeare. I hope you like it."

"More confidence, Walter. More confidence!" Mr. Gribble encouraged.

"Yes, Dad. I'll start again, okay? This monologue is from *Romeo and Juliet* by William Shakespeare." Margot noticed that Walter did sound more confident after that comment from his father. The ironic part was that he could never be that confident on his own, or at least not that Margot had seen. Walter then began:

"But soft! What light through yonder window breaks? It is the East, and Juliet is the sun!" Walter looked shyly in Margot's direction at this point. "Arise, fair sun, and kill the envious moon, who is already sick and pale with grief, that thou, her maid, art far more fair than she. Be not her maid, since she is envious; her vestal livery is but sick and green and none but fools do wear it; cast it off. It is my lady; O, it is my love! O, that she knew she were! She speaks yet she says nothing; what of that? Her eye discourses; I will answer it. I am too bold; 'tis not to me she speaks." Margot considered the absurdity of the remark that Walter could possibly be too bold, but chalked it up to trying to be somebody he clearly wasn't. She knew she herself had some experience wishing she could be someone different. "Two of the fairest stars in all the heaven," Walter continued, "having some business, do entreat her eyes to twinkle in their spheres till they return. What if her eyes were there, they in her head?" He moved his eyes around, attempting eye contact with each person in the room, as if he was asking each person individually the answer to this question, all the while letting them know his troubles and deepest wishes. "The brightness of her cheek would shame those stars, as daylight doth a lamp; her eyes in heaven would through the airy region stream so bright that birds would sing and think it were not night. See, how she leans her cheek upon her hand!" Walter still looked around at everyone, but his gaze seemed to fall on Margot for a split second more than the others. "O, that I were a glove upon that hand, that I might touch that cheek!" Margot definitely could tell why Walter had picked this piece. He really identified with it. The scary part for Margot was that she felt she identified with it, too. She longed for Peter, just as she could tell that Walter longed for her.

Mr. and Mrs. Gribble stood up immediately, with a resounding applause echoing from not only their corner of the room, but from that of Margot's parents as well. Walter had done a fairly amazing job with that monologue, but Margot would not be the one to let him know it. She just clapped along with the others, and smiled a soft, sweet smile at Walter to let him know she liked it – just not how much she felt her own connection with it.

Walter went back to his unsure, inept, awkward ways, and asked at least five times if it was really good. It wasn't enough that his parents had liked it. He needed to know that Mr. and Mrs. Maples and Margot had all thoroughly enjoyed the performance, and were not just humoring him with their applause and kind comments.

"Walter, dear, that was just great. I must say that I truly did not expect such a performance. You really did a fine job." Mrs. Maples was being more complimentary than usual, as she never would have figured that Walter would have any chance whatsoever to do well with the play. He was better than she expected, and she was letting him know it in every way possible to take away her guilt at not having believed in him in the first place. "I really am proud of you," she continued.

"Thanks, Mrs. Maples. I'm glad you liked it." At this, Walter turned eagerly to Margot. "I know you're even better than me," Walter whispered to her. "Wow us! I know you will!" Walter nudged Margot with his elbow, and prodded her up, until she stood in the same spot that he had to make his performance. She was afraid to follow that. Despite how crazy it sounded, Walter Gribble had done a pretty fantastic job performing, and of all the things that had happened to her this week, the last thing she wanted was to be shown up by Walter's monologue.

It was then that she thought of it. The perfect out to her situation. She opened her mouth to speak and began to hiccup uncontrollably as she recited the first few words of her piece.

"Oh dear, oh dear," Mrs. Gribble said with an apologetic tone to her voice. "It seems that all my pushing has gotten to Margot's nerves and caused this case of the hiccups. It's okay, Margot. Why don't you sit down and drink a nice, tall glass of water? Walter can try scaring you later if the water doesn't help." She chuckled a bit, and watched Margot down half a glass.

"I really can't drink anymore," Margot offered when she saw that Mrs. Gribble was still staring intently at her.

"Nonsense, dear. You must drink that full glass to shake those dreadful hiccups. I trust that your mother agrees that this is the best course of action in a case like this."

At this, Mrs. Maples spoke up, citing the fact that Mrs. Gribble was right, and every time that the hiccups had plagued Margot before, a nice, tall glass of water sped them right along and out of her system.

"Fine, but I'm going to have to go to the bathroom after this." Margot sounded agitated and aggravated, two emotions that were all too familiar to her as of late. She finished her water and excused herself to the bathroom, where she stared into the mirror, depression and worry written all over her face.

"How do I get out of here? What do I do?" Margot asked her reflection bitterly. Then, another idea popped into her brain.

When Margot left the bathroom, she caught a quick glance of Walter's room. It was impeccably neat for a high school boy, except for a Polo shirt and khaki pants strewn on the ground. Margot presumed that Mrs. Gribble had made Walter clean the room just before they had gotten there, but Walter must have changed one too many times after he was done cleaning, as evidenced by the outfit on the floor. As she re-entered the dining room, everyone was practically finished eating, and Margot walked up to her mother, whispering something in her ear.

"No, honey, I don't." Mr. Maples, his mouth still full of the last bite of food that was on his plate, asked what the matter was. Mrs. Maples looked at him as if to make him be quiet, but he didn't get the point.

"What's the matter? Whaddya need?" Mr. Maples' words came out jumbled as his cheeks were chock full of final morsels of Mrs. Gribble's delicious dinner.

"Nothing Clark, nothing at all. Don't worry about it," Mrs. Maples whispered in a rushed tone under her breath. Margot appreciated her mother's discretion, but her father was an entirely different matter. It was then that Mrs. Gribble chimed in.

"Is there something the matter? Can I help?"

"No, thank you, Mrs. Gribble. It's appreciated and all, but..."

"Yeah, Margot, what do you need? I'll get it for you." Now Walter was joining the chorus of helping hands as well.

"No, really, Walter. It's nothing. I just..."

"She just needs to get home. She realized that she didn't feed the dog, and if Roxie doesn't get fed soon, she's apt to throw up all over the house. It's happened one too many times for my liking, to be honest. We better go."

Nice save, Mom! Margot thought that was the perfect story. Her mom was actually a pretty great cover artist. She didn't really know that she was just covering up to get Margot out of the Gribbles', but nonetheless, she was saving the day.

"Don't worry, dear, I fed Roxie about fifteen minutes before we left." There it was. Her dad's complete lack of understanding rearing its ugly head.

"Wonderful! Now you don't have to leave so soon!" said Mrs. Gribble.

"Well, that's not all. I really have to go home. Come on, Mom, you understand."

"Yes, Margot. You're right. Come on, Clark, we have to go. That medicine at home will help Margot's hiccups, and it wouldn't hurt to check on Roxie anyway, since she's been sick lately."

After much more back and forth in the conversation, Margot finally pulled Mrs. Gribble aside, and whispered quietly in her ear, "Mrs. Gribble, please understand. It's that time of the month. I'm trying to be discreet, but you have to meet me halfway!"

"Oh, gosh. I'm sorry. I didn't realize." Her voice, although calm and sweet to Margot, was rising in pitch ever so slightly. "I must have something for that."

"For what?" asked Walter eagerly.

"Walter, just stay out of it, please." Margot was about to burst from her insane desire to get out of the Gribbles' house.

"I can't, Margot. I just want to help. Let me help you."

"I have my period! Okay? Just let me go home and rest. I'm irritable. Haven't you noticed?" She was pinning her emotional turmoil on something that was not even truly happening at the moment, and wasn't bound to happen for another couple weeks, but no one knew that besides her, and she wasn't about to let it become common knowledge.

Walter turned a shade of red that she never thought she'd seen before. He looked utterly befuddled as to how to respond. Margot took this opportunity to make a dash for the front door, as her mom quickly thanked Mrs. Gribble for dinner and her dad looked as though he was about to have a stroke from this new revelation about his daughter's further loss of childhood innocence.

As soon as they were in their car, Mr. Maples drove off, leaving another crazy night in their wake.

SEVENTEEN

To Margot's dismay, the weekend came and went quicker than she would have hoped. She couldn't begin to grasp how the most awful experiences in her life knew just how to take their sweet time to play out, and the only respite she had flew by in what seemed like an instant.

School on Monday was rather uneventful, which Margot found a great relief. Kipperton was too much of a nightmare lately. She had managed to avoid all interaction with Max, Lisa, Carolyn, and the rest of their impossibly annoying clique for the day. Even Walter was strangely out of school, which made Margot happy that she didn't have to contend with him asking her how she was. She also didn't have to watch him put his foot in his mouth as he brought up the one thing she would rather die than hear about in school – her period. She found it oddly irritating that he wasn't in school, however. She wondered where he was, but didn't truly want him there. She just couldn't get over the nudging feeling that he was sick or something. She silently cursed Walter and his niceness, as it was provoking her to actually find reason to care for him. After all, she considered him at least partially responsible for her lack of a social life.

I'll call him when I get home to see how he is. Wait! I can't call him. Do you know what he'll do if I call? If he is sick, he'll snap right out of it. He'll tell me that the loving tenderness of my voice and the sweetness of my call have healed him, or something insane like that. Or he'll ask if I can come over and feed him chicken soup, or bring his homework by. His mother will probably get on the phone and tell me that I'm his girl and he's been asking for me. I won't have the nerve to tell her I can't come because her son is sick and all, so I'll go. Darn my niceness! Darn my sensitivity! I...

"Come on, move it!" The sounds of hurried, annoyed teenagers entered Margot's ears as she was pushed into the first open seat at the front of the bus. "What's the holdup, huh? Why you moving so slowly?" The kids on the bus were unrelenting in their continual prodding of Margot to move. Even after she was situated in her seat, they were still sneering at her and telling her off for not moving fast enough to get on the bus. Since Margot had had a fairly uneventful day, she chose to let this aggravation slide by. After all, one day of peace and quiet seemed in order.

Once home, she tried to remain distracted to keep from calling Walter. Nothing seemed to keep her busy enough. She felt guilty, and in order to alleviate this unwelcome emotion, she picked up the phone. Just as she was starting to dial, she heard something on the other end of the line.

"Oh, sorry mom, I didn't realize you were already home. I'll just..."

"Margot?" The voice on the other end of the line did not belong to Mrs. Maples. It was a male voice.

"Yes?" Margot asked before realizing that she didn't have any idea who it was on the other end or how they happened to be on the extension.

"Margot, it's me."

"Me who? Who are you and what are you doing on my phone?"

"You picked up the phone. I called and you answered. Funny, huh? You act as if you didn't even hear the phone ring."

"I didn't. And who *is* this?!"

"Gosh, Margot, it's me. Walter."

"Walter? Oh. Hey. I was just about to call you." Before the words were completely out of her mouth, she knew that she could never take them back.

"You were about to call me? Wow, you've got to lend it to fate, huh? I call, you don't hear the phone ring, and you pick up to call me, but I'm already there. It's destiny, I tell you!"

"Why were you calling, Walter?"

"Oh, uh, you see, I wasn't in school today."

"I noticed," Margot responded with a tinge of sarcasm etched in her voice.

"You did? Well, you see, my great-aunt passed away this weekend, and the funeral is tomorrow, so my mom had me running errands all day with her to help her get ready for the wake. I was wondering if you could tell me what the homework is since I couldn't get it myself. Is there any group work that needs doing?" Walter asked this last question with a note of excitement in his voice, as he desperately wanted any reason – any reason at all – to work with Margot outside of school.

"The only homework was to complete page forty-five in your math textbook and write a summary of the portion of *The Great Gatsby* you're to read for homework tonight. You should have the reading schedule."

"Yeah, I do," said Walter.

"Besides that, it's just that the auditions are tomorrow. I'm sure you'll be fine, though."

"Really? You think I'll be fine? What makes you say so?"

Margot was annoyed. She felt that Walter was just fishing for compliments, but deep down, she knew he truly wasn't. He wanted her to be impressed with him, and he just wanted to hear her say that she really thought his monologue would be well-received.

"Come on, Walter. You did a great job the other night. Don't be silly. You're sure to impress Mr. Richardson and the rest of the Thespian troupe running auditions."

"I wasn't that great," Walter said. "You're the one who's going to be great," he gushed.

"I really don't think so. I suppose I practiced and all, but yours was just right. You had it down pat, and I don't know if I can be as good as you."

She could hardly believe that she was complimenting Walter. Walter Gribble. It was almost too much for her to take. Yet it was all the truth. She tried to think of a way out of the call, but it seemed like they were having a heart-to-heart moment that was unavoidable.

"Do you want to practice your monologue on me?" Walter questioned.

"Eh, really, no. I think I'll just perform it tomorrow. Actually that's what I'm working on right now. I better go."

"You sure? I'll listen to you anytime, Margot."

She believed him. Not only because he seemed to be falling head over heels for her, but because he seemed to be a genuinely nice guy. She didn't want to appreciate his friendship, though. She quickly devised a plan to get off the phone, as she felt she had fallen into a "Gribble trap" and stayed on the phone for far too long. It seemed like just the tactic Mrs. Gribble might use to get someone to listen and stay intent on a conversation they were having with her. Compliments and offers to help. That was the Gribble way. It seemed sweet and not the least bit harmful until you were locked in their grips, unable to tear yourself away from the impending doom of always having to have them around you.

Okay, Margot realized she was overreacting when she thought up this last part about the "Gribble way," but she didn't want to allow herself to develop any types of feelings for Walter, especially those of friendship. If she became too friendly with him, he would surely think it could lead to more.

"Gotta run, Walter. The oven timer just went off and I don't want the potatoes that I put in for tonight's dinner to burn. Bye!"

Before Walter could utter a single syllable, there was a click, and all that could be heard was a dial tone.

EIGHTEEN

"Next!"

Margot shuddered. She was noticeably nervous. Days and nights of preparing now brought her face-to-face, so to speak, with this moment.

As soon as Joey Miller is done, it's me. Oh gosh...

Her thoughts trailed off as Lisa and Carolyn could be seen snickering and pointing at Joey's stutter-filled rendition of Mark Antony's "Friends, Romans, countrymen" speech from *Julius Caesar*. Walter had already gone. Mr. Richardson had smiled slightly and called his performance "intriguing" – whatever that meant. Mr. Richardson was no great judge, after all. He didn't say exactly what he thought. He kind of left you up in the air, wondering if his comment leaned you more in favor of a positive outcome or a negative one.

Margot was the tenth one on the list to perform that day. Lisa, Carolyn, and Cassie were set to try out not much later. She was hoping that by the time she got out there, Lisa and Carolyn would be fed up with their fun and leave to go prepare for their own auditions. Of course, Margot knew that her luck had a limit – none at all. They were bound to be out there, ready and waiting for her to invariably mess up. Cassie was nowhere to be seen – she was probably practicing – just what Margot wished her two sidekicks were doing.

When her time came, Margot approached the stage as if in slow motion, savoring the moments before her ineptitude became all too apparent.

"What, may I ask, is your monologue, Ms...." Mr. Richardson hesitated, not sure of Margot's last name. She was already flustered, and was becoming aggravated by the lack of professionalism that she felt Mr. Richardson was showing. After all, she had introduced herself to him when she signed up, and he had already said her name once to ask her to take the stage.

"Oh, here it is. Yes. Maples. Margot Maples. What monologue have you prepared?"

Margot took a deep breath and heard an almost inaudible whisper usher forth from her mouth.

"What did you say? You must speak up."

Margot could tell that Mr. Richardson was almost on edge. Many of the auditions had not gone so smoothly, and he seemed set on finding the most professional actors he could. Little did he know, or care to remember, that he was still in a high school and not sitting front and center listening to auditions at one of the great New York theaters.

"My monologue is from 'Pride and Prejudice.' It's recited by a girl named Lydia."

Mr. Richardson glanced up, almost as if a note of surprise had registered on his face, and made a motion with his hand for her to begin.

Margot looked down as she had seen some of the other students do when they auditioned, took another deep breath, and looked up calmly, with a sedated expression.

"My dear Harriet, you will laugh when you know where I am gone, and I cannot help laughing myself at your surprise tomorrow morning, as soon as I am missed. I am going to Gretna Green, and if you cannot guess with who, I shall think you a simpleton, for there is but one man in the world I love, and he is an angel. I should never be happy without him, so think it no harm to be off. You need not send them word at Longbourn of my going, if you do not like it, for it will make the surprise the greater when I write to them, and sign my name Lydia Wickham. What a good joke it will be! I can hardly write for laughing. Pray make my excuses to Pratt, for not keeping my engagement, and dancing with him tonight. Tell him I hope he will excuse me when he knows all, and tell him I will dance with him at the next ball we meet, with great pleasure. I shall send for my clothes when I get to Longbourn; but I wish you would tell Sally to mend a great slit in my worked muslin gown, before they are packed up. Goodbye. Give my love to Colonel Forster, I hope you will drink to our good journey. Your affectionate friend, Lydia Bennet."

When Margot finished, she looked down again, and the audience sat silently, seemingly waiting on Mr. Richardson's response so they could find some common ground with him and heighten their chances a bit by acknowledging his stance on everyone else's auditions. Margot felt relieved to be done, but worried about how the monologue could potentially give new ideas for ways to taunt her.

"Thank you, Ms. Maples. Thank you very much. Please exit stage left and wait in the back until all the auditions have been completed. We will announce callbacks then."

Margot did not know what to make of this. The audience looked confused and baffled as to whether or not they should clap as she exited, or snicker and sneer as she did the walk of shame to stage left.

"Margot! Oh, Margot, how did you do? I'm so sorry I couldn't be out there. He said to wait back here. Oh, but you know that. You wouldn't be back here otherwise."

Walter was rambling like he had never rambled before. And he knew how to do it with the best of them. Margot attributed his fervent babbling to nervousness. He wanted to get into this play to try to change his image. He probably thought he'd be cool if he were an actor. Margot didn't want to break it to him that she couldn't see him being one of the cool kids, but deep down, she knew how he felt. This play could solidify or break her fragile standing in the freshmen class and the school as a whole. She needed to make it, or else Carolyn, Lisa, and Max would win. Win what, Margot didn't know. But she did know that she didn't want them to have the fortune of having whatever it was.

NINETEEN

Margot had a sleepless night. She had been called back to the stage by Mr. Richardson and presented a monologue to memorize for her callback audition the next day. She guessed that about seventy percent of the students who auditioned were called back to the stage shortly after their first performance to receive one of the handful of monologue choices. They were all eager to try and wow Mr. Richardson once again. Of course, of the girls, Cassie, Carolyn and Lisa had also been called back.

After school Wednesday, the biggest surprise of all was that Walter had been the first one brought back to the stage. Margot didn't know what to make of any of this. Was there an order that Mr. Richardson was following? Was he calling back the best first and the worst last? Or was it the opposite, and Walter was at the bottom of the barrel and she was at the top? After all, she had been called back as the final contender for a spot on the callback list.

Mr. Richardson had made it clear that after the second monologues were read, he would choose fifty percent of the callback list and those students would make up his second and final callback. If you were to make it to the second callback, you would have to read a dialogue with another student. The student would be decided at Mr. Richardson's discretion. The second callback list would be up first thing Thursday morning by the theater door, dialogues would be presented on Friday after school, and the final cast list was supposed to be up on Monday, immediately before first hour.

Margot knew that several sleepless nights and very long days were ahead of her, but she braced herself and tried to think positively. Heck, trying this new tactic couldn't hurt.

"Dad, do you think you can drop me off by the theater wing today? I want to see..."

"The cast list! Of course! Margot, sweetheart, I just know you'll make it. You have always been our shining star, after all."

"Daaaaaad. Quit it, okay? It's not even the cast list being posted today. It's just the second callbacks. Calm down, alright? I don't need to be any more nervous than I already am."

"Sure, honey. No problem. No problem at all." Mr. Maples quieted himself down, but Margot could still see a half smile on his face as he went back to eating his cereal.

When he dropped her off at school, Margot said a quick goodbye and tried to be as calm as possible as she opened up the door and stared down the hallway at the bulletin board that was about to share her theatrical future (or lack thereof). She quickened her pace a bit when she actually entered the school, but just as she was about to approach the board, Carolyn and Lisa appeared, bringing her level of nervousness up about a hundred notches. They faced her, arms crossed, with evil grins lining their faces.

"Oh, you want to see the board? Are we in your way?" The sarcastic sweetness of Carolyn's voice echoed in Margot's ear. She was almost tempted to talk back to her in the same baby-sweet, ridiculous voice, but she mustered up her strength and merely said, "Yes." She was unable to keep eye contact, however. They were staring her down, and she did not feel comfortable looking either of them straight in the eye.

"We'll move," Lisa added with a nonchalant air to her voice. "Just don't think you'll get top billing, Margie. We're the stars, alongside Cassie. No one can change that. It's the way it's always been and the way it always will be."

Margot really wanted to make it clear that she knew that neither she nor they could ever get top billing in this play. Based on all the auditions they had watched, their chances were slim. The pickings were very good based on Mr. Richardson's cuts from the original auditions, and Margot didn't want to kid herself into thinking she could ever be good enough to be the lead. Disappointment was something she was too familiar with to think that a chance was even in the cards for her. With this knowledge in mind, she pushed past the two girls who were taken aback by Margot's audacity to even touch them.

"I made it. I made it," Margot whispered to herself at least half a dozen times before it fully sunk in. Carolyn and Lisa were still behind her, uttering deliberately demeaning insults about the way that Margot looked, or how her audition was just a fluke, or some other such nonsense. Margot completely ignored their words, as she was totally consumed by the vision of her name on the callback list. The one thing it did not list, however, was the name of the person she would be doing her dialogue with the next day. The sheet of paper said that the match-ups would be posted by lunchtime, and they could all pick up the dialogues at that time to begin practicing. Mr. Richardson had made several notes of reminders, including how he expected those who made it to spend that night practicing their dialogues with their partners, and the following day, immediately after school, they would perform their dialogues in front of everyone. He would post the final cast list on Monday morning.

When lunchtime arrived, Margot was eager to get back to the theater wing, but seemingly out of nowhere, Peter appeared.

"Hey, Margot."

He knows my name. Oh gosh. What do I say? What do I say?

"I just wanted to let you know that I thought you did a great job up there yesterday. Did you make the final set of callbacks?"

"Uh-huh."

"Well, I'll be there later to watch. I thought about auditioning, but it was definitely a long shot, so I didn't even bother. You're really good."

Peter Mulvaney is talking to me. He just stepped out of nowhere and appeared before me. It's like he was sent from heaven. He's talking to me.

"Well, I guess I'll go then." Peter seemed taken aback by Margot's lack of words. He smiled the most adorable smile Margot had ever seen and started to walk away.

"Oh, Peter!" Margot didn't know what had come over her. She had yelled out his name, yet she had nothing whatsoever on her mind to say. She was drawing a blank, and he was staring at her, waiting for her to speak.

"Thanks," she said, unsure of herself. Peter smiled again and continued to walk away. As soon as he was out of Margot's line of sight, her thoughts enveloped her.

Thanks! Thanks! What in the world was I thinking? He was actually talking to me. Talking to me, Margot friggin' Maples, and I, because I am so utterly and unbelievably stupid and dumb, said all but two words to him and probably had the stupidest, most ridiculous smirk on my face the whole time because he was standing there in front of me. I so blew my chance. So totally blew it. He must think I'm dumb or something since I can't form more than two darn words together.

Before Margot had a chance to continue her internal rambling, she realized that lunch was almost over, and she still needed to make her way to the theater bulletin board to see whom she had been partnered with for the dialogue.

When she got there, she scrolled her finger down the list, reading the names two by two.

Walter Gribble and Cassie Shearer

Joey Miller and Lisa Quinn

Mark Altman and Leslie Cooper

Margot could see the pattern. Boys and girls. Just another thing to make her cringe. She was not like the Cassie Shearers of the world, perfectly poised and ready to talk to boys. She thought about what had just happened with Peter. She was definitely not ready for this. After musing about how she couldn't believe that Joey had actually passed to this stage of the audition competition, she glanced down the list and continued reading. After noting several more pairs of names, she noticed a note at the very bottom of the page that read:

We seem to have an odd person.

Margot knew what Mr. Richardson meant here. There was an odd amount of people who received the second callback. It sure made it sound as though someone was a bit strange, though. Margot realized before continuing that it must be her rotten luck when her eyes made contact with the most astonishingly appalling seven words ever to be set in front of her:

Carolyn Dippet, Max Poler, and Margot Maples

She was at a loss for words. Of course she would have to be the very last person listed to make her the odd person. It was only a matter of time before that new nickname made the rounds. She couldn't get over her shock, especially about Max's name appearing there. He hadn't even auditioned.

Margot marched down to Mr. Richardson's office as fast as she could, braving the hordes of students who never knew that there were two sides to the hallway and the middle did not have to be taken up with their incessant chatter and overloaded baggage.

"I'm here to pick up my script," Margot stated in the most polite tone she could muster.

"Here you go." Mr. Richardson barely glanced up at Margot as he handed her a few stapled sheets.

"Oh, uh, Mr. Richardson? I have a question about this script." He made the same motion of his hand that he had when he gestured for her to begin her first audition, and she guessed that meant it was okay for her to continue.

"Well, out of curiosity, how did Max Poler end up in my group? I didn't even see him audition yesterday."

"That's right. You're in his group. Well, you see..." Margot braced herself for what was to come. She knew there was no feasible way to change her group or to get Max kicked out of the audition, but she had to ask. It was the only thing she knew to do in this instance.

"He asked me a couple days ago if it would be okay for him to audition immediately before the rest of you. He had an important family event that was going to keep him from the auditions, and I let him do it, based on the circumstances. Good thing, too. He's quite talented."

Margot looked defeated. She had let it all sink in, and she was stuck with the dreadful fact that she was not getting rid of Max so easily. Why was he so able to make people like him and think he was the nice, wonderful boy that he most certainly wasn't?

"Is there a problem?" Mr. Richardson looked up for the first time since Margot had set foot in his office, and looked genuinely interested in Margot's response.

"Oh, uh, you see, well..."

"Yes?"

"It's nothing. Nothing. Don't worry about it. I just didn't understand why there had to be three people in the group. I mean, I get that there was an odd number of people who made these final callbacks, but..."

"You're just getting nervous. Stop rambling and start practicing those lines. You really impressed me the last couple days. Otherwise you wouldn't be in here talking to me right now and picking up this script. Go to class and meet up with your group after school so you can practice. I'll see you tomorrow."

Margot walked out of his office quietly, but with an underlying wish to suddenly and inexplicably become defiant and demand that he switch her to another group. Not only was she with the inexcusably nasty Carolyn Dippet, but the nauseating thought of being stuck with Max made her insides turn inside out. She just had to get through this audition. She was not about to let Max ruin the one good thing that could potentially make this awful freshman year better.

TWENTY

Margot walked reluctantly back to her locker, picked up her books for her next class, and headed down the hall. She was dreading heading toward chemistry, but of course it was next on her schedule. Of course it was the only one all day that Margot had with both Carolyn *and* Max. She knew they must have already found out the casting match-ups for the dialogues. She didn't know how they were going to react, and she definitely did not want to find out.

As the bell rang, Margot crossed the door's threshold and took a seat. She slouched down, hoping to avoid the scrutiny of two of the biggest thorns in her side. Mr. Carlysle began lecturing, and Margot tried to become fully engrossed in the discussion of the periodic table. The only chemistry Margot really cared about at that moment was the lack of what she had with Carolyn and Max, so she found herself in dire hopes of a change of topic. When Mr. Carlysle segued into the states of matter, all that Margot could think about was how getting into this play mattered more to her than anything. She couldn't think of a better way of ruining her chances than pairing her with those two.

"Don't forget about the quiz tomorrow on the elements. Fifty points toward your final cardmarking grade," Mr. Carlysle yelled over the suddenly raised voices of twenty-five freshmen when the bell rang. Margot jolted upright, seemingly coming out of a daze, when Max approached.

"Here's the deal, *Margie*. Carolyn and I, we're making the play. No two ways about it. You up your game or life will be worse than you know it now."

Margot tried to consider how much worse it could get. She was already a Walter-lover, an inexcusable klutz, a Daddy's girl, and probably, in the eyes of many, a card-carrying member of the losers club. But there was one thing she couldn't deny – Max would find a way to make it worse. Ruining people's lives was his specialty, and nothing could stand in the way of what gave him the utmost pride and joy. Conceited was not quite enough to describe how highly he regarded himself.

"Did you hear me, Margie? Every time he used this nickname, which she hated, it sounded even worse than all the times before combined. If you ruin this for us, you might as well kiss high school goodbye. Transferring districts won't even save you from the humiliation you're going to feel."

Margot was torn. She desperately wanted to be in the play. If she pulled off the audition, the chances of Max and Carolyn pulling it off too were pretty high. Cassie was surely a shoe-in, having been in every play as far back as Margot could remember. Obviously high school was a different ball game, but experience was experience, and if elementary and middle school counted for anything, Cassie should certainly have high hopes. Walter would probably make it – after all, he had made both callbacks, and he had done just as well each time she'd heard him present his piece. She'd be stuck in the same unbearable circle all over again if she made this play. But it was all she ever wanted. How do you balance extreme and utter hatred for the majority of your castmates with your longing, desperate desire to do something you love? It was tearing her apart inside. Finally, Margot spoke up.

"Don't ruin it for me either, Max. I'm counting on this just as much as you."

"*Don't ruin it for me either, Max. I'm counting on this just as much as you,*" he repeated in a mocking tone. "Just don't screw it up, loser. Meet us in the theater hall right after school or we're leaving without you."

"Leaving for where?" Max didn't even take the time to hear Margot's question. He just walked away. Carolyn trailed behind, her nose high up in the air, but her eyes lingering on Max. She glanced at Margot quickly and sniffed her nose in her direction, but then went back to following Max like the lackey she was.

After two more classes, the end of the day couldn't have come sooner, which thoroughly depressed Margot. She would have rather stayed in study hall with the gum-popping, hair-twirling popular girls and the boys who were fawning over them than face her own fate.

She went to her locker and threw her books in, making sure not to lose her script in the process. After she had her backpack squared away, she meandered down the hall and turned reluctantly down the theater hallway. This wasn't how she pictured it. Reluctant was not the emotion she wanted to feel for what should be the most wonderful of days. She wanted to feel joy, but Mr. Richardson had squelched her chances of that by placing her with Max and Carolyn. The same Max and Carolyn who were nowhere to be seen in the hallway. It had only been five minutes since the bell rang. Margot knew that they couldn't have left already. Max hadn't even been at his locker when Margot arrived at hers. Luck of the draw – her locker had to be right near his. Then she saw them, exiting through the doors at the other end of the hallway and piling into the back seat of Mr. Poler's Range Rover. She wanted to scream and yell their names to wait for her. She quickly weighed the scales in her head, balancing the prospect of sheer humiliation for needing them to wait and realizing that she was better off without them. The fact that she saw them smile evilly as Mr. Poler drove off tipped the scales in favor of the latter.

Whatever. Don't let it bug you, Margot. They're not worth it. You don't need them. Oh god. But you do. You do need them. How can you have a conversation with two other people without the two other people? Should I run after them? How perfect would that look to Max? Margot Maples basically bowing at his feet to get into his father's car. No way. I'll just have to practice on my own. Yeah. That's what I'll do. They're not beating me. I can't let it happen. I'm going to memorize each and every line in that script and whenever there's a pause during the callback tomorrow, I'm going to jump in. They're not going to know what hit 'em. I'm confident. Confident, confident, confident.

However, Margot knew that no matter how many times she said the word, it didn't necessarily make it real. It was like wishing for a million dollars. Just because she wanted it and kept saying it didn't mean she'd ever get it.

TWENTY-ONE

"Margot! There's a call for you. From a boy!" Margot hoped against hope that her dad had put his hand over the receiver when he'd yelled that last part. He just sounded so skeptical, like there had seemingly been no chance of a boy ever calling, and this was the breakthrough Margot had been waiting so patiently for.

"Okay, Dad. Who is it?"

"A boy. Just pick it up," he said hurriedly, likely wanting to get back to reading his paper.

Margot wanted to say "duh," but knew her dad wouldn't pick up on her sarcasm, so she picked up her phone and yelled down to her dad to hang up.

"Why am I not surprised that I'm the first guy to ever call you?"

Max. She should have guessed he would call to make her life that much worse after they'd left her in the lurch after school.

"What do you want, Max? You got what you wanted."

"Angry much?" He was talking in a haunting tone. He knew just what to say and how to say it to make Margot's stomach churn and her whole body tense up. "I just wanted to make sure you realized we'd left without you."

"Yeah, I got it. If I can give you credit for being a jerk, you can give me credit for knowing that you are one."

"I think I hit a nerve." Margot could hear Carolyn snickering in the background as Max talked.

"Bye, Max. I don't need you anyway."

"Oh, I think you do. That's why you have no chance tomorrow, and Mr. Richardson will know why after we tell him you flaked on us and didn't show up for our group rehearsal."

"What?! You've got to be kidding me. I was there. You saw me through your dad's car window!"

"Carolyn and I waited patiently until 2:29 and then walked out the door. I said right after school, didn't I? And school lets out at 2:25, doesn't it?"

Margot was fuming. She had shown up at 2:30 and he knew it. He knew that she had to stop at her locker. He had obviously banked on that fact, and now he was using it against her.

"You can't... you can't..." Margot had begun to stutter. She was so lost for words and shaken up by Max's threat that she could barely get a hold of herself.

"Bye, Margie. Hope you enjoy the view from the bottom. We love looking down on you." With that, there was a click on the other end of the line. Margot was so angry. She hadn't even had the chance to hang up on the scumbag.

All of a sudden the phone rang again. Expecting full well that it was Max, she picked up the phone and slammed it down without even hearing his voice on the other end of the line.

"Margot, who was it?" Mr. Maples yelled upstairs over the sounds of gunshots echoing from the TV. Margot's dad was really into cop dramas. It was about the closest Margot figured that he would probably ever get to an action-packed life.

"Just a wrong number, Dad. Don't worry." Margot was trying to sound cool and not rattled, but she was everything but. Then the phone rang again.

"Listen, Max!" she started yelling before the phone was even next to her ear. "You're not going to get away with this! I'm going to..."

"Margot! Hey, Margot!" Margot calmed down for a split second, which was enough to hear the voice on the other end of the line and realize that it was not Max's. She was horrified. Despite wanting it to be anyone but Max or Walter, she secretly hoped that maybe it was Walter. At least she knew he wouldn't judge her for being so worked up over Max. He was too smitten with her to care.

"Margot, are you there? It's me, Peter."

Oh. Oh my god. Peter. Peter. I need to curl up in a ball and die right now. The last thing I wanted was to have Peter hear me scream. That's the last thing you want the boy you like to hear. You as an angry, irrational, stupid girl who doesn't know how to control her emotions. Maybe if I stay really quiet he'll think he has the wrong number. But he already heard me talk! Shoot! Well, you can't sink much deeper. Just talk to him. Go ahead. Talk. Why aren't you talking? This is too long a silence. It's awkward and awful and...

"Margot?"

"Yes?" Margot hiccupped into the phone.

"It's me, Peter," he repeated. Then, after Margot didn't respond right away, he added, "Peter Mulvaney."

Me. Peter. It's like he thought I should know his voice. I wonder if I called him and said, 'It's me, Margot,' if he'd think of me like I'm thinking of him right now. Probably not. Probably...Shoot! You're doing it again. Talk!

"Oh, hi Peter."

"Who were you yelling at?"

"Oh, no one."

"It sounded like you were pretty angry at Max. If it's Max Poler, I totally don't blame you. What did he do now? He's just such a dimwit sometimes. Trust me, I know."

"What do you mean, you know?"

"We used to be best friends. You knew that, didn't you?"

"Oh, I guess so. It's been so long that I guess I'd forgotten," Margot lied. If there was one thing she knew, it was Peter's life. Anything and everything Peter Mulvaney was one of the few social channels she subscribed to.

"Yeah, he was such a jerk to me starting in middle school, and then he met up with Cassie and they started going out. He's been a jerk ever since. Funny, because she seems really nice. I guess that's why they say opposites attract, huh? You want to talk about what he did to you? I'm a good listener."

Margot didn't know what to make of this. Peter had definitely not called out of the blue to swap Max horror stories. But he also had spent the last several seconds going on about Cassie Shearer, Margot's supposed polar opposite.

"I don't want to bother you. That isn't what you called about anyway. What's up?"

"Well, I wanted to know if you wanted to get together for that study date we talked about."

Study date! Oh my god! Oh my god!

"Remember, I thought we could talk more about *Gatsby* since I don't want to get behind on understanding the chapters, and before you know it, there'll be a quiz or test or something else. Walter told me about you two, so he can come along and study too if he wants."

Walter. Yet another pain in Margot's angst-filled life.

"Nothing's going on between me and Walter." The words had shot out of Margot as if nothing rang truer. She sounded so confident and sure of herself.

"Oh. Sorry. It's just that Walter..."

"I know what Walter said. He's mistaken."

"Oh, okay. Well, you and me then. How about sometime next week? Maybe Monday? I can come over to your house if that's easier for you."

Umm... oh gosh... I... say something!

"I'll have to ask my parents. Can I tell you tomorrow?"

"Sure. If your house doesn't work, my mom said you can come here. So, just let me know."

"Okay."

"Thanks, Margot. Hope it works out."

"Bye." As Margot hung up the phone, she turned into her over-analytical self and tore apart their conversation looking for clues as to how much Peter liked her.

A study date. He already asked his mom about whether I could come over. He called me. He was willing to talk to me about Max. So he wasn't in a rush to get off the phone. He might have just been trying to be nice. No. Why would he take the time to talk to me about something that's bothering me if he didn't like me? This is too good to be true. Something must be wrong here. But he called me! Me. Margot Maples. This is just too good...

The phone rang again. Walter. Margot realized that her too-good-to-be-true idea was quickly picking up steam.

TWENTY-TWO

"I heard what Max did to you today."

"What do you mean? How did you hear?"

Walter had a noticeable tinge of regret in his voice. He had told Margot outright when they got their partner assignments for the dialogue that he wished he had been placed with her.

"Hey, you want to join me and Cassie? We can practice twice. I'll go through the lines once with her and then with you. We can go back and forth like that so that you have a dialogue prepared. I can just do it for Mr. Richardson twice."

"Oh. Well, Walter, that's okay. I don't want to cause you any extra work or anything."

"Oh, no! I'd be happy to. Cassie's coming over in a few minutes, and I'm sure she won't mind."

"Cassie's coming to *your* house? You're not meeting at the library or something?"

"Are you kidding, Margot? You know we can't practice at the library. We've got to read lines and everything. I offered my house and she said okay. It'd be better if you came too, though. I'm sure she'll want to help you out."

Even though Margot and Cassie had shared a "heart-to-heart" in the bathroom that awful night at Benino's, Margot was not sure she was quite ready to be in a room with the one person who had it all (if you could call having Max a part of 'having it all'), and Walter, the person who thought he had it all after having accidentally kissed Margot.

"I'll think about it, Walter. Okay?"

"Margot. You've got to make the play! Mr. Richardson gave you a second callback. That's major! I can't do this play alone. I just can't."

Walter was sounding a bit too desperate for Margot's liking.

"Walter, did you listen to yourself at auditions? You hit it out of the park. You were great. You don't need me. Get it through your head that you actually have some talent." Margot didn't want to get his hopes up too high, but she wanted him to realize that he actually could be something without her. Maybe then, and only then, would he let up on his incessant admiration of anything Margot.

"Aw, thanks Margot. I guess I should maybe give myself more credit. After all, I got a second callback too. So, you coming over or not?"

Margot realized that her confidence-boosters were lost on Walter, as long as he had the potential opportunity to get Margot to his house. It didn't even seem to be registering with him that he was going to have the most popular, prettiest girl in the freshmen class in his house any minute now. That's when Margot heard a muffled dinging sound on the other end of the line.

"Oh, Margot, that must be Cassie. See you in a few, okay? I'll tell Cassie you're coming!"

"Walter, wait, no, I'm not..." She didn't want to admit defeat, but she knew that before she had even begun speaking, Walter had hung up the phone in his eagerness to open the door for Cassie and let her know that his "best girl" was coming over too. Okay, maybe he hadn't actually called her that on his own yet, but Mrs. Gribble was sure to wear off on him soon enough.

I hope Cassie doesn't mind. She seemed nice and all in the bathroom. I guess her life really isn't as perfect as she'd like, but so what if her parents aren't all smiles all the time? She's pretty and popular and talented. I have to call Walter and tell him I'm not coming. But then Cassie might think it's because of her. Who cares, anyway? I guess I do if I ever want even the slightest, most miniscule chance of gaining any type of popularity at all. Whatever. I'll go, I guess. I don't have partners anyway. Maybe Mr. Richardson will take into account that I was a team player. Or maybe he'll just think I left my group in the lurch to join a group I preferred. God, this sucks! I'm an awful decision maker. But if I ask my parents what to do, they're definitely going to say I should go to Walter's, and then they're going to say they'll have a talk with Max's parents because what he did was rude and inconsiderate. I guess Walter is the lesser of two evils. Whatever, I'll go.

Margot showed up at Walter's house twenty minutes later, questioning her decision to have ever left her house in the first place. Her parents had, as she had expected, balked at the idea that she practice the dialogue on her own when Walter was so generous as to welcome her into his group. She rang the doorbell only to have Mrs. Gribble open it within half a second. Margot was sure that she must have been spying through the window, waiting for Margot to arrive.

Mrs. Gribble began to speak at such a quick rate that Margot had to grin and bear it. There was no quick way out of talking to Mrs. Gribble. Anyone and everyone knew that.

"Oh, Margot, I'm so glad you're here! Walter and that Cassie are upstairs. She's pretty of course, but our Walter only has eyes for you. Oh, well you know that. Why don't you go upstairs and make sure they're sticking to business, if you know what I mean. We can't have anything coming between the two of you."

"There isn't anything going on between us. Just leave me alone already about it, okay? There is no *our Walter*. He's yours. Only yours. Just get it through your head already. What's it going to take?" Margot wished that those words had come out of her mouth. It would have saved her so much potential strife. Instead, she had to deal with Mrs. Gribble's incessant chatter over Margot and Walter's nonexistent relationship that was, in Mrs. Gribble's estimation, destined for eternal greatness. Instead, Margot said, "Oh, thanks Mrs. Gribble. I guess I'll go up."

Walter's house was a trilevel, so Margot walked up a few stairs, noting that just a couple doors down was the bathroom where she'd concocted her plan to get out of dinner the previous week, and was just outside Walter's room when the creaks in the floorboards gave her away. Before she knew it, Walter was rushing out of his room to welcome her.

"This way, Margot. Come on in."

95

"Thanks, Walter. I wouldn't have figured out to keep following your voices without your help." Margot didn't fear using sarcasm around Walter. It just didn't phase him. He was too busy being happy over her arrival.

"No problem. Cassie's in here. We just got started a few minutes ago."

Margot walked into Walter's bedroom. It was quite large, with a plain blue bedspread and off-white walls. There were a few small piles of clothes set off to the side by the laundry basket, which was almost overflowing. His computer monitor was set to a screensaver that kept flashing the time. Margot didn't like that part. It meant she had to be reminded just how long she had been not only in Walter's house, but his bedroom. She was surprised by just how very ordinary his room was. She half-expected Star Wars posters to line the walls and framed pictures of their kiss to be sitting on his nightstand and dresser. That "special" picture, however, was reserved for everyone to see, standing proudly on the mantelpiece, to what was obviously Mrs. Gribble's delight. She also figured that the night she'd seen his room last week had been a fluke based on how messy it was today. He was obviously an average teenage boy in terms of his not-so-tidy habits.

"Hey Margot. What's up?" Cassie seemed very nonchalant about Margot showing up. She didn't seem like she was in a rush to get the whole thing over with, but at the same time, she looked like she was eager to get started.

"Nothing much. How are you, Cassie?" Margot felt a bit strange. She knew it was weird and all talking to Cassie, but she didn't know how much Cassie knew about her being there instead of with Max and Carolyn. She must have seen Margot's name on the same line as Max's on the callback list. Why wasn't she asking what had happened? Margot had the scary thought that maybe, just maybe, Cassie was in on the whole thing too, and one way or another, Max had figured that he would ruin Margot's chances at the play. Margot realized she may have been jumping to conclusions when Cassie offered her a compliment.

"You did a really good job yesterday at auditions, Margot. I think you're a shoe-in for one of the lead roles."

Margot tried her best not to blush. Cassie Shearer, the most popular girl in the ninth grade, was impressed with her. Margot Maples. There had to be a "but" coming. She just knew it.

"But..." Margot was torn between happiness at being right and fear of Cassie's revelation about just what Margot might have done differently to ensure her the lead role. "But I know I just wasn't good enough at all. Mr. Richardson was just being nice when he put me on the callback list. There's no way I'll make it."

"You've got to be kidding, Cassie," Walter chimed in before Margot could respond. "You were great. You both were great. You know, we can sit here wondering if we were good enough, or we can get to be good enough by practicing some more. Whaddya say?"

"Yeah, Cassie. Walter's right." Margot immediately regretted the words as they sprung out of her mouth. Walter's gleeful smile was almost blinding as he stared in her direction.

"Well, you were really good," Cassie said to Margot. "That's why Max and Carolyn left you behind today. Don't tell them I told you this, but Max was scared you were going to take the main part from me. Carolyn says she's worried about me too, but I think she wants the lead role for herself a bit. Max is set on the two of us getting the lead roles. He says it'll be like we're Romeo and Juliet, even though we're doing *The Taming of the Shrew*. I told them what they did to you was wrong. I didn't even know they were going to do it."

"Whatever. No big deal. I'm here now, so it doesn't really matter anyway. As long as you don't mind me tagging along."

"Mind! We couldn't be happier to have you here!" Walter was too boisterous, like an eager puppy. Cassie sensed it too, and tried to calm him down a bit.

"Hey, Walter, can I have a glass of water? I hate a dry throat when I'm practicing lines." Cassie wasn't afraid around boys. You could tell. She did and said everything in such a laid-back, carefree way. Even though it was only Walter and not someone like Peter or any of the other cute boys in school, Margot envied Cassie's overall demeanor. She was just so cool and confident.

"Oh, sure Cassie. How about you, Margot?" Those same puppy-dog eyes landed on her, and she shook her head, hoping against hope that he'd leave the room as quickly as possible. Before he had the chance to swoon over her any more, he was gone. Surely he'd be back before anyone had the chance to check the time on his screensaver.

"Sorry again, Margot. Max can be a jerk sometimes. I definitely know it." Cassie tried to hide it, but a note of regret registered in her voice. She didn't seem completely happy with Max, or maybe Margot's ears were deceiving her. Margot concluded they must have been, because there was no way that anything could break up Max and Cassie. They were unbeatable together – or maybe she meant unbearable.

"Whatever. Let's just practice, okay? Which lines did Mr. Richardson give you guys to practice with?"

Cassie showed Margot the lines. Walter came back with the waters and they drank, whetting their palettes for their further adventures in dialogue. Walter ran down the hall when he realized Margot didn't have the same lines as them, and used the copy machine attached to his dad's printer to make her a fresh copy.

Mrs. Gribble knocked on Walter's door at least five times over the course of the two hours they were practicing. She kept saying things like, "Margot, are you cold? Walter can give you a sweater," or "Oh, Walter. You're just so great. I've always known you were a great actor. Margot really brings out the best in you. You two are sure to get the lead roles." The worst part of that one was that she said it when Walter was practicing with Cassie. Cassie was really good, too. Margot could tell that, despite Cassie's and Walter's positions on opposite ends of the popularity spectrum, they worked well together. They seemed like they could potentially win the roles of Katherina and Petruchio, or Kat and Patrick as Margot liked to think of them in the movie version of *10 Things I Hate About You,* a takeoff on *The Taming of the Shrew*. It was unsettling, really, for Margot to see Walter's acting ability. He really did have it in him, despite how much she hated hearing Mrs. Gribble's incessant reminders of that fact.

The kicker was when Mrs. Gribble came back and said, "Margot, dear, I talked to your mother just now and she said that it would be fine if you stayed for dinner." Margot hadn't asked to stay for dinner, so the look of shock that showed up on her face must have been very noticeable. There was no mention of Cassie from Mrs. Gribble and no words directed at her, except for Mrs. Gribble's polite, "Nice meeting you, dear," upon Cassie's departure.

Margot stayed for dinner, even though she had been tricked into it. She couldn't believe her mother would sell her out like that. How could she? However, she couldn't really blame her mom. Mrs. Gribble was a true enigma. You had to go along with her or you felt crappy. But when you did go along with her, you felt even crappier. One way or another, she gave you such a hard time about it that you had to feel exasperated. It had the capability of wearing you out rather quickly.

When she got home, she looked over the dialogue one last time and finished up her homework for the next day before lying in bed to think for a while.

Tonight was okay. Cassie's sure to get the lead role. She was nicer than I thought she'd be. I guess she really isn't that bad. I'll probably end up as one of her friends in the play who has all of three lines. I'm not cool enough to play Bianca. She was the cool one – Kat's sister – in the 10 Things *movie, and I know I'm not capable of that level of coolness. Maybe the freshmen play was a bad idea. If I get out now, no one can say anything bad about me. Max and Carolyn will say bad things no matter what, so there's no point in staying in it to spite them. But they obviously thought I was good enough, or else they wouldn't have left me. Well, that's what Cassie said anyway. I can't let Peter down, though. He told me I did a good job at auditions. No, he told me I was REALLY GOOD. Really good. I can't let him down. After all, we're going on a date Monday night. A date. A date! Ehhh, I forgot all about that! I have to worry about too much stuff! That's just like me, too. Getting all worked up over all this stuff and driving myself crazy. Why do I always do this to myself? I'm such a dummy! Well, I've practiced already, so I guess it can't hurt to try out. I've gotta ask mom about Peter coming over Monday. Oh god. I hope she says yes. Even if she doesn't, I guess I can go to his house. Peter thinks of everything. He's so great. And cute. And sweet. And wonderful. And cute. And... shoot! I'm rambling. To myself. That's not a good sign. I think I might be losing it. Just what I need. Okay, Margot. Relax. You're in this to win it. You've got a play to join and a study date. If things go right, maybe I won't just be studying* Gatsby *with Peter. Maybe I'll be studying him.*

Even as she heard those last few words inside her own head, she knew how absolutely ridiculous they sounded. Her chances of getting anywhere with Peter Mulvaney Monday night were just a dream that would surely never come true.

TWENTY-THREE

Even the hostile stares of Max and Carolyn weren't enough to bring Margot down on audition day. Margot's mother had told her that Peter was welcome to come over Monday night. Mrs. Maples seemed incredulous at the fact that he and Margot hadn't become friends sooner, mostly because Mrs. Maples seemed to have been very good friends with Peter's mother back in school. They had grown apart over the years. At least that's what Margot supposed since she couldn't recall hearing Mrs. Mulvaney's name mentioned. Mrs. Maples thought it would be a good idea to have Peter's parents over as well, but Margot nipped that in the bud, citing the idea that this was actually supposed to be for studying and not chit-chatting all night. Mrs. Maples didn't need to know that Margot's inner intentions were to have a little less conversation, a little more action with Peter. It was an absurd idea anyway to even think that anything like that would happen, but Margot just couldn't shake the thought out of her head. Ever since the previous day when she had laid in bed thinking about how she had forgotten to ask her mother about Peter, she was lost in a trance of potential possibilities for the way Monday night could go. The anticipation was utterly killing her, and when Mrs. Maples said that it was no problem for Peter to come over on Monday night, Margot almost leaped out of her skin out of sheer happiness before letting her mind recoil into worry and fear over what could potentially go wrong.

The elation Margot felt over Peter continued into the next day when she thought she might have aced her audition. Walter and Cassie did a great job together, Margot had to admit once again, and Walter did the audition a second time, as he had promised, in order to allow Margot the chance to show off her talent too.

Margot had gotten to school early that morning to tell Mr. Richardson that she had switched groups, and she hoped Mr. Richardson didn't mind. She told him that she was all for being a team player, but Max and Carolyn were never ones to be on her team in anything. They admittedly would do everything in their power to hinder her from getting a role, and she oh-so-badly wanted to be in this play. Mr. Richardson told her that it was okay this one time, but casting was casting, and if she did make the play, she would have to put up with whomever ended up playing opposite her.

"Oh, sure thing. Thanks so much, Mr. Richardson. I really appreciate it. I hope you like my performance." Margot jetted out of the room before he could give her any more of a lecture about being the bigger person or any other such nonsense.

Walter, Cassie, and Margot performed first, followed by Max and Carolyn, Joey Miller and Lisa, Mark Altman and Leslie Cooper, and the rest of the callback list. Margot couldn't believe that she would have to wait through more sleepless nights to find out the results. But her day continued to go well when she ran into Peter on the way out of school.

"Hey, Margot. How did callbacks go?"

"Oh, uh, fine. Thanks for asking." Margot was flustered. She was hoping to run into Peter. Actually, it was all she ever did hope for. But this time she had something to tell him.

"My mom said you can come over. If you still want to." Margot added a bit of up-talk to the end of her sentence. She didn't want to make it seem like he had to come. She wanted him to want to come. Even though he had been the one to suggest their "study date," she didn't want to make him feel as though he was obligated, but secretly she was overly concerned that he would find some way to back out of it.

"Great. Can't wait. *Gatsby*'s going to be a piece of cake once we're through with it."

"Oh, and she said you can come for dinner too if you want, but I'm sure that you're..."

"Sounds good. My mom has a pretty routine schedule for what she makes each day. It'd be nice to have a change."

Margot couldn't believe her ears. Not only was Peter accepting the invitation that he himself had originally made to come to her house, but he was adding more time to it by saying yes to her mom's dinner offer. This had to mean something.

"So, what time should I come?"

Throwing her nerve into high gear, Margot said, "I thought maybe you could just take the bus with me after school that day. That'll give us the most time before dinner to get started on studying. How does that sound?"

"I've gotta check with my parents. Can I call you later about it? My mom has me running some errands today, so not sure what time I'll get back. My parents are still stuck in the Jurassic age and haven't gotten me a cell phone yet, so I have to wait till I'm home to ever talk to anyone anyway. You'd think they'd get that I'm in high school now and a phone would actually come in handy." Margot marveled at the fact that she again was not the only person in the world with parental distress – and no cell phone.

He's going to call me. Me. He agreed to dinner. He didn't try to back out of studying. What could this all mean? And why am I talking to myself? He's standing right here in front of me! I keep doing this to him. Sooner or later he's going to think I'm a real ditz. I've got to stop. Only talk to yourself when you have free time, Margot! Peter Mulvaney is standing directly in front of you trying to have a conversation and you're talking to yourself. AAHHH! Stop it! Go back to Peter!

"Sure, uh, yeah. Sounds good. Just let me know later."

With that, Peter said goodbye, and Margot rushed home to wait by the phone. At least it took away from having to think about auditions for part of the night.

Two hours later, Peter had yet to call, and Margot was starving for dinner. She decided that it would be okay to sit down with her parents to eat. Her mom had called to her three times while making dinner to tell Margot what time to come down for the meal. Margot was just fearful that the exact moment she sat down with her parents was when the phone would ring. Margot's dad would most certainly want to answer it and would undoubtedly say something unflattering or embarrassing. But Margot realized that the phone was the least of her worries. Even though she was excited about Peter coming to her house, she knew that it would provide her parents with the perfect excuse to become even more "parental" than they already were. They knew just what to say and how to say it in such a way that Margot would suffer from inner torment the whole night long. Plus, they would have to sit through dinner where Margot knew her father was bound to ask ridiculous questions, like what Peter wanted to do when he grew up. She had to be sure to remember to tell her father to take it easy on Peter. She didn't want to scare him off.

Luckily, Margot survived through a physically calm, yet mentally unnerving meal before rushing back upstairs, citing the extra homework that she had and her nerves over auditions for her quick exit. Shortly after returning to her room, the phone rang.

"Hey, Margot. My mom didn't want me to use the phone until everyone finished dinner. And my little brother knows how to take his sweet time, asking for seconds and thirds. He can be really annoying."

He doesn't sound upset about talking to me in the least. I shouldn't have worried so much about him calling. I can't keep doing this to myself. He obviously likes me enough to take the time to call. He could have just as easily blown me off.

"Oh, no problem. I didn't even realize the time." Margot didn't want to let on that she had been waiting desperately all night for the call.

"So, Monday still good?"

"Yeah. For you?" As soon as she said it, she realized that it was a stupid question. Of course it was okay for him if he was asking if it was okay for her. *Duh, Margot!*

"Yeah. Can I still catch the bus with you?"

"Sure." It was then that Margot heard a dog barking in the background. "Is that your dog?" Margot didn't want to sound too pleased, but she was happy to know they both might have a dog, which would give them something in common.

"Yeah, his name's Buddy. He's a golden retriever."

"We have a German Shepherd."

"Cool. What's his name?"

"It's a her. And it's Roxie. She's a lot of fun."

"I love messing around with Buddy. He loves it when I chase him around the house. Sometimes he stops short and looks back to see if I'm still following him. I think he could run around like that all day long. Whenever I sit down to rest after chasing him, he stares at me like I'm the biggest wimp ever."

"Roxie's a lot like that, too. She chases squirrels and rabbits around the backyard for hours at a time. Sometimes we have to go pull on her chain to get her to come back in the house. I swear she could live outside if we let her. She already has a food bowl and water container out there. All she needs is a doghouse and she's set."

"She sounds like fun. Can't wait to meet her."

And she can't wait to meet you. Why are you so perfect? We have such an easy time talking to one another. It's just so, what are the words I'm looking for? Meant to be. Meant to be like Romeo and Juliet. Well, maybe not like them, because they had to die for their love, but like some other famous couple in history that loved without loss and shared common interests. Is there even anyone with so perfect a life? I don't know. But if there isn't, I'm going to buck the trend and make my life that perfect. I just have to. I owe it to myself to have something good happen!

"Should we go over anything besides *Gatsby,* you think?" Peter segued.

"Ummm, not sure. Let's think about if we need to and you can bring stuff with you if you want. We'll see how much time we have."

"Works for me. Which bus are you on again?" Peter questioned.

"Route 23."

"Wanna just meet in front of it after school?"

"Okay."

"By the way, good luck Monday," Peter added.

"With what?" Margot asked uncertainly.

"The play."

"Oh, yeah, thanks! I thought I'd forgotten a quiz or something. I've been practicing for auditions for so long, but my nerves are still going crazy waiting."

"I'm sure you did great. Don't worry." Even though Margot knew that Peter's words could never change her overwhelming nervousness, they still made her feel good inside. "You totally deserve a part," he continued. Margot felt herself blush internally and her lips curved into a smile.

"Thanks, Peter."

It feels so good to say his name.

"Nerves can be totally annoying. I'm totally an impatient person. I guess we have that in common."

We. We. We. It's my favorite pronoun. It stands for me and Peter!

"Yeah, waiting sucks. My anxiety usually is over-the-top." She paused for a second, and when Peter didn't say anything, she continued, "I should probably go. But have a good weekend, k?"

"Yeah, you too, Margot. Talk to ya later."

Margot wished she could savor the tenor of Peter's voice for a while longer, but she felt like she would eventually say something wrong, so she got off the phone and fell back on her pillow, contemplating the sheer happiness that she felt over Peter's use of "we," how he said "talk to ya later," and how he asked if it was okay to spend an even longer amount of time with her. What had started off as an after-dinner study date had turned into dinner and a study date, which had turned into an after-school, dinner, and study date triple header. Margot was in such a good mood at this point that the thought of the play, even though Peter had mentioned it, was not foremost in her mind. All she could think about was – yep, not hard to guess – Peter.

TWENTY-FOUR

Margot couldn't believe it. Not only did she have her triple header evening ahead of her, but she had made the play. As understudy for the lead role! It didn't even phase her that Max had gotten the lead male role. Even though she knew he didn't deserve it, she was so caught up in the greatness of her achievement that she let everything else slip her mind for the time being. She could dwell in disappointment at a later date. This was the time for celebration. She kept thinking back to Peter's comment, when he said, "talk to ya later." She couldn't wait and could hardly contain her excitement as she thought about spending time discussing her success with the boy she liked most.

The bubble popped when Walter approached Margot, just as thrilled with his casting as understudy to Max as Margot was with her understudy role to Cassie's lead.

"Margot! Did you hear? We're the understudies. I can't even believe it. I totally didn't think I was even that good." Walter's modesty was becoming overly irksome to Margot. He was good and he had to know it. She had told him herself. She wanted to believe that it was just an issue of poor self-esteem that was holding him back from believing how good he was, but his self-esteem seemed to shoot up whenever Margot was around, so she wasn't so sure. Nevertheless, she played into Walter's happiness because she wanted to keep her high going for as long as possible. Especially through the night so that she and Peter could discuss her new role in the play.

"Yeah, I heard, Walter. Congratulations."

"You too! This is just so exciting. We get to practice together and everything. Since Mr. Richardson posted on the casting sheet that the first read-through will be Wednesday after school, I thought we could get together today or tomorrow and go over the play. How about tonight?"

"Oh. Well, tonight doesn't work for me."

"Why? What could you be doing that's more important than this? Shakespeare said, 'the play's the thing' and now it's our thing together! We've got to practice in case Cassie or Max gets sick or has stage fright or something. I mean, we have to be prepared."

Walter's over-excited nature was becoming a nuisance yet again. Margot felt she had to speak up.

"Walter, listen to me. I think we can wait till the read-through on Wednesday to start practicing. We'll have enough time after that to work together." Margot worried that this response had inadvertently caused Walter to think that they could spend all of their free time after Wednesday together to practice the play. However, before she had the chance to rephrase what she had said, Walter chimed in.

"You know there's a chess club meeting after school today, right? I'm so happy we decided to do the club together. I'll see you there, right?"

Margot was thinking of so many things she wanted to say to Walter right then and there to get him off her back. She couldn't say those things to his face, though. Not only would she have to deal with the guilt she would undoubtedly have over her words, but word would no doubt get back to Mrs. Gribble who would in turn talk to Margot's mom, who would certainly turn on Margot for her lack of etiquette. It didn't stop her from thinking those thoughts, however.

First of all, I didn't join the chess club! You added my name to the roster and gave me a position without any say on my part! And anyway, I can't go. I have a study date with Peter. Yep. That's right. A date. And Peter and I talked on the phone last night about the play and our dogs and stuff. So get it through your head. I like Peter! Just leave me alone already.

What came out of Margot's mouth was entirely different, though. "I can't go to chess club today, Walter. I have plans after school."

"But... but... the meeting..." Walter's stuttering did not serve to make him any less annoying.

"I didn't even know about it till just now when you told me."

"It was on the announcements last week."

"I must have missed it. Sorry, Walter. Gotta go to class. Congrats on being understudy. See you tomorrow."

As Margot walked away, she saw a look of devastation on Walter's face. She couldn't believe that her absence from a chess club meeting that she didn't even join on her own could warrant that much of a reaction from Walter. She figured she had saved him even more strife by not mentioning her date. He would probably take that as a full-frontal attack on their alleged relationship.

The remainder of the day was mostly uneventful, except for a person every now and then who would wish Margot congratulations over her casting feat. She couldn't decide whether each person was truly happy for her or if they would have been the kind to gloat if they had been cast in the role instead. Still, she sucked it up and made it through the majority of the day with a smile on her face.

Things might finally be turning around. My mom always said, "When it rains, it pours." I think she was talking about when boys would start to like me. I really found that hard to believe, especially because no boys ever like me. But Peter likes me. Maybe. At least a little. Right? Stop questioning yourself. He has to like you at least a little bit if he wants to come over. And early, too. Not just the required study time. Dinner and before dinner too. That's gotta mean something. It has to. And now the play. I don't think I'm popular yet, but maybe I'm getting there. Maybe.

"Daydreaming, Margie? You must think you're cool or something now that you're Cassie's understudy. Don't get too comfortable, all right? Mr. Richardson must have been out of his mind casting you for that role. Or maybe he knew just what he was doing. Making you second best. I always thought of you as third or fourth best, or even lower on the list than that, but I guess as long as you're not first, everything is right with the world. You better stop daydreaming if you want a shot at keeping that role of yours. I hear you're already on thin ice."

"What are you talking about, Max?"

"From what I hear, you told Mr. Richardson that Carolyn and I stood you up. Well, you see that that didn't keep me from getting the lead role, did it? But you, you're just an understudy. A nobody. A wannabe." The wannabe part struck Margot as particularly hurtful. She knew all too well that she *was* kind of a wannabe. She wanted to be popular and liked, but she did not, under any circumstances, want Max to know how much she really, truly wanted that status. That would be social suicide – that is if she had a social life to throw away in the first place.

"Whatever, Max. Just leave me alone and be happy for yourself. That's what you do best anyway."

"Ooh, good comeback." Max's sarcasm was not lost on Margot. She only wished Walter would pick up her sarcasm like she could pick up Max's. Yet, she didn't really wish the kind of hurt that Max inflicted on her on anyone else – not even Walter.

As Max walked away, Margot knew he was inwardly gloating to himself about his effect on her. She did not want to let him get to her today, though. All that she needed was to be in a bad mood when she met Peter by the bus after school. It would be no way to spend their first date, if you could even call it that. Margot was beginning to doubt that anything in her life could go just right without some outside force having to do everything in its power to spoil it for her.

Why can't life just go my way for once? One time. That's all I ask. Today was supposed to be great. And I'm going to make sure it stays that way. Don't let Max get to you!

No matter how many times Margot ran that last phrase through her mind, she knew better than anyone that it was next to impossible. Max was a leech who did everything possible to ingratiate himself into the lives of those he felt superior to. Margot's mom had taken a psychology class a few years prior and had told Margot that people who demeaned others just to feel better about themselves were typically cowards. She said that her psychology teacher had said that they only felt the need to hurt others because they didn't feel confident enough about themselves. Margot doubted that Max lacked any kind of confidence. He was overly certain of himself, and Margot knew that he truly believed he was better than her. There was no lack of self-assurance on his part. Of that, Margot was even able to be confident. It was one of the few things in life that she felt strongly about.

As the last class of the day began to wind down, Margot was getting more and more excited for her after school meet-up with Peter. Before class was over, she asked the substitute teacher for a pass to the bathroom. She wanted to be sure her hair wasn't mussed up, and that her lip gloss was on ever so slightly, but not quite enough that Max or anyone else would be able to say anything snotty to her if they were to see it. Feeling okay enough with her appearance, she left the bathroom and made her way back to the classroom before the bell rang.

Well, I guess I look okay. There's not much more I can do. I wonder if I should wear my hair behind my ears or not. Oh gosh. The bell's going to ring and I have to decide. I guess it looked okay in the mirror pulled behind my ears. But sometimes it looks better the other way. Eh, what does it matter anyway? If he likes me, he likes me, right? No! That's not right. I have to look good. Cassie always looks good. Any boy in his right mind would notice her. Well, except Walter. Oh, stop it! Don't think about Walter at a time like this! I'll never look as good as Cassie. This is as good as it gets. Well, there's the bell. Here goes nothing.

TWENTY-FIVE

Margot walked as fast as she could, through the hordes of anxious students who wanted to make their escape as quickly as possible from what they considered to be yet another long, exhausting day in their never-ending school lives. She fumbled with the combination on her lock before finally getting it to open after not one, not two, but three failed attempts. It seemed that just because she was in a rush to get outside and meet Peter that people had to find reason to allow their backpacks to swing aimlessly, causing her to stumble over, which in turn caused her to have to repeat the combination until she finally got it right. The sound of the lock snapping open was music to her ears, but the sound that followed it was what Margot considered to be the beginnings of a headache.

"You're sure we can't meet today after school, Margot? I was really looking forward to starting to practice."

"Walter, you just found out you got the part today. How long have you been looking forward to this?"

"Well, since this morning." Walter looked humbled. He had a look on his face that Margot knew too well. She used it quite often to get her way with her parents. She was not going to fall victim to it. Especially today, of all days.

"I've really gotta go, okay? I'll see you tomorrow. We'll have plenty of time to practice. See ya!"

"What about tomorrow then?" If nothing else, she had to give him points for persistence.

"I have a lot of stuff to do around the house tomorrow. I promised my parents. Wednesday will be here before you know it and we'll have the read-through, okay? Really gotta go! Bye!" She rushed off before he had the opportunity to bombard her with another request. She didn't know why she was trying to calm his nerves. She determined that it must be because she was happy for him and didn't want to squash his joy in the moment he had been cast as understudy, probably the most prestigious role he had ever earned in his life.

At the same time, though, Margot knew that she had hurt Walter's feelings. Numerous times today, in fact. But she sucked up the guilt she knew would be boiling up inside her, and she picked up her pace.

There he was. Peter. He looked so cute. Margot was a bit surprised to see him there. In the back of her mind, she wondered if it was all a dream she'd had, or a ruse made up by her nemesis, Max, to make her feel like a total nincompoop. But he was really there. Waiting for her and no one else.

She smiled widely and approached him.

"I thought you might not come," Peter said in what Margot considered the cutest "I knew you would, but I'm trying to be funny" kind of way.

"Well, here I am." Margot felt more confident than usual, but that didn't keep her from starting to let the butterflies back in. She knew she had to keep her willpower up if she wanted to seem calm, cool, and collected. "We better get on. Rick gets annoyed if people wait outside the bus too long."

Did I just say 'Rick'? How can it possibly look that I'm on a first-name basis with the bus driver? I am a complete and total doofus.

"No problem. It looks like most of the busses are filling up fast anyway. Before you know it, we'll be the only ones left outside."

That's not a big deal to me. I'd love to be alone with you anywhere. At least you didn't catch my stupid mistake. Just don't make any more. Pull yourself together and just be happy that you're with him. It's like your dream come true. Don't screw it up!

As the bus pulled away from the curb, Margot saw Walter through the double doors at the end of the hallway where her bus was standing. He had a slight grin on his face, like something had gone his way. She found herself wondering what that something was, but forced herself to not think about it. Any time she spent thinking about Walter was time lost thinking about Peter. She saw Bobby Bishop approach him, probably so they could walk to the chess club meeting together. Before she had a chance to be seen staring at them, she turned to Peter, whom she found to be sitting right next to her.

"I know I was across the aisle, but it looked like you were looking at something interesting out the window, and I just wanted to see what it was. What were you looking at?"

Margot was more than flustered. Peter was sitting so close that his boyish smell was lingering in her nose. It was the most heavenly scent she had ever had the privilege of smelling. Before she could be more taken in by it, she said, "Oh, it was nothing, really. Sometimes I just stare off into the distance."

Sometimes I just stare off into the distance?! What the heck are you saying? Great, Margot. Really fantastic. What the heck is wrong with you?!

"Yeah, I know what you mean. After a long day, I sometimes like to relax a little too."

I can do no wrong by him. He ignores my 'Rick the bus driver comment, and he's not annoyed that I seemed uninterested in him while I was staring out the window. And he said we'll be together for a while tonight. I know, I know. Of course we'll be together because we're eating dinner and studying, but when it came out of his mouth, it was like time stood still in that moment.

Margot and Peter spent the next ten minutes until their bus stop sitting quietly, once in a while turning to smile timidly at one another. Some boys in the back were creating farts under their armpits (seniors, no less – no wonder they were still riding the bus at eighteen), and a few sophomore girls were giggling incessantly over some note that they were passing back and forth.

When the bus came to a stop, Margot, Peter, and a few others straggled down the aisleway and made their way onto the street. Margot's house was a block down, so she and Peter began to walk.

When they got to the house, Margot couldn't wait to get inside. She and Peter would be alone. It would only be for a short hour until her mom got home, but she still was over anxious. Her hopes deflated when she opened up the front door and Roxie's leash wasn't hanging on its chain. Either Roxie had been dog-napped and everything else in the house had been left intact, or one of Margot's parents was home, since they were most certainly destined to be yet another inhibiting factor in the never-to-be romance that was Margot and Peter.

Sure enough, five minutes later, Roxie came bounding through the front door, down the hall and into the kitchen where Margot and Peter sat, eating some freshly baked cookies that Margot figured her mother must have come home early to bake and set on the table. They were good – Margot couldn't deny that – but they were not supposed to be there. Just like Margot's mom wasn't supposed to be there, and their day wasn't supposed to turn out like this. As she tried to suck it up, Mrs. Maples launched into a full-on question and answer session with Peter.

"How's your mom? Gosh, it's been years since I've seen her. It's amazing, isn't it? We live in the same city, our kids go to the same school, and we haven't run into each other. Is she on the PTA?"

Moooom! Only elementary school parents do the PTA anymore! You're making me out to be even more of a geek than Peter probably already thinks I am. Just be quiet. Please??!!

"Um, well, she does do the PTA, but for my brother's school. He's at Perry Middle School."

"Oh, of course. Of course! It makes sense that she'd stay on the same PTA committee, since you went there and your brother started. When did he start there?"

"This year. He's three years younger than me."

"Nice. Well, we must make sure to get together sometime. Tell her I said hello and that I'm looking forward to getting to see her again."

"Sure thing. So, Mrs. Maples, what's for dinner tonight?"

"Well, Peter, that's a good question. I've been going back and forth all day. Chicken or fish. Fish or chicken. It's the never-ending conundrum, isn't it? Well, I think I decided on chicken breast with baked potatoes and a steamed vegetable. Does that sound okay?"

Mom, I can't believe you said 'breast'!

"Yeah, really good. Thanks again for having me."

"No problem. Margot never brings a boy home, so this is a special treat."

Oh...my...god. I think I just died a little.

At that point, Margot knew that the evening was lost. Her parents were going to steer the evening in the wrong direction. No doubt when her dad came home he would just pick up where her mom left off, leaving no embarrassing stone unturned.

Margot still tried her utmost to change the subject, telling Peter that they should really get to studying before dinner so they'd have at least some of their work done before eating. However, before Margot could get Peter up the stairs to her room (where she was hoping they would do their "studying"), her mom had the brilliant idea that they should make use of the new patio furniture.

"It's just sitting there, and we might as well use it, or else what was the point in buying it?" She had repeated this numerous times over the last few months since they had bought it at the beginning of the summer, and Margot knew that there was no deterring her mom from pushing something when she had it on her mind. So they ended up sitting right outside the kitchen window, in full view of Margot's mom as she cleaned potatoes next to the kitchen sink. It was like a nightmare come true. This was the worst possible turn of events for an afternoon that Margot thought would be the beginning of something great with Peter. Something great *without* parental supervision.

But then Margot's mom pulled the screen door open and stuck her head out.

"I forgot the vegetable. Can you believe it? I have to run down the street to the market. I'll be back in a few. Will you kids be okay without me?"

"Mom, I think we'll be fine. We're in high school after all." Margot's tone had an obvious note of aggravation in it. She was trying to show her mother how annoyed she was with her. However, her mother was not picking up on Margot's disappointment in her early arrival and insistence on keeping a close eye on them.

"All right then. Back soon."

When Margot heard the garage door close, she jumped at the chance to ask Peter if he'd rather move inside. The weather outside was fairly nice, but the sun was beating down, and despite having all this nice, new patio furniture that Margot's mother made sure got its proper usage, there was no umbrella to shield them from the sun's rays.

"I really don't mind it out here, but if you'd rather go inside, we can. I'm good either way."

"I think we should go inside. The sun's a little hot, don't you think?"

"I guess. Okay, let's move then." Peter was indifferent to the issue, but he didn't seem annoyed in the least about moving, so Margot made quick work of it. Before she knew it, they were sitting side by side on the living room couch, instead of across from one another at the circular patio table. When Peter's shoulder brushed up against Margot's as he started to reposition himself, she felt a tingle run through her from head to toe.

"Sorry about that," Peter said apologetically.

"It's okay. So, do you understand more about *Gatsby* now?"

"Yeah. It really is like a soap opera. I know you said so, but I didn't know how a writer from the early half of this century would even know anything about soap operas. I mean... well, you know. Obviously there weren't soap operas in the twenties, but he really knew how to stir up trouble and write about romance. I wonder if he had a girlfriend or anything."

"Actually, his wife's name was Zelda."

"Oh, he was married. Well, I guess he must have known a thing or two about romance then. That probably helped him out a lot when he was writing."

"Yeah. I'm sure it did. Well..."

"Uh, Margot, I had something I wanted to ask you. You see, the homecoming dance is coming up, and I..."

Just then, with impeccably awful timing, Margot heard the garage door leading into the family room fly open, and Margot's mom called out for help. Apparently Roxie was trying to make a break for it. She had one paw in the door and the other out, and nothing any of the three of them did was making her walk away from that door. The neighbors' Shih Tzu was yip-yipping across the street, and Roxie wanted to play.

After that, the moment was gone. Peter seemed to have either lost his nerve or completely lost interest in asking his question about the homecoming dance.

Is he really going to ask me out? No way. No friggin' way! Don't count your chickens, though. Take a deep breath and think about this. The freshmen class is responsible for decorations. Maybe he joined the committee and he wants some help hanging crepe paper or something like that. Shoot! That's probably it. Just my luck. I actually find a boy I like who mentions the homecoming dance to me and he doesn't even want to ask me. I'm such a loser. But I don't know for sure yet. There has to be a way to get him to talk about it again. Darn my mom and her stupid timing. I swear she takes tips from my dad on how to perfect all those annoying tendencies that bother me so much!

"Kids, if you don't mind, I actually could use some help setting the table. Once it's set, you can go back to studying, but it might as well be done so we can eat when your dad gets home, Margot. I'd really appreciate it." Even though Margot's mom had ruined the question-asking moment, Margot obliged and began handing Peter plates. Once the table was all set up, fancy napkins and all, Margot asked her mom if it was okay that they get back to studying. When Margot's mom looked outside and started to beckon them that way, Margot told her they had set their stuff up in the living room and would be working in there. Mrs. Maples looked a bit upset that her prized patio furniture was missing out on some prime use, but she made peace with the idea with a reluctant "okay."

The next hour or so passed by pretty quickly. All talk was on *Gatsby*. Peter seemed like he had something he wanted to say, but every time it seemed he was about to say it, Mrs. Maples stuck her head around the corner and asked if they were okay. Even though he was being as nice as possible to her mom, she wished he'd look annoyed, too, and that way he could begin to feel comfortable talking to Margot as though her mother wasn't even there.

Dinner actually went smoother than Margot thought. Her dad seemed to have had a rough day at work, so he wasn't much for conversation. He asked a few questions here and there so as not to make Peter feel unwelcome, but the questions were more about what Peter thought the weekend weather would turn out to be, and if he knew if any sports games were on that night. Margot was flabbergasted. She knew her father would inevitably regret having had his shot to pin down each and every answer to each and every question imaginable that he could have asked Peter, but she didn't push the issue.

At about eight o'clock, Mrs. Maples came into the living room.

"Peter, I better be getting you home. You did say you would need a ride, right?"

"Oh, um, sure. I guess I did say that when you asked me at dinner. But I can walk. You don't have to take me."

"It's no problem. Besides, I can't let you walk home when it's getting dark out so early now."

"Really, Mrs. Maples. It's only about eight blocks down and three streets over."

"That's too long and you know it. Pack up your stuff. I'll wait in the kitchen."

"Okay. Thanks a lot. But you really don't have to."

Mrs. Maples exited to the kitchen and Peter began to say goodbye to Margot.

"I wanted to ask you something, but can I call you tomorrow? Your mom's ready and I don't want to keep her waiting. Honestly, my mom probably wants me home already anyway."

"Sure. Call me tomorrow." The words rolled off Margot's tongue and made her feel that same tingle run through her once again.

"Okay. I will. Congrats again on the play, Margot. And thanks for all the *Gatsby* help. I know I'm ready for that test next week. I might have a few extra questions, but I'll be talking to you."

With that, they said goodbye, and Margot watched through the slits in the living room drapes until her mom and Peter were out of sight. Yet another night of prolonged waiting and hoping was on the horizon for Margot. This anxiety was not good for her. She was sure she would never get used to it, either.

TWENTY-SIX

These last couple weeks have gone by in a haze. Play practice followed by Walter's insistence that we practice some more followed by some more play practice. But here's the best part. My best friend Ashley is coming to visit. She says that since the freshmen play is being put on during a week she has off from school, she can come to see it. She knows I may not have a chance to actually be on stage or anything, but she wants to come anyway! I'm just so excited. She's the only thing that kept me sane through most of middle school. Maybe with her here, I'll be able to calm down and relax a little more. A lot more would be even better.

It's too bad she can't make it to the homecoming dance too. You know, I thought Peter would ask me to it. I was just so sure of myself. I guess that's what I get when I actually think I have a shot. Shot down. Ironic, huh? Well, I guess I wasn't really shot down by Peter. I didn't ask him and he didn't ask me. What he did want to ask me was if I could help him out by telling him what girls like and figuring out what one particular girl likes – Cassie Shearer. The one thing standing in my way of getting to Peter. Okay, okay, don't get all high and mighty on me. I'm not so stupid that I don't realize my chances with him are pretty slim. He obviously only likes me as a study partner. But he probably wouldn't have asked my advice on girls if he didn't see me as one. What am I saying? Duh! Of course he knows I'm a girl. Any idiot could tell that, at the very least. But he thinks I know what I'm talking about when it comes to girls. That must count for something.

Whoa, Margot, don't get your hopes up again. He just wants your help impressing a girl he has no chance with, but who would certainly be lucky to have him. She's not all bad, I guess. She did talk to me in the bathroom that one night at Benino's and didn't tell her aggravating lackeys that I was in there failing to regain my composure. She even tried to make me feel better by telling me about her parents. I shouldn't be so selfish about Peter. The thing is, though, that Peter doesn't seem to be too fazed by the fact that Cassie is dating Max. Max Poler. The bane of my existence. The lowest of the low. And, let's not forget – Peter's old best friend. Maybe Peter's just good at hiding how he feels, like I'm doing keeping how much I like him a secret.

How they were ever friends in the first place is just beyond my comprehension. Max is such a dimwitted pest, and Peter is... well, he's Peter. Sweet, kind, wonderful Peter. Except he isn't proving to be too smart himself. What does it take to get him to notice me? One minute he seems like he likes me and the next he doesn't. Maybe I'm just looking too far into it all and he has always just liked me as a friend. Why else would he ask me for help with Cassie? He could just ask me out.

I'll just be positive. Ashley will be here before I know it, and the homecoming dance is next weekend, so I get to spend the next few nights with Peter. That's really why I couldn't say no to him in the first place. He looked so cute asking me for help and telling me he wanted to go over how to best talk to girls and how he could find an opening to talk to Cassie without Max around when we get to the dance. I would've been a fool to say no to night after night alone with Peter, talking. It's weird, though, that he says he has a hard time talking to girls. He doesn't have a hard time talking to me.

TWENTY-SEVEN

The night of the homecoming dance arrived, and Margot had made sure to dress herself up to be the absolute prettiest she could be. Whereas it took most girls, especially those like Carolyn and Lisa, hours on end to hone their look of perfection, Margot had spent the majority of time on her hair, only putting on a dab of blush and a reserved amount of lipstick, noting her mother's past instructions about makeup. *It's better to look like you're not wearing any at all*, she would say. This had never made sense to Margot, as she didn't understand the purpose of putting any on if it looked like she wasn't wearing any, but she still took her mother's advice to heart and was quite pleased with the results.

To her delight, even though she and Peter were not going on a date, Peter had said that he would pick Margot up to go to the dance. She could hardly contain herself, but she tried her utmost to do so as she didn't want her father getting all defensive and upset. His only daughter, the one who had been kissed a mere few weeks ago, was going out on a date with a *different* boy than the one who had kissed her. This would have been too much for him, so she had told him that it was a group of them going together and Peter's mom was driving everyone. It was a little white lie, but it was protecting her father from unnecessary upset, and it was protecting her from the results of that upset.

Little did she know that her fictional group was about to become real.

Next thing she knew, the doorbell rang and she almost skipped down the stairs, so happy that Peter would be standing on the other side of the door, surely looking super dapper in his suit and tie. With a smile etched on her face, she opened the door, only to find none other than the notoriously unflinching in his attempts, yet non-comprehending in the results, Walter.

"Walter, *what* are you doing here?" Margot asked as kindly as she could as the smile disintegrated from her face.

"Taking you to the dance, of course," Walter said as he entered the vestibule and smiled at her.

"What? I never said I was going with you."

"Yeah, you did. Last week I asked you in the hall on our way out the doors to the busses. You said 'sure,' remember? Well, when I got home that night, I went shopping for this new suit. My mom's waiting in the car to take us. Are you ready?"

Margot reflected back on the last week. She couldn't believe that she would have said 'sure' to Walter's proposal to go to the dance together. And now Mrs. Gribble was outside waiting for them? This was too much. Too much to process. Too much to deal with. And Peter. Peter would be here any...

Ding dong!

"Oh. That's probably my mom wondering what's taking us so long. She wanted to take pictures, but I told her to wait in the car and she could take them when we get to school. It'll be better there, anyway, with all the homecoming decorations and everything. I'll get it."

Walter went to open the door. Margot finally remembered the moment that Walter was sure had been the one in which she said yes to him and the dance. All she had been trying to do was get rid of him. She was on her way out to her bus and he kept pestering her with question after question about whether or not she knew her lines well enough and if she wanted to practice some more. He said a few more things after that, but Margot had seen Peter across the way and was trying to get to him quickly before he got onto his bus. When he did, she hurried more quickly, Walter still fumbling along beside her. When she was about to enter her bus, she said in renewed haste, "Sure, Walter, okay. See you then," thinking he was talking about play practice. Had she really fenced herself into a real, live date with him? Her luck was surely at the bottom of the barrel now. She couldn't see him making this up. He was smart, but not cruel. That was Max's forte, not Walter's.

On the other side of the door, to Margot's surprise, was not Peter nor Mrs. Gribble, but Mr. Maples, coming back from his walk with Roxie.

Walter pet Roxie while Mr. Maples explained how he had left his key in the house and couldn't remember the code to the garage door. That's when Peter showed up. And finally, to make the party oh-so-complete, Mrs. Gribble.

"Margot! You look so pretty," Mrs. Gribble shrieked. Peter, not really fazed by all the people in the Maples' entryway, smiled timidly at Margot with a half-puzzled expression on his face. It took Walter all of three seconds to notice him.

"Eh, Margot, what is *he* doing here?" The words bore so much heat that Margot pretended not to hear Walter's question. She just started walking backward, retreating into the kitchen as Walter stared desperately at her for an answer and Peter got bombarded with questions from Mrs. Gribble.

"Oh, are you meeting your date here too? You look so nice. It's just so refreshing to watch you all get ready to go out for the night. This must be so exciting for you kids, huh? You know, it wasn't so long ago that Mr. Gribble and I... well, I won't date myself, but just a short while ago we were going to our first homecoming."

Peter took this all in stride. He was truly a good sport. Margot heard Mrs. Gribble's incessant talk and then heard Walter try to stick Peter with what Peter would most certainly deem appropriate questions, when what Walter was doing could only be defined as ribbing. Margot didn't know that Walter had it in him to tease someone else so mercilessly. At least she thought he was being quite merciless, even though he was merely trying to stake his claim on who he was sure would end up being his date that night – Margot.

"Yeah, Peter, you look *really nice*," Walter offered. "You know, Mom, Peter here isn't even in the play. I guess not everyone is meant for the theater. Margot and I are having so much fun doing it together."

Peter, finally catching on to Walter's insanely juvenile jealousy, poked right back at Walter with, "Yeah, every time Margot talks with me about the play, she goes on and on about how hard everyone is working on it. She's even run her lines by me. She sure is great."

Walter, despite agreeing with Peter on this point, did not want to give in just yet. Then, Margot reentered the room, citing her need to grab her purse from a pile in the basement as the reason for her sudden retreat.

"Why don't we go?" Margot said to nobody and everybody at the same time. Everyone stared at her, wondering just whom she was talking to. "You see, Walter," she said a bit patronizingly, "I'm helping Peter out with this thing tonight."

Walter, who normally would have put on a defeated face, found courage in this statement. "Oh, this *thing*, huh? What thing?"

"I really can't say, okay? It's kind of pers…"

Just then, Peter interrupted her, saying, "You know what, Margot, why doesn't Walter come with us? It's okay. I mean, I don't mind if you don't."

Margot wanted to shoot Peter a withering stare. She wanted to let it be known to all that stood in her house at that moment that she would not, under any circumstances, tolerate another night of Walter Gribble. Despite this not being a date with Peter, she wanted every spare minute with him and him alone. After considering all this, she was surprised to hear herself say, "Yeah, okay. Sounds fine to me, I guess."

Walter's spirits brightened instantaneously. He no longer looked jealous, but rather proud. He was upset that he wouldn't have Margot to himself, of course, but if Margot wanted to help Peter, the least he could do was be there with her. That way, no funny stuff could happen and Walter would be able to keep an eye on his competition.

TWENTY-EIGHT

I've only mentioned Peter to Ashley a bit so far. She knows him, of course, from middle school, but every time I bring him up, she has to tell me about Brad, this new boyfriend she has who is so totally head over heels for her (her words). It's not that Ashley doesn't care about me and my problems – even though sometimes it feels that way. Ashley's just always been like me. Semi-cute with a sweet personality, but no luck with boys. Now that she's actually got somebody, she should be able to flaunt it, I guess. But I never thought, in all the time we've been friends, that she would end up with someone before me. In a perfect world, we would both have boyfriends who adore us and buy us boatloads of chocolate and flowers. I know it sounds cliché, but it's a cliché I'd love to live.

You might think that I wouldn't want to be compared to those female Disney characters, because a lot of people think that they exhibit all those typically female stereotypes that women should not be proud to boast about. But I would give anything – ANYTHING – to meet my Prince Charming and have him whisk me away to the ball. Or the homecoming dance in this case. Peter was the closest I could get to a date, besides the ever-present, ever-annoying Walter.

You know what? I've come to the conclusion that I don't care if Peter and I had to go as friends. At least it wasn't as enemies. And Peter didn't have to ask me. But he did! He asked me. To help, of course. But asked nonetheless, and that's a step in the right direction. That's seeing it as the glass half full. But then Walter showed up. What an awful mess he constantly makes for me! Maybe I shouldn't have looked so flabbergasted to see him at my door, but what was I to do? He had to know that Peter was my "date." And who am I to tell him that it was just as friends? What he doesn't know won't hurt him. At least that's what I keep telling myself to keep the guilt down. When Walter first saw Peter it was at first a look of slight defeat, but then it morphed into a type of anger, like he was plotting revenge against Peter for his backstabbing ways (at least that's what it looked like when watching the wheels of Walter's mind at work, but who really knows the mind of a Gribble besides a Gribble?).

It's just that I don't know what to do about Walter anymore. Anytime I say anything that makes him upset, it just makes him try harder to win me over. Why doesn't he just get it that I don't want to be won over? I mean, I guess I can see what he's trying to do. I'm trying to do kind of the same thing with Peter. I want him to notice me and to like me. Well, he already seems to like me at least enough to ask me to the dance. Yeah, yeah, I know. As friends. Well, if he didn't like me, he wouldn't ask me to come over to my house to study. If he couldn't stand me, he'd probably be all about not hanging out with me. So I guess I'm thankful for that. Actually, no guessing about it. I AM thankful for that. Walter is different. I don't want to hang out with him. At least not like I do with Peter. I know it must be making him feel bad, and I hate making people feel bad because I always end up with a guilty conscience. Especially after what happened to Walter at the dance. I mean, he's always in these situations that make me feel for him, and I can't do anything but be nice and try to make him feel better.

I think it's something my mom ingrained in me from the time I was little. I bet her mother did it to her too, and she felt she had to pass on the guilt or else all would be lost. It's like a mother's intuition. They just know how to pick at the little things about you or the things that you do that they can make you feel guilty about. Like when I don't get a huge project done within a week of when it was assigned, even if I have three weeks till it's due, my mom pressures me to get it done, because why should I wait and procrastinate? I might as well be done. Even if I have other things to work on or places to go (not that I really do, but my mom doesn't have to know how totally sucky my social life is right now, does she?), she makes me feel so guilty that I'm more than halfway done and not just finishing it up. I hate guilt. I promise, here and now, that I will never, ever make my children feel guilty. It's a powerful technique, though. I'll give it that much. My mom always has such power over me, and my dad succumbs to it, too. He's so complacent and carefree about most things, so I guess it's easy to throw guilt at him. He just eats it up since he wants to make everyone happy all the time.

So, I guess what I'm trying to say is that I feel guilty. Guilty about pushing Walter away, guilty about wanting to strangle Mrs. Gribble every time she opens her mouth and tells me that Walter's "best girl" is so great and we should really come over for dinner again soon, guilty for not telling Peter how I really feel and making him think that I really want to help him win Cassie over (even though getting back at Max for countless torturous moments might make that guilt subside a little), guilty for placing myself in situations that are so ugly in nature that there is no way out of them unless I hurt someone in the process. The really nasty part of the whole thing is that that someone usually tends to be none other than me.

TWENTY-NINE

"Margot Maples." A junior girl scanned the list marked "FRESHMEN" in big, bold, capital letters, as if they had to make it absolutely clear how lowly they were in the school totem pole. The junior girl – her name was Carli, with a heart over the "I" in place of a dot on her nametag – handed Margot her ticket and turned to Peter. She looked like she'd rather be anywhere than at that table greeting hordes of freshmen and not dancing with her sure-to-be-popular boyfriend. At least that's what it seemed like from the super athletic looking guy standing behind her, glancing over her shoulder every twenty seconds, it seemed, to see how far along she was with the freshmen list. There were three other tables for the different grades, and Carli looked like nothing more than a robot, going through the fluid motions: *Name?* Checkmark. *Here's your ticket. Have a good time.* It was as if the freshmen were an afterthought, Margot noticed as she scanned the faces of the people manning the sophomore, junior, and senior tables. They all had balloons and smiley-faced student workers. The freshmen table was nothing more than Carli and her less than ecstatic attitude.

"Okay, all set," said Peter, Walter following closely behind. "What should we do now?" Peter glanced over at Margot as if all the answers were at her beck and call. She fought the urge to shrug her shoulders, not wanting Peter to think she didn't care about his mission. She had chosen to accept the responsibility of being at his side for this action sequence, and she wanted to milk it for all it was worth so she could have the maximum amount of time with him. The fact that Walter was along for the ride was an unpleasant addition to her plans, but she would have to make do.

"Why don't we go in and see what's going on? We can't really have a plan until we see who's here, what they're doing, and all that kind of stuff.

Whaddya think?" Margot tried to sound as calm and cool as she could, but she was getting more and more nervous by the minute as they waited to enter the gym. She knew when she had taken on the task of helping Peter that it would put her in close *proximity* to Max, the king of awfulness, but even that hadn't scared her off. She was determined to see this through and prove to Peter that Cassie was not meant for him, despite how nice she had been to Margot herself in the bathroom that day at Benino's.

To her surprise, when Margot walked into the dance, Max, Cassie, and their gang of merry followers were nowhere to be found. Margot surmised that they must have wanted to be fashionably late – whatever that means – but they were already fashionably late themselves, having arrived forty whole minutes after the dance started. Margot excused herself for a minute, telling Peter that she had to use the bathroom, while Walter listened in intently on their conversation, trying to eavesdrop most unsuccessfully.

"Sure thing. I guess it's kind of like reconnaissance anyway," joked Peter. "Maybe you'll see her in there." Margot made a half-smile and turned away, dejected at how desperate Peter seemed to be to find Cassie so quickly. She hadn't even had much time with him to herself. Walter had ruined the ride over. He and Peter had quibbled a bit over whose car they would take – Mrs. Gribble's or Mrs. Mulvaney's – but Mrs. Gribble won out, as she always seemed to miraculously do despite everyone's determination to not allow it to happen. Mrs. Mulvaney didn't seem to have a problem with losing. She just stuck her hands out the driver's side window to fix Peter's tie before she left, while Peter fidgeted away from her grasp.

Once in the bathroom, Margot found herself alone. She had just sat down in the stall when the door creaked open, and giggles could be heard.

Why does this always happen to me? What is it about me and bathrooms? It's just my luck!

It was just Margot's luck – her bad luck – that brought Lisa Quinn and Carolyn Dippet into the bathroom at that moment.

Giggles pervaded the space inside the girls' restroom.

"So, ya think there's a chance he'll ask me to dance?"

"Are you kidding? It's so obvious he likes you. He couldn't stop staring at you through all of play practice the last few times."

"Well, with *her* around, I can't get near him. You can distract her, can't you? You're so great at coming up with plans, Lisa."

Their slurred speech made it hard for Margot to understand them too well, but as unobtrusively as she possibly could, through the gap in the stall, she glanced out and saw Carolyn holding on to the porcelain sink, trying to keep her balance.

"Okay, you ready?" Carolyn asked Lisa with annoyance lacing her voice, like Lisa should have already answered before the question was even asked. Lisa glanced up, smoothed out her light blue eyeshadow with each pinky finger, and blotted her lips from the rose-colored lipstick she had just put on.

"Yeah, I'm coming." Margot heard a bitter twinge of regret in Lisa's voice, like she didn't want to be Carolyn's sidekick. But she followed closely behind anyway. Before the door creaked shut, Margot heard Max's voice telling the two girls how nice they looked. When the door did finally close completely, she heard his muffled laugh on the other side.

Ready to wash up and get back to Peter before any more time was wasted, she wondered if and when she would break the news to Peter about Carolyn trying to make a move for Max. At least that was who she assumed Carolyn was talking about. It was something that they could potentially use to their advantage to get Peter closer to Cassie, but did Margot really want that? Besides, Max, being the dog he was, would become so territorial over Cassie if anything were to tarnish his name in front of her that the war would be on before anyone knew what hit them.

Before Margot made it back into the gym, she spied Max out the window, stuffing something into the inside of his suit jacket. She couldn't make out what it was, and truthfully, she tried to tell herself, she didn't care. But curiosity, as it has a habit of doing, was getting the best of her. She knew she would be keeping one eye on Max for a little while longer that night, which bummed her out because it was one less eye she could focus on Peter.

"Hey, you're back," Walter said, a bit too cheerfully. "Everything okay?"

Not really wanting to delve into the soap opera-esque scene that had just taken place in the bathroom and outside the school window, Margot muttered that there was a long line, which Walter and Peter were more than apt to believe as it was a well-documented fact that girls' restrooms were notorious for just such an occurrence. The boys were always able to just walk in and do their business, but the girls had to wait not-so-patiently for their turn.

"So, what's up?" Peter asked curiously, looking all around for what Margot could only assume were signs of Cassie. Out of the corner of her eye, Margot saw Max, but she lost him behind a group of kids before she could follow him any more closely.

"Eh, nothing really. Carolyn and Lisa were in the bathroom, but no Cassie. Maybe she didn't come," added Margot hopefully. More time for her and Peter was about to be had. Getting rid of Walter was the only barrier to that happiness.

"Oh, I saw her over there a while ago. I think maybe she walked out to go to the bathroom when you were coming back in. I'd hate to ask you to go back, but..."

Not wanting to hear Peter ramble on and on any more about Cassie than she already had to pretend to want to listen to, and putting aside the fact that she had just been in the bathroom and didn't want to look like a loser who had to go twice in a two-minute period, Margot quelled Peter's almost nagging nature and said she'd go back in the bathroom and see if Cassie was there. Lo and behold, she wasn't. Thankful that she had averted another "bathroom moment" with a girl she really didn't want anything to do with, she pulled the bathroom door open and turned the corner, running right into none other than the one and only Cassie Shearer. Margot had to admit that Cassie did look amazing. Her hair was done up in a bun with tendrils falling softly on her shoulders. Her dress was a pale pink color with a hot pink bow tied around her waist. It was form-fitting, to say the least, and Margot found herself haunted by pangs of jealousy for the trim figure standing before her.

"Hey Margot, you look really great. Love the heels." *Great. What guy looks down there? You look great all over and I'm stuck with great heels. Whoop de doo.*

"Yeah, thanks. You look great too. Love the color." Margot pointed quickly at Cassie's dress, and Cassie smiled kindly, unlike what Margot could ever picture Carolyn or Lisa being capable of.

"It doesn't look right. I told my mom that I at least needed spaghetti straps. It doesn't fit me right..." and then Cassie got quieter, "...up here." She glanced down at her chest, and Margot couldn't believe she was in the middle of such a personal conversation. It was like something out of another dimension, where the popular girl tries to be sweet to the lowly, dorky minion. Besides, Cassie was being modest, and it was nice to talk, but Margot didn't want to let Cassie be the friendly one. Her desire for Peter was something that had to overtake her friendliness in that moment.

"I should get back, but it was nice talking to you," Margot said in as polite a tone as she could muster in order to get away quickly.

"Oh, you're here with people?" Cassie asked, not at all meanly. Margot thought about how those words would have sounded coming out of Max's mouth: *"You're* here with *people,"* he'd say, snidely. How he had gotten a girlfriend as nice as Cassie was beyond Margot's comprehension.

"Yeah, I should get back to Peter. He's probably wondering where I went."

"Peter Mulvaney? Oh, he's such a nice guy. He picked up my books for me once when I dropped them in the hall. He always seems to be around when I drop something or trip or something like that. He must think I'm a total klutz."

Not wanting to correct Cassie, but at the same time feeling guilty for wanting to let her drown in humiliation for her not-to-be-believed klutziness, Margot stayed quiet. She couldn't seem to break loose from this conversation with Cassie. To tell the truth, she had always dreamed of the day when the popular girls would want to talk to her, get her opinion on things, and share their innermost secrets because they just felt that comfortable. Now that the time was here, she was doing everything in her power to get away. Was this what she really wanted? To get away from Cassie in order to get back to Peter? Peter who didn't even like her and wanted to be with the ultra-gorgeous, sweet-as-pie girl who stood in front of her? It was all just too much to take in at once. Margot found her mind jetting from one thought to another...to another...to another...

"Margot? You okay?"

Realizing that she had been swept into a daze of her own creation, Margot quickly drew herself out of it and said, "Oh yeah, I must not have eaten enough. I'm getting a little light-headed, that's all. I should go grab some punch or something. See ya later, okay?"

"Yeah, I'll stop by and say hi to you guys in a little while." Again, she wasn't talking about Margot and Peter like they were below her. Her tone was anything but patronizing. Margot wondered if maybe Cassie actually liked her as a person. But it couldn't be that easy, could it? To be liked and well thought of by someone as popular and pretty as Cassie?

As Margot made her way back into the dance, she spied Max talking to Carolyn, Lisa, and a few boys whom she had seen around, but she couldn't remember their names. They were always hanging around Max, like he was a god or something. It was kind of revolting, to say the least.

"Margot! Thought you'd never come back. I was just heading over to get a drink. Want one?" Walter was giddier than Margot could ever remember him being. "The punch is so good, you know? And I noticed you haven't had a drink yet. You know, you look really pretty tonight."

"Thanks, Walter. You look nice too." *Why did I say that? He's going to take it the wrong way. Why oh why am I so stupid?*

"Really?" Walter asked in sheer exasperation at the idea that Margot had complimented him. Then, under his breath, Margot heard him mumble, "I knew this new cologne would work."

"You know what, I actually *am* thirsty, Walter. If you don't mind getting me that drink, I'll just go wait for it over by Peter, okay?" She had made sure not to say she'd wait for him, but for the drink. She didn't need him misconstruing any more of what she said as grandiose compliments or acceptances of dates in Walter's imaginative brain.

"Sure thing." Walter's speech sounded a bit slurred, but Margot was in so much of a rush to get back over to Peter and away from Walter that she ignored it. Then, out of the corner of her eye, she saw Max and his gang of miscreants chatting away on the other side of the refreshments table where the cookies and cakes were. Carolyn and Lisa were giggling a bit, but Cassie looked a bit puzzled. It seemed strange that Cassie wouldn't be in on whatever joke was playing out among that group. She was too big a part of it to be unaware of something. Then, Max whispered something in her ear and they strolled onto the dance floor. Cassie caught Margot's eye and smiled pleasantly. However, as the slow song continued and Max was more in her line of vision, he stared at her with a sneer. Even when she turned back toward Peter, she could still feel Max's eyes boring into the back of her head. Peter seemed to be fixated on the same sight in front of them.

It was only when Walter reappeared with the drinks after having shuffled anything but effortlessly through the crowd that Peter emerged from his anxious, wishful thinking. Margot knew full well that Peter wanted to be on that dance floor with Cassie. Max was a thorn in Peter's side and had been so ever since they had stopped being friends. It was hard enough for Peter to muster the courage to merely smile at Cassie on top of wanting to talk back to Max more than anything. He wanted Max to be just a blip on his radar, a mere constellation in his overall existence. But he was so much more than that. He was a nuisance who reared his ugly head any chance he got just for the shot to make Peter feel weaker and awful about himself. It had been so long since they'd been friends, and Peter still didn't understand just why Max had it out for him. Margot felt the same, but neither Peter nor Margot knew the full extent of each other's animosity toward Max, so they couldn't discuss it much.

"Here's your drink, Margot." Peter looked over at Walter, expecting that there would be a drink for him too. There wasn't one. Walter looked a bit contemptuously at Peter, even though his eyes were darting back and forth across the room like he couldn't keep them still for some reason, and Peter told Margot he'd be right back after he grabbed something for himself. Walter looked satisfied. Another battle won, he thought.

"I don't get it," Margot said to no one in particular, even though Walter was listening most intently and hanging on to her every word. "Cassie was cool first. You'd think that Max was just riding on her coattails all this time, but it seems like he's trying to edge her out or something. It just doesn't make sense."

"Yeah, no sense."

"He's just such a witless moron, you know?" It seemed like Margot had forgotten to whom she was speaking until Walter threw in another, "Yeah, for sure." She realized that he had absolutely no idea why she was talking about this but that he just wanted to have something to talk about with her. He also seemed to be inching closer with each word she said. But it wasn't the kind of inching closer that girls dream about. Heavens, no. It was that awkward, geeky, I'd-trip-on-my-own-two-feet-if-they-weren't-attached-to-me kind of inching. After all, Walter was anything but a dating savant. He was working harder than Margot had ever seen him work, and he looked quite uncomfortable in his efforts, which made Margot wonder how he would ever have luck with any girl.

"Oh, Peter, you're back!" Margot exclaimed a bit too eagerly. She regretted sounding so happy, but Peter didn't seem to mind. However, it only served to make Walter scooch more in her direction. He was almost elbow to elbow with her, and Margot was having a bit of deja-vu back to that infamous day at Benino's when all possibility of popularity had been flushed, almost literally, down the toilet.

Margot had made sure that the conversation she had had with Cassie earlier did not come up as Peter was going on about how pretty Cassie looked. She felt kind of guilty that she wasn't telling Peter about it, after Cassie had been so nice and all, and had even known Peter's name and how nice he had been to her, but she couldn't help it. Something inside of her was making her bottle it up and store it away.

After what seemed like a whole ten minutes of Peter talking about Cassie (it was only three, really), Cassie must have felt her ears burning, because all of a sudden she was headed over their way, Max *not* in tow.

"Hey, Margot. Walter. Peter."

It took almost everything Peter had in him to keep his mouth shut. If he hadn't been trying, it would have been wide open, hanging on that last word that Cassie had said – "Peter."

"Hey, Cassie. Haven't seen you lately. Not since we practiced for the play together." Margot noted that watching Walter talk to Cassie was weird. He wasn't acting anything like how he acted when he was around Margot. He seemed more like a normal guy. Dweeb-like, of course, but pretty normal nonetheless. "I gotta get something to eat. And something to help it go down. Want anything, anyone?"

They all looked at Walter and shook their heads, and he darted off to get the next installment of refreshments.

"So, Peter, what's new? It's so nice that you guys came to the dance, but it's pretty lame, don't you think? I mean, they don't even have colorful balloons. They're just black and white."

"And red all over! Like a newspaper! Was that the joke?"

Cassie turned around, realizing Walter was already back, and not quite understanding what he was talking about.

"Red all over! A newspaper gets *read* all over. Get it? Huh? Huh?"

"Walter, I thought you were getting yourself some more snacks," Margot blurted out. At least having Walter there with the three of them made the triangle a bit less precarious. She couldn't understand why she was trying to get rid of Walter in that instant, which led her to question her sanity a bit for wanting to keep him there at all.

"Oh yeah, be right back." Walter seemed a bit dazed and confused, but Margot chalked it up to his strange habits.

"Lame, yeah." Peter's overly delayed reply to Cassie's long-ago question about the dance didn't stop her from continuing right where that conversation had left off.

"I know, right? Wanna get out of here? We can go to my house and hang out."

"Wh…what?" Margot was happy, but at the same time completely confused. "What about Max and Carolyn and Lisa and all the other guys over there?"

"I'm just bored. Besides, they won't realize if I'm gone anyway," Cassie said in a slightly more muted tone of voice.

"Hey, what's going on over there?" Margot wouldn't normally speak up for Walter, but she could see him getting pushed around by Max and his jerky friends and didn't want to somehow get blamed for letting them use Walter as their punching bag. She might have also felt like she owed him one. After all, she had kind of said yes to his proposal to go to the dance together. Even though it was totally against all she had ever wanted to do, she couldn't deny that he had plainly asked her, and it was only her fault and her fault alone if she hadn't actually been listening to what he said. Despite how much it pained her to realize this was really the truth, she still felt for Walter. He didn't deserve to be pushed around. Especially not by Max Poler and his ridiculous gang.

"Cassie, can't you do something? I mean, he *is* your boyfriend, isn't he? Tell him to leave Walter alone or something." Cassie looked slightly defeated, as if she knew that if she walked over there in that instant, her cool kid status would be revoked. "Well?!" Margot spoke up more loudly in Cassie's direction.

"Um, sure, yeah," Cassie said, and then she threw a smile back on her face. It seemed like she had been deep in some kind of contemplative thought. She really didn't seem to want to go see Max. It appeared like she'd rather hang out with Margot and Peter and let Walter dangle at the mercy of her so-called friends, but she somehow got up the nerve and walked over.

"Max, leave him alone, alright? What has he ever done to you anyway? We can go like you wanted to."

"So now you want to leave with me, huh? This dweeb here was saying that you're going to *his house*." The last two words were said with a fair amount of consternation.

"He's got it wrong. I did go to his house. For the dialogue prep. Remember? You knew about it." Max didn't want to let on that he had been okay with Cassie hanging out at Walter's house, but he also didn't want to lose his own "cool" status. He wasn't about to let Cassie get the upper hand in the conversation.

"I said I'd go with you. What more do you want from me?" Cassie didn't look thrilled to be saying the words that were coming out of her mouth, but she seemed to have thrown her pride by the wayside to get Max to leave Walter alone. It was then that Margot glanced next to her to find that Peter had started to make his way closer to Cassie, well into Max's line of vision and the not-so-metaphorical line of fire.

"What's your problem, Max?" Max looked around as though he couldn't believe his ears.

"Mulvaney?!" Max's laughter permeated the room and caused some kids who were dancing to the hip-hop beat to turn around and ogle a bit at the ensuing action.

Seeming to have realized that he had spoken the words aloud, Peter looked as though he would give anything to disappear in that moment. Max was inching closer, looking as though he would give his right arm to hear Peter repeat himself so he could punch him out.

Somehow, out of the nothingness that hung heavy in the air, Peter repeated, "What's your problem? Trouble hearing, too?"

With the sudden nerve that was welling up inside of him, Peter seemed to have lost consciousness of the fact that Max, even though not much bigger than Peter, was quite a bit stronger, and definitely a lot more confident in himself. These two traits were sure to win Max any fight against Peter, and Peter knew that, as did the rest of the freshmen class that was ganging up around the sidelines waiting for the action to start.

That's why it came as a total surprise to all around when Peter balled up his fist and threw it directly at Max's face. The awful part about this was that despite the look of shock mingled with uncertain defeat on Max's face, Peter's fist fell just a few inches short of its destination.

THIRTY

It all happened in what seemed like a split second. Margot covered her eyes, Cassie yelled at Max, Walter mumbled some incoherent words with a slight look of bemusement on his face, Peter looked dumbfounded by the results of his first attempt at anything violent, and Max just smiled before hurling his own fist straight toward Peter's gut. But before it could connect, the booming voice of Dr. Perkins could be heard moving its way through the throng of entranced freshmen.

"Break it up! I said break it up! Unless you want detentions all around!"

"Oh, hi Dr. Perkins... sir." Max made sure to add the obligatory "sir" when he saw Dr. Perkins' stare make its way toward him.

"Isn't it convenient that you're here right now," said Max in his snottiest tone. But Dr. Perkins didn't even notice. He immediately launched into an interrogation about just what was going on.

"You see sir, well... I think it would be best if Mulvaney here told you what was happening. I mean, he is the one who tried to hit me. I was just standing here, minding my own business, and..."

"You're a liar." Cassie didn't even know she had said it. It left her lips in such a matter- of-fact tone, and it had happened in a mere instant. "You're a liar and you know it. Dr. Perkins, Max pushed Peter to try to hit him. He and I were in a fight, you see, and I wouldn't leave with him, so..."

The triviality of the ensuing explanation was not lost on Dr. Perkins. He cared about his students more than he could say. But their private lives and relationships were not even a blip on his radar and he wanted to keep it that way. Delving into the personal lives of countless teenagers would surely drive him to an early grave. He had to see what had happened for what it was and what it was alone. He couldn't have his judgment clouded by various freshmen students' distaste or affection for one another.

"Just tell me what happened here. I need to know so I can dole out the consequences. Remember that freshmen meeting we had? Well, this is a perfect example of how the freshmen class can go awry when not guided through the appropriate channels of discussion over aggression. Mr. Mulvaney, is it? Did you try to hit this boy? I mean, something had to have happened to gather such a crowd of onlookers."

Peter didn't know what to say. He was flabbergasted as to just how he had gotten to this moment. It felt as though all eyes were on him. He wanted to turn around and sprint away, but he knew that the repercussions from that would be disastrous, both reputation-wise and discipline-wise. He had to come up with some words, but they were lost on him.

"I, uh, I..." Before any more mumbles could issue from Peter, Dr. Perkins made a decision.

"Okay, this is what's going to happen. I want to see you, you, you, you, and you in my office. The rest of you go back to dancing, if that's what you can even call it anymore." Dr. Perkins seemed a bit old-fashioned in his tone just then, no doubt due to his having grown up in the 70s when disco was the rage and dancing wasn't just grinding up against each other like he had been witnessing the last several years.

In the next moments, Max, Peter, Cassie, Margot, and Walter all followed Dr. Perkins down the hall to his office. It seemed like a long, drawn-out walk, roaming the hallways of the school with no knowledge of just what would happen next. Margot still didn't understand why she was involved in this. She had never been to the principal's office before, except for that one time in middle school when the principal awarded her with a certificate for earning no tardies on her attendance for a whole semester. This visit to Dr. Perkins' office seemed like just the opposite of a happy occasion.

"Okay, I want all of you to sit down in those seats over there. First things first, I'm going to call your parents. Then we can get down to the bare bones of what happened here tonight."

As Dr. Perkins was about to turn the corner into his office, the five of them sat down, Max leering at the rest of them with contempt, and the rest of them staring right back – even Cassie, who was just as angry at Max as the rest of them were. Walter, however, was off in his own world. As he went to sit down in the fifth and final seat in the main office, his balance wavered, and he fell backwards, snickering as though something hilarious had just happened.

"Walter," Margot whispered, "get up! Don't you know where we are?! What on earth is making you so silly?"

Walter got his composure back a bit and sat in the seat, just as Dr. Perkins rounded the corner once again. After asking for each of their names, he said, "Okay, you first, Mr. Poler. Dial." Max walked up to Dr. Perkins, but before he picked up the phone, he made one more plea for his case to be heard.

"Dr. Perkins, you have the wrong guy. This isn't my fault. I was just on my way to tell you the punch tasted spiked, and that's when Mulvaney came up with this group here and told me to shut up. When I told him what I was planning on doing, that's when he hit me. Why else do you think they're all so against me? Four against one seems pretty unfair, don't you think? I think they're trying to cover up for each other. I mean, look at Gribble over there. He's clearly wasted."

That's when it hit Margot. Walter's slurred words, his upped confidence, his interest in continuing to get more to drink. And then she remembered the most important detail of all – Max stuffing something inside of his coat pocket through the window after she had heard Lisa and Carolyn talking with their own slurred speech in the bathroom. It was Max. He was behind it all. He was the one who had spiked the punch. Most of the dance was probably getting wasted already, but Walter was the only one who was going to get caught. Margot wanted to say something. She wanted to tell Dr. Perkins to look in Max's coat pocket and find what was surely a flask of something alcoholic.

"Which of you is Gribble?" asked Dr. Perkins incredulously. The thought that someone had spiked the punch under his watch was not something he was at all happy about and not something which he was going to take lightly.

"I'm Walter, sir. That's me. Walter Drib... I mean Gribble. Ha! I'm funny." Max looked anything but defeated in this moment. He had a look of supreme courage and outright ease as if he had clearly won. That's when Margot realized that getting her nerve up was the only way to stop what she considered to be Max's reign of terror on her and her group of hard knocks.

"Dr. Perkins! Walter might have had something to drink, but I know he didn't do it purposely. Max must have been the one to spike the punch. I saw him earlier, stuffing something inside his coat pocket. You have to believe me."

"I don't have to believe anything, Ms...."

"My name is Margot Maples, and I'm telling you, he's innocent."

"Don't you find it awfully curious, Ms. Markles is it, that you're so blatantly attacking Mr. Poler right now? I mean, you're terribly defensive for a supposedly innocent bystander in all this. Why do you care so much about Mr. Gribble's innocence?"

It was in that moment that Margot deeply considered the question before her. Had it been posed by Walter himself, she would have surely done everything in her power to get away from him in that instant. But she couldn't ignore Dr. Perkins. He was the school principal, and she couldn't help but be scared that being defiant could be terribly costly to her. Her year had not started out well. Everything was down the drain so far, save her understudy role in the school play. That was the only thing really keeping her sane. That and Ashley coming to visit. She wasn't getting anywhere with Peter, and Walter was just as annoying and clingy as ever. She didn't know why she was trying to help him, other than the fact that she knew he was innocent, and like the good person she was, she wasn't going to let him take the fall for something stupid that Max, of all people, had done. It wasn't in her nature, and she wouldn't stand by and let it happen. The problem was, she didn't know how to prove it other than saying that Max had the alcohol in his pocket. Or so she thought. It could have been anything that she had seen him put in there. It could have been Carolyn or Lisa who had the alcohol smuggled in a purse. She was taking a shot, even if it was a long shot, and she was determined to see it through.

"Maybe I'm defensive. But I don't think it's right to see someone that I know and like..." Everything seemed to stop for a moment as Margot realized the words she had said. She realized not only that Walter was looking at her longingly, through glazed eyes and a dizzied expression, but that she had actually come to care for the wreck of a dork Walter really was. He was annoying, sure. Bothersome to no end. Aggravating and anything but understanding of her feelings toward him. But he was her friend. He would stand up for her, and she had to stand up for him. She knew she'd regret it. She knew he'd find a way to make her sorry she had done it. But there was no stopping it now.

She continued on, "...well, it's just that if you check Max's coat pockets you're sure to find something in them. Trust me."

"This is unbelievable. You can't possibly believe her, Dr. Perkins." Margot marveled at Max's words and how easy it was for him to act innocent.

"Okay, okay, enough already. Just take a seat there and we'll wait for your parents to come."

Margot was flabbergasted at Dr. Perkins' lack of interest in the situation. He had them down in his office and he seemed to be wanting to get to the bottom of things, but he looked intent on waiting for the parents to arrive. The only thing was that they hadn't called them yet.

"Uh, Dr. Perkins...sir? We haven't called our parents yet," Margot offered.

"I knew that," Dr. Perkins said, not so believably. He seemed to just be standing there waiting for the buzzer to the office door to ring.

After they had all called their parents, it was only a matter of about ten minutes before they started to arrive. An overly worried looking Mrs. Gribble came in first, followed by Margot's parents, Peter's mom, and Max's dad.

"Oh honey! Are you okay?" Mrs. Gribble asked anxiously. "I was waiting in the car around the corner from the school reading my book. I didn't want to go home if for some reason you needed me to pick you and Margot up early from the dance." Walter didn't seem too fazed by any of this, but Margot was horror-struck. Now she not only had Max upset that she was ratting him out, but she had him thinking that she had actually come to the dance with Walter.

"What's going on here? We're all here and no one seems to be saying anything to explain what's happened. Why is my son down here? Can someone explain this to us, for heaven's sake?" Max's dad was a bit over-dramatic, but it stands to reason that that's what you get when you have a lawyer for a dad. Always looking for the accusation and the evidence.

"Mr..." Dr. Perkins stopped short, not remembering Max's last name.

"Poler. Fred Poler."

"Well, Mr. Poler. Your son here has been accused by Ms. Marbles of spiking the punch bowl and having a bottle of some kind of liquor in his pocket. As I do not feel comfortable going through your children's pockets for items, I ask that you look for yourself so we can get to the bottom of this."

"It's Maples, Dr. Perkins. Margot *Maples*." Margot didn't know why she had spoken up, but she didn't want to be just another person in the crowd in this scenario. If this was happening, she was going to take at least some of the credit for bringing Max down.

"This is preposterous. What could possibly have made this girl here accuse him of something so ridiculous? My son is 14 goddamn years old. He'll be 15 in a few weeks." At this point, Mr. Poler looked proud. He looked as though his son was guilty of nothing and never would be. Margot pondered how it was obvious now where Max had gotten his hideous attitude. It was also no wonder that he and Peter had had to stop being friends. Peter was nothing like the Polers. They were so stubborn and self-absorbed.

"Could you please just do it, Mr. Poler? We're wasting more and more time here." Mr. Poler then reached into his son's coat pockets, with an air of complete defiance. When his hands became visible again, a couple of crumpled tissues and a ticket stub were all that could be seen.

"I could have sworn..." Margot started. But Mr. Poler was quick to cut her off, turning on his lawyerly tone and pushing for what he obviously considered a cross-examination of the accuser.

"So, Ms. Marbles, is it?"

"Maples." Margot was taken aback by the tone of arrogance in Mr. Poler's voice and the look of it on Max's face. The expression on Max's face showed something more, though. It seemed to hint at a bit of "gotcha."

"You accuse my son of spiking the punch and bringing liquor onto school grounds. It stands to reason that you yourself might be guilty. Why are you so anxious to blame someone else?"

"Because it was him!" Margot blurted. She was being careless, she knew, but she didn't know how else to get it across to everyone that he had done it.

"We should check her too. After all, my son had to go through it. Why shouldn't she?"

"My daughter is innocent. What right do you have to check her?"

"What right did you have to check Max here? But no one said not to. So I'm saying to check her."

Walter, dreary-eyed, turned to his mother right then. "Can we just go home? I don't feel good." He then went into his pocket to grab a tissue to blow his nose, but instead came out with a teeny tiny bottle of some kind of liquid.

"What's that? Walter!" Mrs. Gribble was beside herself with uncertainty. "What do you have there? What is that?" She kept repeating the same thing over and over, but it was all she could think to say. Everybody turned and looked. It was the same item that Margot had seen Max stuffing into his pocket. But it was in Walter's pocket now. And a snide smirk was plastered on Max's face while his father looked as though he had cracked the case.

"Well now we're getting somewhere," said Dr. Perkins.

THIRTY-ONE

Walter was suspended for two weeks. His mother looked like she would have to be shocked back to life when she saw that tiny bottle of vodka emerge from Walter's pocket. She couldn't believe it. Margot, Cassie, and Peter knew it couldn't be true. And Max was in the free and clear, other than the fact that he and Peter had been dealt a day's worth of after-school detention and a stern warning about their behavior. Dr. Perkins had made it abundantly clear that any more fighting would result in a suspension.

"It's going to be okay, honey. School will get back to normal before you know it. Just find Margot. She's sure to get you through it. My Walter is a fighter. Aren't you, dear?"

"Sure, Mom," Walter said in the most understated of ways. He was usually much perkier around his mom, but he knew that the last two weeks had been the low point of his life, and he didn't want to even think of reliving them through the kids at school. His parents had finally decided that they believed him, despite their shock and amazement at his drunken state at homecoming. Margot, Cassie, and Peter had even gone over to visit Walter during his two-week "vacation," as his mother liked to refer to it, in order to try to convince his parents that it was Max. Cassie kept coming at them with the argument that he was her boyfriend, and she knew how awful he could be. He was definitely guilty, and the Gribbles seemed to really know it. There was just no way to prove it, so getting back at Max was a lost cause.

It was a funny thing for Walter, walking into school that first day back as the guy who allegedly spiked the punch. You'd think other students would have had admiration for the courageous soul who had attempted to make the dance a little more interesting. But the fact that Walter had gotten caught must have signaled shame to most, as he was being cast sidelong glances from almost everyone who passed him in the hall when he returned after his fall from nerdy grace.

Not only was he an outcast, but Dr. Perkins wouldn't let him come to play practice during his suspension, so his role of understudy had to be recast. Mr. Richardson had felt terrible about this. He for some reason saw Walter as having tons of acting potential, so at the first rehearsal they had on Walter's first day back, Mr. Richardson offered him the role of understudy to the understudy. Walter was so happy to even have a chance at still being in the play that he almost hugged Mr. Richardson. Margot couldn't help but smile (quickly and under the guise of a joke another student had just told), because she knew that Walter was innocent and he didn't deserve the treatment he was receiving. She couldn't tell anyone that, though, or what little she had left of a reputation would most probably be forever tarnished.

Max showed up to rehearsal as smug as ever. Margot wondered to herself how he could be so cunning as to have been able to sneak that little bottle into Walter's pocket, but instead of using his cleverness for good, he had to be an all-around jerk.

"Hey, Margot! Over here!" Cassie was almost shouting over the throng of students in her path. "I wanted to catch you before you got on your bus. I thought we should practice our part some more. I mean, since we both know it so well, it makes sense for us to help each other out." Ever since homecoming, Cassie had been friendlier to Margot. Not that she hadn't been friendly before. But it was somehow different. Margot thought that it could have to do with Cassie's disapproval of Max and their newly strained relationship, but the fact was that Margot still sometimes saw them roaming the halls together, chatting as if nothing had even happened. It didn't make sense to Margot, but like it or not, she thought Cassie was nice, and she didn't want to put any strain on what could potentially be a newly formed friendship with someone who was actually considered at least semi-popular.

Cassie never mentioned Max around Margot, but despite Margot noticing them hanging around each other, she never saw any affection between them. It was as if they were being required to be with one another. But the chemistry was severely lacking.

Mr. Richardson noticed this in play practice one day. He even tried having Margot take over the role of Katherina for a bit while Cassie sat down. Having worked with his share of actors and actresses, he would often note that "Relationships have their twists and turns. No one is perfect. But the show must go on!" These words did not help to quell the discomfort that Margot felt playing against Max's Petruchio. She even considered having to play against Walter, and felt a bit more unhinged at the fact that she didn't feel quite as much discomfort at that thought. The only thing that kept her sane at play practice anymore was Peter's presence. He wasn't there for her, of course. At least not fully. He wanted to see Cassie. He felt ever that much closer to her now that they both shared at least a hint of disdain for Max.

The play was coming up in little less than a month, and Margot was getting slightly nervous. Not only did she have to make sure that she had perfected her lines to a tee, but she had to anticipate Ashley arriving. She often found herself lying in her bed at night, making entry after entry into her journal, reflecting on the irritation that she felt when she had talked to Ashley lately.

All that Ashley ever talks about anymore is Brad. Brad this and Brad that. I am happy for her. Really. I mean, she deserves to have a guy. I deserve to have a guy. Yeah, yeah. I know. I should be happy for her. She is my best friend. I just feel so distant from her. She seems happy about coming to see me, but all she does all the time that we talk is rant on and on about how much she'll miss Brad. How they just had their one month anniversary. All I have to say to that is...well...I won't say it here. I wouldn't want to sour these pages. I mean, this is a place that I come to talk about my innermost secrets. You'd think I could let loose and say whatever I want. I just don't want to say it, though. I kinda wish she didn't have Brad and we could have it be just like old times when she comes. But instead of being excited and thrilled about her upcoming visit, I'm terrified of having to listen to her talk day in and day out about how happy he makes her, and how she's a better person since she's met him, and how she's already planned out the next ten years of her life with Brad, culminating in what will surely be her version of a fairy tale wedding.

Having had enough of the pity party she felt she was throwing for herself, Margot grabbed the phone to call Ashley, thinking that maybe, just maybe, they could have a regular talk about something other than Brad. But instead, Ashley's voicemail message began playing in Margot's ear.

"Hey! You've reached Ashley. I'm out right now. Leave a message, and I'll get back to ya as soon as..." Before Margot could hear any more, she ended the call, unsettled by her realization that she didn't care to talk to Ashley anymore, especially if she was likely with Brad at that moment. Margot only knew what Ashley had told her about Brad, as she hadn't had the pleasure (or displeasure) of talking to him yet. She had also seen his picture. Ashley had scanned it into the computer and sent it via e-mail. As soon as Margot got it, Ashley bombarded her with question after question about all the aspects of Brad's cuteness that could possibly be ascertained by looking at the photo.

"Adorable. Positively the cutest guy you've ever seen. Right, Margot? I mean, who can deny it?" Margot couldn't honestly deny it. Brad was cute. Cuter than she ever thought she or Ashley would have a chance at getting. He was also a year older and on the school's football team. That was another point that Ashley brought up on a more than regular basis. Dating a football player is no small potatoes. Bragging rights come along with the territory.

All of the talk of Brad and the football team and his cuteness had begun to wear on Margot more than she had cared to believe it could. He was Mr. All Star, at least to Ashley, and anything (or anyone, namely Peter) that Margot even considered bringing up seemed to pale in comparison to Ashley's hunky dory love life. That's why Margot hadn't mentioned Peter yet. Just as she was reveling again in her pity party, the phone rang.

"Margot! It's Ashley!" her mother yelled from the bottom of the stairs.

"Okay. Thanks, Mom!" Margot responded. "I'll get it up here." She reached for the phone much slower than she normally would have. It was right on the other side of her bed, but even though she had just called Ashley for the purpose of trying to see if they could have a normal conversation, she knew it wasn't possible. This was evidenced quickly enough.

"Margot! We're out right now. But I saw you called and I didn't want to make you wait to hear back from me. We just finished up dinner, and now we're in line at the movies." Margot didn't want to note that it was a school night. She knew that that would seem like the dorkiest thing to possibly say in this situation. But she knew that her parents would never in a million years let her go out to dinner and a movie on a school night, especially when it was already 8 o'clock and they hadn't even started the movie. Then, Margot realized that it was even an hour later where Ashley was in Canada, and couldn't believe that Ashley's parents were really allowing this. That is, if they even knew their daughter was out. Since Margot hadn't hung out with Ashley in a while, she didn't know if Ashley had possibly become the sneak-out-of-my-room-to-hang-out-with-my-boyfriend type. It worried her that her best friend could potentially have changed so much, but she set those thoughts aside and continued her chat.

"Cool. Whatcha seeing?"

"Oh, some action spy thriller flick. Brad is into that stuff, and I just want to hang out with him, you know? What's new with you?"

"Just finishing up some homework and playing with Rox…"

"Oh, Margot, you won't believe this!" Ashley interrupted.

Margot feigned interest for what seemed to be the millionth time since Ashley had started being attached to Brad's hip the month before. "What is it, Ash?"

"The guy at the concession stand is yelling at me to get off the phone. I guess there's a no-cell policy here in the lobby. Such a stupid rule. I mean, really? No talking? I'm not in the movie yet or anything. Whatever, I guess. Can I talk to you later? I have to go. Call you tomorrow?"

"Yeah, sure," Margot said in the most unexcited voice she could muster. It didn't seem to faze Ashley, though. She just threw in a quick goodbye and a happy-go-lucky "talk to ya later," and hung up before Margot had the chance to say bye back.

If this is what it's going to be like when she gets here in a few weeks, I really would rather her just not come at all, Margot thought wearily to herself.

THIRTY-TWO

"Peter, you'll be home after school today, right?" his mom asked.

"Nope. Not right away. I wanted to go see the play rehearsal today. It's coming up in less than two weeks now, and they've been doing actual dress rehearsal. Plus, I'm on the props committee." Peter had joined the props committee a couple weeks before when some of the props guys had been caught getting high in the parking lot behind the school after practice one day. There had only been four people on the committee to begin with, and the three guys who were kicked off didn't do much to help the committee stay strong. They were responsible for getting everything in order, and no matter how much of a control freak the main girl was, she basically looked like a frenzied, out of control animal every time anyone tried to give her anything new to add to the props pile. The three guys hadn't really been too much help when they were around, but by having them there, the girl at least looked like she wasn't going nearly as crazy. Peter had joined just to calm her nerves. Plus, it gave him the chance to be closer to the action.

"Okay. I'll ask Mrs. Carson if she can have Billy over for a little bit after school. I know he and Chris have a project to work on for science anyway."

"Sounds good, Mom," Peter said in his most non-interested-but-will-act-interested tone.

"How's the play going, anyway?"

"Pretty good, I guess. The two main leads have been getting into more and more fights lately, though. After what Max did at the homecoming dance, Cassie isn't really happy with him." Peter smirked. It served Max right to lose Cassie. It was obvious she was too good for him, at least in Peter's estimation.

"You two used to be such good friends. It's too bad that you can't find a way to be close again." Peter shrugged off his mom's cluelessness. She didn't really understand how upsetting Max could really be. He had never really explained why he had started to push Peter away, and Peter had taken a while to get over the hurt he felt losing his best friend.

"I don't know, Mom. But I think the tension between everyone is actually helping the play go better. Cassie is playing the lead, so she's the "shrew" in the title of the show, and apparently in Max's opinion. It doesn't help that Carolyn and Lisa are also in the play, and they're treating her crappy too."

"Don't say crappy, Peter. It's not nice."

"Whatever, Mom. It's true."

"It doesn't matter."

"Fine. They're not being too nice to her. Is that better?"

"That tone won't help, either, Peter."

"Fine. Sorry. The point is that nobody is getting along so well outside of the play, but the show is coming along. It's kind of exciting to watch it all come together."

"I'm glad you're enjoying yourself. Maybe next year you can try out for a part." Peter didn't respond to this, but walked over to the fridge, grabbed his lunch, and headed toward the door. Mrs. Mulvaney was busy putting some paperwork together on the kitchen table.

"Bye, Mom. Gotta go."

"Have a good day, honey. Love you."

"Yeah. Love you, too." Peter headed out the door, excited for the day to end so he could get to play practice.

***

With less than two weeks till the play, Cassie got up the nerve one day to approach Margot and ask for her help.

"Margot! Hey, wait up, okay?" Margot slowed down, a rush of nervousness coursing through her. Even though she'd been talking to Cassie lately, it had only been in regards to the play. She didn't know if she knew what to say to her outside of that context.

"Slow down. You look like you're going a mile a minute. What's up?" Acting nonchalant around Cassie was still difficult. Margot even avoided calling Cassie by her name, resorting to "Hey you" or the simple question of "what's up?" to keep from having to say her name. It was as though she thought that saying it would make Cassie instantly dislike her. Like she'd say it wrong or someone would overhear her and think her unworthy of saying the name of someone popular when she was on the opposite side of the reputation spectrum.

"I was just wondering if you wanted to come over and practice some lines. You did such a good job covering for me when Mr. Richardson asked me to sit out. Max was just getting on my last nerve, you know?" Margot most certainly did know, but she didn't want to be all over-the-top angry at Max because she worried that if Cassie ever decided to make amends with him, anything she said against him would be used against *her*. Even if not by Cassie, by Max if he ever found out. It was the last thing she wanted to happen.

"Yeah, I know," Margot improvised in an attempt to steer clear of that topic of conversation.

"So, wanna come over? My dad is out playing poker tonight, so you won't have to worry about my parents, well, you know." Margot couldn't help but remember the awful display that she had witnessed at Benino's between Cassie's parents. Cassie seemed so forlorn at the time about the situation, but she seemed to have gotten past it, or at least it came across that way, since Cassie was so calm and welcoming of Margot to come over.

"Okay, I guess that sounds good. Running lines a few more times can't hurt. I feel like every time I do that I start to have an easier time remembering them."

"Yeah, I know. Some people say that going over them too many times can make your brain kind of forget or something. But it definitely helps me. I guess we're similar in that way."

Wow. Similar. To Cassie Shearer. That's something I'll probably never hear again. I wonder what Ashley would think about that.

"Okay, well, see you later, then. Thanks for thinking of me."

"No problem. Us actresses have to stick together." Cassie smiled and turned to head off in the opposite direction. That's when Margot's overthinking kicked into high gear.

Even though Margot was beginning to think of Cassie as a real friend, she knew that Ashley would find a way to ruin it.

If Ashley for one second thought that Margot was achieving a higher status than she was, Margot knew that despite their years of being best friends forever, Ashley would be haunted by pangs of jealousy until Margot felt like less than Ashley. It was a sad and disappointing cycle that Margot wished she could skip, but Ashley had a way of making her feel this way, especially during the last few months that heralded not only the start of ninth grade, but the start of trying to one-up the only person you never thought would make you feel you had to one-up.

THIRTY-THREE

"It's so great you came over. It's about time I hung out with someone other than..." Cassie trailed off in that moment, but Margot knew she was talking about Max, Carolyn, and Lisa. "I mean, you're a really great person, Margot. It's about time I started hanging out with people like you more. And Peter and Walter, too. They're nice, don't you think? And Peter's totally in to you too."

This conversation was turning into the lifestyles of the strange and stranger. Margot had to do a figurative double-take in her mind in order to take in what Cassie had just said.

"Uh, what did you say?"

"You're all so nice. I mean, I can't believe it's taken me so long to get to be friends with you, Margot. You really get me. It's been a long time since I felt like anyone did. Especially Max." The last two words came out muffled, and Margot didn't feel right about bringing it up any more. She did want to hear that last part about Peter again. Cassie was obviously mistaken. Peter didn't actually like her. He'd been using her to get to Cassie. She thought they were friends, but at the same time, she questioned whether or not he really liked her. I mean, he did hang around her a lot, but he also seemed to be asking about Cassie all the time. She could see that Cassie was hurting, and the last thing she wanted to do to their new and fragile friendship, which Margot was still in awe was actually happening, was bring up a sour subject in Cassie's life or bring up questions of her own. If Cassie wanted to talk about it, she would. But Margot still had to ask to be sure.

"Did you want to…" Margot suddenly paused, unsure of whether or not to continue. She finally finished, "…talk about it?" She figured this left the conversation open for Cassie to discuss her whole friendship debacle with

Max and the others or what she had just said to Margot about Peter.

"Nah. Let's focus on the play."

"Oh, okay. As long as you're sure."

"Yeah, I guess so. I mean, let's run lines and then we can see if there's time to chat. We need to be prepared, you know."

"Yeah, I know."

The girls spent the next hour and a half before dinner playing out the lines with different intonations, hand gestures, and even accents when they started to get goofy toward the end. They seemed to be really hitting it off. Margot didn't want the day to end. It seemed like everything was so right. She had a friend. Someone who didn't even mind talking to her at school. That was a rare find for Margot. Of course she had Walter, and, she supposed, Peter, but a girl who was a friend and who wasn't Ashley was one of the more awesome things that had happened to her in what seemed to be the neverending first couple of months of high school. Now that she was going to be in the play, and the lead not only wanted to be her pal, but wanted to distance herself from the people Margot disliked more than anything, she felt she had finally struck gold. Now she just had to find out what Cassie meant about Peter liking her.

After dinner, Margot's mom was so quick to pick Margot up that she didn't get a chance to ask Cassie anything more about what she had said about Peter being "totally in to" her. She had to have meant in to herself. He was in to Cassie. That was that. But what could Cassie have possibly meant, then?

The next day at school, Margot was still thinking about the conversation that had so abruptly ended the night before. Sure, they had run their lines over and over and gotten them down to the point where if they practiced any more, they would probably think that the play was real life. Margot wanted to invite Cassie over to see if it was all just a fluke. She figured she'd say no and look at her like she was out-of-this-world crazy to think she would ever be caught dead taking the bus to Margot's house. But she needed to know if that was true. She needed to find out if Cassie was just like all the rest of the kids whom Margot knew she never had a chance to get to know because of their preconceived notions about her own reputation and status.

To Cassie's credit, she turned out to be everything Margot had hoped for and more. She accepted the invitation, almost too quickly, and said that coming over sounded awesome. *Awesome*, thought Margot. *It'll be awesome.* Getting together with Cassie was turning into what seemed to be like an all-out event. Margot had butterflies in her stomach and wanted to be sure she had picked out the right outfit. She didn't want to scare Cassie away. She needed to impress her so she wouldn't lose her. They planned for the next night.

And soon enough it had come. The night was upon them, and Margot made sure that she had lines running in her head so she would be able to ask about Peter in the most nonchalant and subtle way possible. She didn't want Cassie to think she was overeager. She had seen Cassie and Max leering at each other across the stage while they ran their lines, and she didn't want to throw too much sunshine and happiness Cassie's way while Cassie was clearly hurting from her break-up with Max. Strangely enough, once she was over, Cassie brought it up herself.

"So, what do you think of Peter?"

Margot was caught off-guard and didn't know how to answer. She had had it all worked out. What she would say, how Cassie would answer (certainly by saying she had shared false information and didn't know what she was talking about), and then they would just hang out and talk about school and the play and other goofy stuff like friends did. Luckily, Margot was saved by the phone ringing.

"Uh, I have to get that."

"Sure thing. I'll just look through your stack of magazines. That okay?"

"Oh. Yeah. No problem." Margot was flustered. She ran to the phone and picked it up.

"So, next week already. So excited!" Ashley. Margot felt like she was losing balance. First she had been blind-sided by Cassie's question about Peter, and now she had to waylay what could potentially be a big problem if Ashley were to find out that Cassie and Margot were now friends and Cassie was actually over at that moment!

"Hey, Ash. What's up?"

"Everything okay? You sound a little weird." Margot knew she did. Whenever she got flustered, her voice tended to take on a higher pitch.

Ashley was well aware of this. Margot knew she shouldn't feel guilty. Ashley was popular too, with Brad and the rest of her so-called friends at her new school. But it was just in Margot's nature to feel guilt. She thought back on all the things her mom had made her feel guilty about over the years.

"Everything's fine. Yeah. Just hanging around. You know what? Can I talk to you later? I'll call you in a few hours."

"Sure. I guess that's fine." Now Ashley sounded a bit bothered. "I'll talk to you later."

"Is everything okay?" Cassie seemed genuinely interested as Margot hung up the phone.

"It was just my friend Ashley. I'll call her later. I didn't want to be rude while you're here."

"Ashley... Ashley..." Cassie repeated the name a few more times as if trying to figure out whom Margot meant. "There was a girl named Ashley who you were friends with at Perry, right? Is that the one who was just on the phone?"

"Actually, yeah," Margot said, utterly surprised that Cassie remembered not only Ashley, but the fact that Margot had been friends with her. "She moved away and is going to a new school now. She's coming to visit next week in time for the play."

"Totally cool. I'd love to see her."

"Yeah, totally cool," Margot repeated in a rather lackluster tone.

"Something *is* wrong." Cassie couldn't be fooled. It was clear from Margot's tone and facial expression that all was not well in her world.

"It's just. Oh, whatever. Never mind."

"No. Margot. Tell me what's up. We're friends, aren't we?" Margot fought her urge in that moment to have her eyes well up with tears and start sobbing. She knew she should be happy. She was hanging out with Cassie. But she was also terribly hurt by what she had convinced herself Ashley would be like when she got off the plane with her incessant talk of Brad, her "one and only."

"Well... okay. Ashley and I were best friends, you know? And when she moved to Canada, we said we'd talk every day and text and e-mail and all that stuff. But then she went and got a boyfriend. A football playing boyfriend who also happens to be tall, dark, and handsome. And I'm stuck here... with nobody. I mean, you know. I have my parents, and Roxie, my dog, but..."

"Are you kidding?" Cassie couldn't help but interrupt. "You've got me too. Am I the only one here who considers us friends? Every time I mention it, you seem to brush it off. Do you not like me or something? I mean, why did you invite me over anyway if you don't even consider me a friend?"

"I'm self-conscious, okay?" Margot was keenly aware that she sounded defensive now. She didn't want to be the dorky girl she knew she really was. Especially not with Cassie there... in her room, no less. "I didn't know if you were my friend or not. I know you keep saying it, but I'm not used to popular people liking me."

Cassie looked dumbfounded, which in turn made Margot feel slightly bad, but also slightly peeved.

"Popular? You think I'm popular?"

Margot wanted to throw out about a dozen "duh" responses to Cassie's questions, but she restrained herself and led with, "Uh, yeah. Don't you?"

"I guess I can see why you say it. But to tell you the truth, I'm just as self-conscious as you." Margot didn't want to believe this, but then she thought back to the night of the homecoming dance when Cassie asked Margot for her opinion on how her dress looked, and how she said that it didn't fit her quite right. Margot couldn't fathom how someone as beautiful and sweet as Cassie could even for a second not understand her reputation being leaps and bounds greater than Margot's own. But then she thought about Cassie's parents, and how looks weren't necessarily what Cassie meant.

"I mean, if popular is hanging around with Max and the rest of my old friends..."

Margot noted the use of the word 'old' in Cassie's thought process, and she decided to end the conversation so Cassie wouldn't get too exasperated over the whole thing.

"I don't want to get you upset. Why don't we talk about something else? If that's okay, I mean..."

"Okay," Cassie said with a slight whimper tacked on. "What do you want to talk about?"

"Well, I don't mean to just come out and say it, but what did you mean when you said that Peter likes me? That's what you said, isn't it?" Margot wasn't giving Cassie the time to get a word in edgewise. She knew she was talking a mile a minute, and she felt like she wanted to know the answer that Cassie would give, but at the same time, she was worried that if she stopped talking, Cassie would take it all back and say that it was all just a cruel joke and she was trying to get back at Margot for being mean to Max or some nonsense like that. Margot realized that her self-consciousness and ability to see the negative in each situation was keeping her from being true friends and confidantes with Cassie, but she was too scared to let herself be happy. So, she continued, "I really don't think he does. After all, he was just having me help him to get to you. He didn't feel comfortable talking to you himself. Especially because he used to be friends with Max and all, and now Max is, well, you know. I don't want to get into it too much, but why would you say something like that about Peter liking me? It's just too ridiculous to even believe, right? You were joking, weren't you? I mean, it's really not funny, but I think it has to be a joke. Or maybe..."

"Margot!" Cassie didn't know any other way to get Margot's attention than to shout. Margot wasn't even looking at Cassie. It was like she was having a conversation with herself and trying to convince herself that there was just no possible way that any boy could possibly ever like her. Minus Walter Gribble. He was just someone she was going to have to deal with for a while. "Just calm down. Relax for a second. I'll tell you why I said what I said if you'll just stop. Okay?"

"I just..."

"No. You have to stop. Can I just say something?"

A silence overtook the room and Margot looked at Cassie distressed, as though the worst news ever was about to cross her lips and make its way into Margot's eardrums.

"Now that I've got your attention..." Cassie said with a grin. "If it's so obvious to you that he was using you, why not think about it like this? You've told me about the times you guys have hung out together already, right? So, why would he take you to the homecoming dance and want to spend time with you both before, after, *and* during it in order to make sense of me? You and I weren't even really friends until just recently. I don't care if you could read minds and know everything I was thinking; no guy wants to spend that much time with someone if he doesn't at least like that person a little bit. I mean, consider Walter. It's clear he likes you too."

"Well, that's kind of more obvious. I know that I'm kind of naïve about when a boy might like me, but he's pretty darn open. Your telling me that Peter likes me as more than a friend is kind of like telling me that Max is being mean to me because he thinks I'm cool. This isn't the third grade, Cassie. Boys are more direct than that in high school."

"Margot. I'm not trying to talk down to you or make you feel like you don't know what you're talking about, but you're wrong. That's *exactly* what boys are like in high school. They never got past the third grade mentally. I'm not saying that Max likes you as a friend. He's obviously a phony and a jerk and why either of us bother worrying about him is beyond me. I wish I had never gotten so interested in him. It's just that he used to be, well..."

"What?"

"You know what? Never mind. That's for another time, okay? Let's finish talking about Peter. He's a nice, great guy. His eyes light up when he's around you."

"They light up when he's around *you*."

"That's because *you're* around. Don't you get it?" Margot was trying to get it. She wanted to understand the inner workings of boys' minds. She figured that this is what men tried to do with women. She always heard it said that no man knows how to understand a woman. She couldn't fathom how this could be truer than trying to understand a ninth grade boy. It seemed like the hardest thing imaginable.

"Okay, if you don't believe me, we'll test this out. After play practice tomorrow, I want you to ask Peter if he wants to come over to your house and study for that chemistry test that we have coming up in a few days. See if he's willing to come. If he is, we'll plot out the rest from that point and see what happens. How does that sound?"

THIRTY-FOUR

Margot couldn't believe she had actually taken Cassie's advice and asked Peter to be her study partner for the chemistry test. She knew in her heart of hearts that he liked Cassie, and she felt as though this was cruel and unusual punishment making her sit through a whole study session next to the boy she likes while he daydreams about another girl. She kept thinking in science terms, about how they had no real chemistry because Peter's was only with Cassie. How Cassie's anatomy was so much more perfect than hers, so why would any boy even bother wasting his time studying with her when he could be studying with Cassie? Margot kind of hated herself for thinking in the ways she was thinking. She knew that Cassie truly meant well. She was trying to help out a friend, and she really didn't seem to have any interest in Peter in that way.

That aspect kind of haunted Margot a bit. She liked Peter so much. But at the same time that she liked him, she wanted other girls to think he was cute too so that if she ever got him, she'd be envied, even if ever so slightly. She knew it was selfish, but she didn't care. She couldn't remember if there had ever even been a time when anyone had envied her in her whole, entire life. If he wasn't good enough for Cassie, was he really good enough for Margot? The fact was that whenever Margot started to think like this, she realized how ridiculous it was. She liked him and that was all that mattered. Just because most of the other girls at Kipperton couldn't see Peter's good looks and sweet personality wasn't her problem. Plenty of them probably liked him for his smarts and his friendly nature, but she knew that those girls only liked him as a friend. She thought he was perfect, and she wasn't going to let anyone or anything tell her differently. Not even her own warped mind that tried to see the negative in every possible scenario.

The fact that Peter said yes to Margot worried her more. Now she had to sit through a night with a boy who didn't even like her. At least not like she wanted him to. And Cassie wanted to give her a "Margot-over" as she had phrased it, in which she would bring out all the best aspects of Margot's appearance and highlight them so Peter would be a fool not to see them and comment on how wonderful she looked. Margot thought it was a silly, bad idea. She didn't need to get all dolled up for a boy and then have him talk about Cassie Shearer all night long. She wanted to be with him, sure. But the way she knew it was going to go was so unappealing to her that she'd rather have been anywhere else that night than in her own living room with her chemistry book and Peter Mulvaney.

Margot decided after school that day that she was going to write in her journal and vent all her frustrations so that she could look back and hopefully feel that she was at least slightly unwarranted in her nervousness and anxiety over the impending study session. She wrote about Cassie fixing her hair and giving her tips on what to say and how to say it so that Peter wouldn't be able to misconstrue anything she said as wanting to be just "friends." The thing that bugged Margot most about all of this was that she hadn't really asked for any of this. Cassie had just pushed it on her. However, she couldn't say that she minded the attention. It was nice to have someone like Cassie fussing over her and making sure she was ready. She just didn't know if she was ready to be ready. Hearing the awful "no, I'm not interested in you" was too much for her to bear. If he tacked on "I think we should just be friends," she thought she might die a little right there in front of him. And if he made matters any worse at all by adding anything about how beautiful or amazing or sensational Cassie was, Margot thought she just might hit him. That wouldn't be a good start to a possible relationship, now would it?

Margot had told Peter to come by at 7, after the Maples' ate their 6 o'clock, like clockwork, dinner. Cassie had planned to leave before dinner started, but when it got to be 5:30 and she was still there, Mrs. Maples took it upon herself to extend an invitation to Cassie. Margot thought for sure that Cassie would decline. After all, it was too risky for her to be there when Peter arrived. It would look like they'd planned it all or something or other would go terribly, miserably wrong, as Margot felt it always seemed to do in her head. She knew she would inevitably be right. She wished she could be optimistic, but her fate as of late was too spotty and irrational for her to feel comfortable making any promises to herself or anyone else about what the future held.

They got through dinner just fine, to Margot's sheer surprise. She assumed that Walter would knock on the door or Max would show up and find some reason to yell at her, or Carolyn and Lisa would just peer through the window, point, and laugh at her impending doom. She knew her imagination was running wild. She knew that her suspicions were unwarranted. Cassie even got out of the house unnoticed by Peter by 6:50. Ten whole minutes before he was supposed to show up. When the phone rang at 6:58, Margot figured this was the kicker. This was what was going to ruin her night.

It was Cassie. Margot had answered the phone so swiftly that it hadn't even finished its first ring. She realized the seriousness of doing this and knew that Cassie was going to tell her what it was. It made her look desperate, anxious, and totally available.

"You want to look available, Margot, but you also want to kind of play hard-to-get." The contradictory nature of this statement was not lost on Margot. She couldn't imagine how she was supposed to make Peter know she wanted him while at the same time making it so that he couldn't have her even if he wanted her. It frustrated her to her very core to not be able to grasp the intricacies of boys, dating, and how girls like Cassie Shearer seemed to know these things and understand them to perfection.

"Okay, okay. But he's going to be here any minute. I'm even more nervous talking about this right now. So, can I go?"

"Oh, I didn't think about that." Margot thought then and there about how of all the things Cassie understood about boys and how to potentially get them, she didn't have the best timing as to when to quell someone's emotions rather than allow them to spike to unknown levels of irrationality. At least there was something Cassie wasn't good at.

7 o'clock came and went. Then 7:05 and 7:10. Margot knew the phrase "a watched pot never boils," but she couldn't help but stare at the clock, and then back at the phone, and then at the clock, and the phone again. He wasn't calling. He wasn't coming. He had stood her up. Then the doorbell rang.

"Oh, hey Margot. Sorry I'm late. My mom made me eat a second helping for dinner because she found out I skipped lunch today. I tried to hurry, but time just seemed to have gotten away..." Margot couldn't help but think how cute Peter looked right then, explaining the situation that she was so glad had occurred. She had been getting nervous, but at the same time relieved that she didn't have to deal with Peter coming over and knowing how to act around him in order to pull off Cassie's plan, while at the same time studying for chemistry. It seemed like a lost cause, trying to fit everything into a mere two to three hours of time in which he'd be at her house.

"What've you been up to today? I mean, after school let out?" Peter asked.

"Well, since Mr. Richardson told us we had to take a day off from play practice because we might over-rehearse, I came home. I mean, what does that even mean – over-rehearse? Do you really think that's possible? I love rehearsing. I can't imagine over-rehearsing."

"I guess he means that he doesn't want you to run your lines so much that you start to question yourself when you say them."

"Why would I possibly do that? If I know them, isn't it better that I keep saying them?"

"I see your point. Just be happy Mr. Richardson was willing to give you a day off from it, though, when there's only one week left till the play starts."

"Yeah, I guess you're right. Plus, Ashley comes next week." Margot kind of regretted saying that as soon as it came out of her mouth, but she couldn't take it back now.

"Ashley Burnham? Your friend from middle school? She's coming?"

"Yeah. You remember her?"

"I had a couple classes with her. I remember you guys used to hang out together by your lockers." Margot felt a twinge of happiness at the thought that Peter had actually known who she was and watched her at her locker once or twice, if not more. "What's she coming in for?"

"Oh, the play. I told her I was in it – well, kinda – and she said she wanted to come. So, she'll be staying here for a week. She has a couple days off school that week for teacher meetings or conferences or something, so her parents figured it worked out okay."

"Cool. I guess you'll be really busy next week then, with the play and Ashley and all."

Margot's over-eager imagination and undying need to understand what Peter was thinking were starting to get the best of her, and he hadn't even been there ten minutes. *He seems upset that I'll be really busy. Maybe he wanted to ask me out or hang out or...something! Eeeks! What do I do?!*

"Yeah, I'll be busy, I guess." Margot realized that this phrasing of her answer was only a re-phrasing of Peter's statement/question to her about her availability, but she got up her nerve anyway. "What kind of plans do you have next week, besides the play and all?"

"Oh, uh, nothing really. It might be nice to see Ashley again. I remember her being pretty cool, and now that we're friends (*eeks!*), maybe you wouldn't mind if we all hang out together. Whaddya say?"

"I don't mind." Margot tried to say it in the most understated, subtle tone she could muster, but it was awfully difficult. Her only wish was that they could hang out at least a little bit more on their own before Ashley actually arrived.

"Maybe Cassie can come too." And the bubble that Margot knew she had been living in was suddenly and sadly burst by the realization that Peter wanted Cassie there. She tried to think positively. *Maybe he wants Cassie there so it'll be easier to, uh, you know what — it's not worth it. I should just give up now and tell Cassie I told her so.* "And Walter. The four of us have been hanging out a lot lately after that whole Max incident." *Did he just redeem himself? Is he trying to say that we're all just friends? Does he just want Walter there because he's trying to stick me with the nerdy goofball that seems to cave in to my every whim just because he is infatuated with the idea of a girl like me who actually pays him any mind? Maybe he thinks it'll be easier to be with Cassie if Walter is there too and Ashley and Walter can keep me occupied while Peter makes his move. Oh, Margot. Get a grip. You're thinking too hard. He's here now, isn't he?*

"Margot? Hey, Margot?"

"Yeah?"

"It looked like you were thinking really hard about something. You haven't said anything in like ten seconds, and I wanted to know if you heard my question. I thought maybe you got focused on something in your textbook."

"Oh, sorry." She didn't know if she really meant it. She wanted Peter to know how annoyed she was with the uncertainty he kept throwing her way. She wanted him to understand the pain of liking someone and not being liked back. It seemed he did kind of understand that. With Cassie and all.

"Margot? I wanted to ask you something else."

"Yeah? What is it?" Margot's hopes of Peter being interested in her were already dashed with the question about Cassie being able to come hang out with them. She felt bad about it because she really did like Cassie. The girl was really being a friend. But at the same time, Margot was hurting, and Cassie seemed to be exploiting that by making Margot find out what was up with Peter and his feelings. Margot knew that Cassie wasn't *really* exploiting her, but she felt like crap whenever she was around Peter now, and that was enough to make her believe her own crazy thoughts.

"I thought we could go out on Saturday night. Just the two of us. To thank you and everything for all you tried to help me with. Sound good?"

Margot was floored. Maybe it was true. When you least expect it, it happens. Her mother had always told her that. She had never truly believed in the power of letting go and finding that something can happen because you're not thinking about it anymore. She had never thought that it could happen as quickly as it just had, at least.

"Did you just ask me out?" The words had come out of Margot's mouth before she could take them back. She realized that it sounded like she was making sure she had been asked on a date when she only wanted to make sure he had really said what he'd said.

"I guess that's what I did," Peter said with a slight contortion of his face that made his dimples pop out even more than they already did.

A slight smile appeared on her face, which she promptly tried to hide. "Sure. Sounds great. Where were you thinking?"

THIRTY-FIVE

"I told you so! If you would just trust me a little bit!"

"But he did ask about *you*. And he said he just wanted to thank me for everything I've helped him with. Which has all revolved around *you*. Sense a pattern here?"

"I see what you're saying, but go with me on this. Maybe he just was talking about me to get to spend time with you."

"Sounds nice, but it's hard to believe. I guess I'm still finding it amazing that he actually wants to hang out with me one-on-one, but that *is* happening. Maybe I should come to terms with the fact that you may be right on the other stuff too."

"Maybe? Maybe?!" Cassie was getting flustered. She didn't seem to know what to say to get Margot to grasp the concept that Peter actually had some kind of feelings for her. "Just take my word for it. I'm almost never wrong."

"But that means you're sometimes wrong. Maybe you're wrong about this."

"Maybe I'm not. Ever consider that? Huh?"

Margot liked the give and take, the back and forth, the friendly banter that she and Cassie were having. Cassie had mentioned Carolyn and Lisa a couple times in the past week that she and Margot had been hanging out more, and the conversation almost always seemed to revolve around the ditzy duo's self-centeredness and backstabbing nature. Cassie kept saying she had wanted out of those friendships for a while, but breaking away was harder than she thought. She was trying to hold on to a reputation while at the same time being who she wanted to be and not what someone like Max thought she should be.

Margot desperately wanted to give her take on the two girls. She knew, though, that if she did, and Cassie ever went back to being friends with the two wicked witches, she would pay. And it would be even more severe than if she talked about them behind their backs when Cassie actually was their friend. She didn't want word to ever get back to those two from Cassie that she was talking ill of them. Because if she lost Cassie, she lost all certainty of safe haven. It was like being in elementary school again, when everyone was playing tag on the playground and Margot was the one whom everyone would be chasing since she was talking so pointedly about each of them in mean, sarcastic ways. *Let Cassie say whatever she wants. If she really feels the way she does, then this won't be an issue. I won't have to worry about those girls bothering me again. Because even if they do, I have a buffer now. Maybe two – if Peter works out. And I suppose I have Walter, too. He's annoying, but at least he's got my back.*

"So, you think you're ready for tonight? You know what you're going to say and all that?"

"What do you mean what I'm going to say? Why can't I just talk like normal?"

"Margot." Cassie tilted her head slightly and shot a knowing glance in Margot's direction, almost as if to say that Margot wasn't really capable of knowing how to converse with a boy on a full-fledged date.

"I thought I'd leave the conversation up to him."

"Okay, first things first. If you leave the conversation up to a boy, and he starts an awkward silence, where does that leave you? You don't want to talk too much, but just enough. Have stuff to say and things to talk about."

"I guess we can talk about the play."

'That's a start."

"And...uh...oh gosh. I don't know! What can we talk about?!" Margot felt herself getting nervous. She had felt fine up till now, but with Peter's arrival looming in the next thirty minutes, she was starting to feel twinges of uncertainty and desperation for Peter to maybe not show up. She really wanted him to, but she thought that maybe lying in her bed and having him stand her up would be better. That way she could get used to the awful rejection she was sure to face countless times in the future by all the other boys she was sure would think of her as nothing more than a nerd, or even worse – a friend. That was the worst. To be thought of as a friend. The next worst thing was to be likened to a sister. Margot hadn't had that happen to her yet, even though she assumed it was bound to – most likely by Peter.

"Okay Margot. I think you'll be okay. I don't want to make you more nervous than you already are."

"Nervous? Don't be silly. I'm okay." Cassie knew this wasn't true. Margot's tone was uneven and her face gave away her anxiety as she tried to smile, but was only able to grin slightly. But Cassie didn't want to throw Margot off any more, so she told her to be herself, because she was really a great girl, and to let Peter lead the way since he had asked her out in the first place. If he got stuck, she should just come up with something to talk about.

"You're smart, Margot. I'm sure it'll work out just great. Trust me."

Trust you? Trust you? How can I trust someone like you who could have any guy she wanted – including the one I want? Why should I trust you?

"You trust me, don't you Margot?"

Do I trust you? You've helped me out tonight even though I'm jealous and skeptical of you. You know these things but continue to do your utmost to make me feel as though I'll be okay tonight. I guess I trust you. I don't think I ever would have before. But now...

"Yeah. I trust you. Look how much you've helped me tonight."

With that, Cassie said goodbye and made her way out of the house. Of course Peter showed up just as Cassie was walking down the driveway. She played it cool and told Peter that she was just dropping off some play material that Margot had asked her for.

"Really nice seeing you." Peter smiled as Cassie walked farther away.

"You too, Peter. Margot's looking forward to tonight."

"Yeah, me too." Peter suddenly remembered where he was and turned toward the door. "It should be a lot of fun."

"Yeah. Have fun tonight, okay? You two are cute together."

Watching through the slightly open window screen, Margot could have yelled at Cassie for that remark. *What could she possibly be thinking telling him that we're cute together! She's trying to make him realize what a mistake this is. I know it!*

"Yeah, she is kinda cute," Peter said, and a dimple appeared on his cheek. A smile!

Whaaaat? Did he just say I'm kinda cute?

As Peter turned around to head to the door, Cassie looked up, saw Margot in the window, and gave a thumbs up and a huge smile. Margot knew it was meant to say "told you so." She didn't know if she should believe it 100% just yet. There was still plenty of room for trouble to occur. Peter could bring up Cassie and how great she was to come over and be with Margot as she was getting ready. And maybe he was thinking that he really should have invited Cassie to come along, because they were really the ones who were meant to be together. Margot knew her nerves were getting the best of her, but she couldn't silence them. It was almost as if they were eating her alive. Then the doorbell rang.

Gaining her composure, Margot reminded herself that he probably thought of her as just a friend. Then she opened the door. Even though she had already seen him through her window as he walked up her driveway and talked to Cassie, she had to revel in just how cute he really was. He was wearing khakis and a button-down shirt.

"Hey, Margot. You okay?" Margot blushed, realizing that she hadn't even said hello yet and Peter had been standing there for at least a few seconds since she had opened the door.

"Yeah, I am. You look nice." *I can't believe I just said that!*

"You too." *He thinks I look nice too!* "Ready to go? My mom's waiting in the car and she said that she'd drop us off at Benino's. I thought I heard you say once that you liked it there. *He's listening to what I like! Even though that horrendous accident with Walter happened there, I'll take it!*

"Yeah, let's head out. Mom! I'm leaving!" Margot's mother made her way down the hall, wiping her hands on a dish rag.

"Have fun, you two. Oh, Peter, don't you look spiffy." *Did my mom just say 'spiffy'? Kill me now.*

"Thanks, Mrs. Maples. My mom said almost the exact same thing." *At least it's a mom thing*, Margot thought to herself. *Even though my mom takes the cake for cheesiness.*

"Make sure you say hello to her for me. What time can I expect you back, Margot?" *Why can't we just get out of the house without her asking so many intrusive questions? I know she's my mom and all, but oh. my. gosh.*

"Uh, I don't know." She realized that she didn't really know what they were doing tonight besides going to Benino's, and even if that was it, she didn't know how long they'd stay there or what would transpire during their time there to make them want to stay out longer.

"Well, Peter, I can't imagine your mother wants to pick you up too late. Did she give you a time that she expects you to be ready for her?"

"Moooom..." Margot nudged her mother while Peter looked a bit befuddled. When her mother looked at her, Margot shot her a look that encompassed not only aggravation, but desperation for the line of questioning to let up. Her mother knew her daughter well enough to know that she was responsible. On the other hand, she had never known her daughter to go out on a date. Homecoming had been different, since it had turned into a group thing, Margot figured. So a little nagging seemed in order, but it was still terribly infuriating to Margot.

"As long as she's home by 11. Okay? Does that sound good?" Margot shot her mom another look – this time one of thanks – and stepped closer to the door as Peter followed.

"No problem, Mrs. Maples. Back by 11. I'll be sure of it." *That could mean two things*, Margot thought morosely. *Either he's eager for the night to be over before it's even started, or he's being the gentleman that I know he is and telling my mother what she wants to hear so he can get in good with my parents and continue to take me out on date after date after...*

Margot's thought process trailed off as they got into the car with Mrs. Mulvaney and started driving to Benino's. The ride was rather pleasant, but quiet. Nobody seemed to be saying anything, other than a mere mention of how beautiful it still was outside even though it was already well into autumn.

"Sorry about my mom needing to drive us. I can't wait till the beginning of sophomore year when I'll get my license. It's really great that I have an early birthday. I don't know what I'd do if I couldn't drive at sixteen."

"Yeah. I know." Margot couldn't think of more to say. She was too busy pondering each and every word, and on top of it, each and every facial and hand gesture, that Peter used around her. *I know I'm reading too much into this, but maybe he wants to get his license so he can drive me around when we go out on dates since we'll be dating next year. Whoa. I have to get a grip. I'm reading way, way too much into this. Or am I? Yeah, I am. But what if...*

When they entered Benino's, the hostess, a girl whom Margot recognized as a senior at Kipperton, led Peter and Margot to a table near the kitchen. The way that the area was set up allowed customers to see the cooks throwing dough into the air and spinning pizzas around in their hands. As they passed the booth where the ill-fated kiss with Walter happened, Margot felt a chill come over her a bit. Thankfully, it went away almost as quickly as it came when they got seated at a two-person booth. When they sat down, Peter smiled, and his dimples appeared again. Margot felt happy. But she didn't want to look too happy. It was just what she needed – to seem desperate and eager. So, she looked over at Peter and smiled timidly, so as not to seem that way.

"It's great that we could do this tonight. I mean, we're hardly ever alone, minus those times you helped me." *He's going to bring up Cassie. And the whole night is going to turn into a 'where might she be?' or 'what could she be doing right now?' This is gonna majorly suck...* "Like if you hadn't helped me with my science or English homework, I don't know what kind of grades I would have wound up getting on my first quarter report card. You're a lifesaver, Margot." *At least it wasn't about Cassie. But maybe he's just thinking of this as a thank you dinner that his mom obligated him to come and have with me since I helped him keep his grades up and so one day he can get into a good college and go off and meet some other girl who's completely the opposite of me, and...* "Really, I'll do anything. Let me make up all the time you've spent with me."

Margot wanted to say, *I wouldn't have had it any other way. Spending time with you is what makes my days fly by. But I wish they wouldn't fly by. Even though I'm sure it means we're having fun. You know what you can do for me? Be my boyfriend and kiss me and hug me and be with me.* And then she would stare longingly into his eyes and hear back from him that everything she had just said was exactly how he felt. He just didn't want to say it in case she didn't feel that way. But she was so brave and strong and wonderful that he knew she would get up her nerve before he ever did. And then she would mention Cassie and how she had been jealous of her, and Peter would say how ridiculous that was and how Cassie couldn't hold a candle to the beauty and infectious spirit that Margot possessed. And how being the understudy to the lead role in the play wasn't a slight at all, but a wonderful way of saying how strong an actress Margot is that she can learn all the lines and be prepared in the case of a sickness or problem that may never even occur, especially since she'd have to play leading lady to Max's leading man if Cassie were to get sick or have some other kind of issue.

But instead of all that, she found herself saying, "It's no problem. We're friends, right? That's what friends do." And she wished she'd really said the other stuff instead. Now he was probably thinking that that's all she would ever want to be. And if he had even possibly been thinking about how great they could be together, it was all shot to heck now. If she just wanted to be friends, he'd just want to be friends, and all the trouble she had gone to getting ready and having Cassie help fix her up would be for naught. At least if she'd said the other stuff, it would all be out in the open, and she could know once and for all if something was going to happen. She wouldn't have to play the game anymore that everyone always talks about and which she knew she would likely always end up losing. That dating game where you never know what the other person is thinking, but you keep going out and trying to figure that person out. But you never seem to. *You're such a doofus, Margot! Get. A. Grip.*

When the waitress came to take their order, Peter asked Margot if she wanted to share a pepperoni pizza. She gladly accepted. It was her favorite type of pizza, after all. Margot found that after they ordered, she became keenly aware of her surroundings. She wondered if anyone saw them there together. She became more and more curious if anyone would think anything more was going on and if maybe, just maybe, word would get back to Peter that they had been on a date, and she'd be around when that happened to hear how he responded. Then, she could know if she could say that she'd finally had her first date.

It seemed too good to be true that she was there with Peter, at Benino's, her favorite restaurant. Despite that awful evening with Walter and his parents, she still loved it there. She felt comfortable and cool, as though her uncertain reputation had remained intact despite the aggravation that she had had that night, and which she had resolved would never have the likelihood of happening again. She was watching her back, being careful – and not getting anywhere too close to Walter, especially at this location of all places. Things were going great. That's when she knew something, anything, was bound to happen to waylay her date with destiny. But nothing happened – at least not right away.

A half hour passed before their food came. The waitress had brought them a basket of breadsticks to munch on before the pizza was ready. They chatted about school and the play and life in general. Margot was surprised at how easily the words flowed out of her mouth as she talked to Peter. It was basically effortless. Moments of awkward silence were few and far between, and when they happened, Peter did his best to fill them with jokes. She enjoyed his humor, and she loved hearing him snicker every time he said something he considered funny.

Just as they were starting to wind down their meal – just as Peter asked Margot what they should order for dessert – a light squeal hit Margot's ears. She looked up, not really knowing why, but feeling deep down that she should have kept staring at her food, or at Peter, or at something else entirely. Looking up was the worst possible thing she could have done, or at least she thought so when she did it.

Kelly Gribble was a mere few feet away from Margot and Peter. She and Walter's dad were being seated just a few tables from them, and Mrs. Gribble, upon seeing Margot, got so excited that she just had to stop by the table, as she explained in her own words.

"Why hello Margot! What a pleasant surprise to see you here. I just had to pop over and say hi!" *Why me?* "Is my Walter around? He must be around here somewhere..." *Does she honestly think that I'm with him 24/7? She's got to be out of her mind.*

In the nicest tone Margot could muster, she said, "Um, no Mrs. Gribble. Not sure where Walter is." She found it deeply interesting that Mrs. Gribble wasn't aware of Walter's whereabouts. She was one of the most overprotective mothers that Margot had ever known – and she had always thought her own mother took the cake for that. That is, until she had met Walter's mom several years ago.

"Well, where is he, dear?"

"I don't know."

"But you're his..." Margot knew that Mrs. Gribble was about to say 'best girl.' She was appalled, flabbergasted, and completely humiliated that Peter was sitting right there, watching this debacle play out right in front of his own two eyes. As Margot was pondering all of this, Mrs. Gribble had turned her attention to Peter as she had cut herself off. "Oh, hello. Peter, is it?" Mrs. Gribble had a tone of indifference in her voice. She seemed to take issue with Peter sitting there. Figuring she would subtly try to push for information on what was going on between Margot and Peter, she hastened to keep talking to them, delaying their discussion of dessert ever so much longer. Mr. Gribble was sitting in his booth, being the kind of person Margot could only wish that Mrs. Gribble would decide to be in that moment, but she knew it would never, ever happen. Peter seemed in a haze, and looked as though he had no idea how to detach himself from the aggravation that Mrs. Gribble was piling on them.

"Walter is such a fine young man, don't you think? So wonderful and loyal. That's why he is so fond of you, Margot. You're so *wonderful*." She had said the last word with a hint of criticism in it as she turned back to Margot. As though she didn't believe it quite as much anymore. Even though it was probably supposed to hurt Margot down to her very core that Mrs. Gribble would disapprove of something she was doing, she only felt a twinge of upset, and that was merely because she wanted to be left alone. She had always been taught to respect her elders. She knew if her mom was there, she would allow this to continue, or she would nudge Margot in the ribs again like she had when Walter and his parents had come to sit with them during their first visit to Benino's this school year.

Every time Mrs. Gribble looked over at Peter's side of the table, she seemed to avert her eyes, as though looking at him would cause her too much pain and heartache, since Walter wasn't the one sitting there. After about five more minutes of letting Mrs. Gribble go on and on about Walter's most wonderful qualities, Peter spoke up.

"Um, yeah, hi." Mrs. Gribble looked over at him as if she couldn't believe he'd interrupted her. Mr. Gribble was still sitting over at his table, probably thrilled that his wife had left *him* alone for any amount of time at all.

"Yes?" Mrs. Gribble asked, elongating the 'e' sound to make it seem the hardest word ever to say.

"Well, you see, we were actually about to decide what to order for dessert. I know you're Walter's mom and all, and he's a great guy, really." At that, Mrs. Gribble tried to stifle a smile, as she knew this was true, but didn't want to show any happy emotions toward this boy who was, in her mind, certainly only trying to upstage Walter with Margot. "But you've been talking for, like, five minutes, and we were ready to order. So not to be rude or anything, because I don't want to be, but do you mind if we get back to our meal?" Mrs. Gribble looked slightly appalled and perturbed. How would she ever continue going on and on about Walter? But she looked at Peter, turned to Margot, told Margot to enjoy her dessert, and added in that she'd be sure to tell Walter that Margot had said hello and was sorry she missed him. Margot hesitated to stop Mrs. Gribble from moving ahead with this plan because she knew it would only cause her to talk for longer.

"Bye then. Nice seeing you." She looked at Margot, took a sidelong glance at Peter, and walked back to her table.

"Sorry. I just wanted to get back to dessert. That wasn't rude, was it?" Peter sounded like he wanted Margot's blessing to have done what he did. He was so unsure of himself, having talked to Walter's mom in that way. "I mean, what I did was okay, right?"

"Are you kidding?" Margot semi-whispered, certain that Mrs. Gribble was doing her utmost to overhear their every word. "I'm sorry I didn't have the guts to do it myself." They both laughed together quietly, snickering at the absurdity of the situation. Margot was sure Peter was thinking that it was just ruining their timing for dessert, while Margot was upset that the last five to ten minutes of her life had been spent listening to Kelly Gribble rather than to the wonderful sounds of her date with Peter.

Everything sounded nice, everything looked nice, and everything felt nice, minus the lapse in conversation they had had due to Walter's mom. *I guess I'm just destined to have life get messed up for me. Nothing ever seems to go as planned. But Peter's still here. And he had the guts to stand up to her. That was pretty awesome. Maybe he really does like me. At least a little. Otherwise he could have just let her keep talking, and he could have said that Walter and I do look like a pretty great couple. Gosh. I wonder what Mrs. Gribble would have done if he would have started agreeing with her and going on and on about Walter's wonderfulness and how he really is the 'best guy' for me.* It was too weird and scary a thought to even consider any further, Margot reasoned to herself. She told herself that at least all was well now, and to try hard not to wonder why Peter had done what he had, but rather to just accept it and be happy about it.

They finished their dessert – two scoops of ice cream, Margot's topped with butterscotch fudge, Peter's with chocolate – and decided they would play some of the arcade games. When Peter's mom picked them up at the end of the evening, Margot made a point to avoid eye contact with the Gribbles, but she could feel Mrs. Gribble's eyes following them out the front door of the pizza parlor.

Mrs. Mulvaney waited in her car as Peter walked Margot to her front door. She had been hoping he would, but she didn't know if his mom being right there, or the fact that he probably didn't perceive the evening as a date, would stop him.

"I had a really good time tonight. I'm glad we were able to do this."

"Yeah, we should do it again sometime," Margot heard herself say.

"Sounds good. Maybe we can do something next weekend." He hesitated, before continuing, "Oh. That won't work. It's the play." Margot was stunned back into reality with that statement. The date of the play had completely flown out of her mind. If it was next weekend, that meant that Ashley was going to show up in just a few days. Time sure was flying.

"Well, we'll figure something out. Maybe we can all hang out at the cast party."

"Definitely." Margot tried to decipher whether Peter's 'definitely' was one that declared certainty because he wouldn't have it any other way, or if it was one that declared, 'well, I'm obligated to you now, so we'll have to go through with it, I guess.' Margot knew she was driving herself crazy, but over-thinking things was her specialty. She didn't see that changing anytime soon.

It was then that Peter started to say good night and walk away. Margot took her key and started to put it into the front door lock when she heard Peter say, "Thanks again, Margot. It really was fun. Hopefully when Ashley comes in, we can do it again." Margot finished turning the key in the lock, said goodbye, and walked inside, almost floating up the stairs to bed.

THIRTY-SIX

He didn't even mention Cassie's name while we were eating. She didn't come up at all. Maybe he just didn't want to upset me. But if he didn't like me, or didn't think I thought anything of going out with him, there would be nothing keeping him from mentioning her and her beauty and grace and all that stuff. I know I like her, and she helped me and all, but I still can't help but be jealous of her. It's stupid. Yeah, really stupid. I know. But how would you feel if the guy you like has always had you trying to figure out what one girl thinks, and then he all of a sudden doesn't mention her and takes you out to eat? Well, you're a diary, so of course this doesn't pertain to you. But if you were real, I know you'd think it sounded crazy. Almost as crazy as me asking my diary what it would think in a similar situation to the one I'm in. Geez, I'm nuts.

Anyway, moving on, he didn't mention her. He only talked to me about stuff that we both seemed to like. He joked and I laughed, and then he laughed, and he was sooo cute. I just can't imagine him getting any cuter unless he walked around with a little puppy dog. And he wants to get together again. When Ashley comes. Oh god. When Ashley comes. Why do I think that's gonna be a recipe for disaster? I mean, I love her. She's my best friend and I would never say anything bad about her. But... she just has a way of making everything about her. And for once in my life, I want everything to be about me. I know that sounds selfish and egotistical and all that kind of self-absorbed stuff, but she is coming to see ME in the play. I mean, if I get a chance to even perform. To stay with ME. To hang out with MY friends. Wow. I think that's the first time I've ever claimed to have friends other than Ash. Wow. I guess Dad was right. High school is maturing me. I won't tell him. He won't be happy that his little girl is

181

growing up. But I am. I guess I am growing up. For heaven's sake, I just went on my first date. My FIRST DATE. I'm calling it that. Even if Peter didn't think of it like that. But I think he did.

Now I just have to figure out how to get it to work out again. How will I work it out in such a way that Ashley won't embarrass me or say something ridiculous or make him want her instead? Or make him want Cassie again? Because Cassie wants to hang out with us too. How am I going to do this? We can hang out with Cassie, but I don't want to do it at the same time that we hang out with Peter.

I never thought I would have such a problem. It wasn't so long ago that Ashley and I were lamenting the woes of never having anyone but each other to hang out with. Now, don't get me wrong. We loved having each other. But we couldn't understand why certain people who had been our friends weren't our friends anymore. It all started in the sixth grade. That was when Miranda Langford moved to town. She was in our homeroom and Ashley and I were quick to be friends with her while everyone else seemed to be sizing her up to see which clique she'd best fit into. Can you believe that? Cliques. In the sixth grade. The power of bullying was and still is strong. Max Poler made his mark in the sixth grade by starting to hang out with the eighth graders. How he did it I'll never know. He was always destined to be popular, I guess. And Cassie followed along, just like the rest of that stupid gang that she doesn't hang out with anymore. I guess I envied them then. I wondered how they did it, hanging out with the older kids, making jokes, and walking down the hall like they were the hottest, greatest, most exciting eleven-year-olds in the whole wide world. I know it sounds ridiculous. That's because it was. Eleven-year-olds haven't even gone through puberty yet, and they're chic and awesome already? Yeah, right. But it seemed to be true, at least back then when we were all in the same sixth grade boat, and they were being saved by the lifeboats when it started to sink and I... well, I was drowning alongside Ashley. At least we were together, but we were miserable together.

Then everything kind of got better. Minus Max being a snobbish jerk to the two of us – especially me – as often as he could. We started talking with Miranda Langford, that new girl. Even though Max and the rest of his lackeys were hanging out on what seemed to be easy street, Miranda was friendly and kind and she wanted to be our friend. She even made fun of the "cool kids" with us. For the whole three months of sixth grade we'd been through so far, Miranda, Ashley, and I had been almost inseparable. We had sleepovers every other Friday or Saturday night, if not every week. We went to the mall, the movies, the park, the zoo, you name it. Life was good.

That is until December rolled around and the Winter Dance was about to be held. The three of us made a pact. Wow. I can't believe I haven't thought of this in so long. And that I've never written this down before. I guess when you suppress something, you really put it out of sight, out of mind. Anyway, back to the pact. We were all eleven-year-old sixth graders who didn't know anything about anything. Not that I know anything now. I'm still in the dark about this whole dating thing. I like it, but I don't like the uncertainty of it. That's for sure. We said that we were all going to go with dates, or we weren't going to go at all. We all basically knew that this was an impossible road to hoe. No boy had ever even shown any interest in us, or chanced a glance our way. We were like the girl version of the Three Musketeers. All for one, and one for all.

Then, Kyle Crews came on the scene. He was a seventh grader who had just transferred over in November of that year from the other middle school in the city. He was quickly becoming a must-have among the girls – even the eighth graders. He had already had his growth spurt, and he even seemed to have a hint of a five-o-clock shadow. It was strange for a seventh grader, but maybe it was just the aura of maturity that he seemed to exude that made it seem that he really had all of these things going for him. The three of us had chanced our own glances at him, but he had never looked back. It was just unrequited cuteness. We all thought he'd go for Cassie or some other more popular girl. That is, until he asked Miranda to the dance. She was just as shocked as Ashley and I were when he approached her at her locker one day and told her he wanted to go with her. Before she could even think about the fact that she had made that pact with us, she was smitten with saying "yes" over and over. She must have said it at least five times while a big smile spread across his face.

She tried to apologize to us. She tried to tell us she was sorry, but when we wouldn't accept her apology for breaking the Winter Dance pact, she got upset. She said she would have understood if we had done the same. She definitely wouldn't have. She was always saying how loyalty is the most important thing, so I think that was really a load of bull. She went with him to the dance while Ashley and I stayed home and watched Grease *and tried to participate in the hand jive dance in the movie in order to feel like we were at least at some sort of social gathering.*

Before we even had a chance to make up with Miranda, her dad got transferred to a town a few hours away, and she was gone before winter break even ended. I don't want this same thing to happen with Ashley. We have to find a way to not let the whole Miranda thing become what happens to us. The fact that Ash is coming to visit is great. We've maintained our friendship despite the distance. I'm thankful for that. I hope she is too.

Maybe I should tell her about Peter before she gets here. I haven't told her that we went out yet. I don't want her to get here and be all upset like I kept something from her. According to her, she tells me everything. I really can't believe that, but I guess I'll take her word for it. That is, until she starts making it seem like I'm not good enough to know something because I don't have a full-fledged boyfriend. That's my biggest worry, I guess. Her making me feel like I'm less than she is. I know she doesn't think she does it, but she does. She's always telling me on the phone all these things that make me feel inferior to her. "One day you'll know what it's like, Margot." "I can't believe it took so long for it to happen to me. I feel so wonderful all the time now." "It'll happen when you least expect it. Just like it did for me." I just want to scream when she says things like that and tell her to just shut up and go away. She's so patronizing about a boyfriend that she's had for what? Like not even three months? And she's making it seem like the world revolves around him and nothing else matters. I mean, I guess it's good that she still takes the time to call me up, but 95% of the call is about Brad. What Brad wore that day, how Brad did in his sports game, what Brad bought her, what time Brad is coming over. I know that if Peter was my boyfriend, I'd be raving all about him too, but shouldn't she be even just a little bit sweeter around me? It's like she thinks I'm saying, "Wow Ashley, tell me more."

Like that song in Grease. *But I'm not. I'm really thinking, "You stuck up snot. Don't you realize I'm all alone and you're making it all that much harder? How would you feel if this situation were reversed?" And she'd act all stupid, like she didn't realize what she was doing. And maybe she doesn't, but shouldn't she realize that I'm not thrilled with what we talk about? I wonder what she can tell me about me from the last few months. All she probably knows is that I'm in a play, and... that's about it. I'm in a play. Wow. Whoop de doo for best friend Ashley. Okay, enough ranting and raving. I better get to bed. Sweet dreams to me. I sure need 'em. Good night!*

THIRTY-SEVEN

"Margot! Let's get a move on. We've got to get to the airport. Ashley will be getting here in less than an hour."

The day had arrived. Ashley was coming, they play was in a mere couple of days, and life was going pretty darn well, if Margot had to say so herself. Peter had called the day after their "date" and asked if she wanted help running her lines. She tried to forget that Walter had called up that next day too, asking if he could stop by and do the same. When she had told him no, even though it was after Peter had asked, he sounded hurt, but at the same time, vehemently eager.

"I'll see you at dress rehearsal, though. Right, Margot? We'll have to run the lines. I mean, in case Max and Cassie have some kind of issue that keeps them both from being on stage. I even asked Mr. Richardson, and he said he might devote one performance to the understudies to be the leads. Wouldn't that be great?" Walter was working his way into being with Margot any way he knew how. Margot had to admire his determination. Especially since he wasn't even the lead understudy anymore, but second understudy ever since the homecoming debacle. However, he was not easily swayed, that was for sure. But she would not be sucked into the guilty feeling she knew would be coming if her mother knew she had turned down a run-your-lines get-together with one of her male counterpart understudies.

She also couldn't deny that it would be pretty great if Mr. Richardson really allowed that to happen. She knew that Cassie would be fine with the idea. Heck, she'd probably even welcome it to allow Margot some time in the spotlight. And it sure wouldn't hurt to have Ashley see her bowing to immense applause after she killed her performance. But Max, on the other hand. He wouldn't have it. Margot knew he would fight tooth and nail to be sure that she didn't get any time to shine. He was just a bully like that. Always putting her down, never letting her feel like she was worth anything. He'd always been like that with her, and Margot still couldn't for the life of her understand how he and Peter had ever been friends. Peter was nice and kind and so incredibly cute. Not that that last fact made any difference in the matter, but it never hurt for her to add it in as a special consideration for herself. The thought of them hanging out together just didn't make sense to her.

Pulling up to the airport, Margot was about to get out of the car when she saw Ashley running toward them, through the throngs of people who were lining the walkway into the security area. She looked great; Margot couldn't deny it. Her hair had grown out, and she was wearing makeup – something she never wanted to wear before, but which she must have given in to for Brad. She always said it took too much time and energy to put something on that wasn't even going to get her noticed. Now that she was getting noticed, Margot guessed it had changed Ashley's mind. Even though Margot did feel happy to see her, she still felt pangs of jealousy for this new life that Ashley had.

"Margot! I can't believe it's really you! I'm here! It seemed like this day would never come!" Ashley's excitement made Margot forget her worries, at least for the time being, and throw herself into full so-glad-you're-here, can't-wait-to-have-things-be-back-like-they-used-to-be mode.

"Ashley, you look awesome!" At that moment, Mr. and Mrs. Maples exited the car, eager to see their quasi-daughter who used to be at their house more often than she was probably at her own home.

"Mr. and Mrs. Maples! Oh, I'm so glad to be back. Is Roxie at the house? I can't wait to pet her!"

All the exclamations kept going as they piled into the car and headed back down the highway and neared the house. As they pulled up the drive, Margot was surprised to see none other than Peter sitting on the porch.

Despite her desire to run out of the car into his arms so she could proclaim how much she loved him, she held back, noticing that Ashley had not yet looked in Peter's direction. As soon as the car came to a stop, though, she saw him.

"Margot, who's that?" Upon looking a little closer, she grabbed her bag and opened her door, trying to get a better look. "Is that Peter Mulvaney?" she asked, her words laced with curiosity.

"Yeah, I guess it is," Margot responded.

"I invited him over." The words rang out loud and clear as Mrs. Maples said them. "I heard him talking the other day with you, Margot, about wanting to see Ashley while she was in. So I invited him to come over. I hope that's okay."

Margot didn't know how to respond. Even though she loved having Peter over as much as she possibly could, throwing him into life with Ashley right away seemed too much. Margot didn't want to ask him to leave, however, so she found herself stuck with the situation. Ashley seemed quite pleased, though, so Margot knew all wasn't lost – at least not yet.

"I haven't seen him since the end of eighth grade. Wow. You didn't tell me you were friends with him."

'Yeah, well, I...'"

"Girls, you better get a move on. He's sitting there waiting, after all." More of that motherly guilt brought to you by a mom who set something up and then expected you to just go with the flow, notwithstanding your own feelings about whatever the issue may be.

Approaching the porch, they waved hello as Peter made his way down the walk to the driveway.

"Long time, no see. Thought I'd come over and chat."

"Yeah. Good to see ya. It's been too long." Ashley was perky, and Margot was happy that all seemed to be going well, at least so far. It looked like Ashley couldn't decide whether or not she should hug Peter, and she seemed to be looking at Margot for cues. This prompted Margot to say they should head inside and drop Ashley's stuff down in her room so they could sit in the living room and chat. This obviously gave Mrs. Maples reason to suggest the patio, but Margot reasoned that it was a bit too cool outside in her opinion, and she'd rather just sit inside and stay warm. Plus, Roxie was waiting at the window, and heading inside was the best bet to make her happy.

Peter stayed for about an hour. Mrs. Maples offered to have him for dinner, but he said that his mother had dinner plans for his family. Margot tried not to look disappointed. The hour had gone by smoothly, and Ashley and Peter were getting along great. She wasn't acting all high and mighty like Margot thought she would. She seemed to be okay with hanging out with Peter, and this thrilled Margot. But she knew that the truth could come out that Ashley was just being nice for the sake of not upsetting Margot as soon as she arrived. That made Margot nervous.

Dinner passed slower than Margot would have hoped. By the time her dad was done questioning Ashley about her new school and how her parents were doing, it was getting late. Ashley had yawned a couple times, and Margot really didn't want to wait until the next day to hear Ashley's thoughts on Peter.

"Mom. Dad. I think we should get upstairs. I mean, Ashley must be tired after her flight." Noting Margot's line of thought, Ashley thanked Mr. and Mrs. Maples for dinner and got up from the table, Roxie following her closely, hoping she'd drop some crumbs or spare bits of food that were possibly lingering in her hand.

"I think I'll get done in the bathroom. I *am* pretty tired," yawned Ashley when she got to the top of the stairs. Margot nodded to her room. Her parents had set up a cot for Ashley on the floor next to Margot's bed. She was hurt that the night hadn't gone exactly as she would have liked, but she understood that it wasn't fair to Ashley to keep her up just to satisfy her own curiosity.

She didn't have to wait until the next day, though. Ashley walked into the room, perky as ever. Margot figured that she had learned to fool parents quite well by yawning and being polite. This made Margot happy, but at the same time, she became terribly concerned about what Ashley would have to say now that she had been blissfully awake the whole time. It took about a half hour of Ashley talking about the flight and her new school and then about her new room in her parents' new house, followed by a bit about Brad, and then just a little more about her fantastic new life before Margot had a chance to get a word in edgewise. She was starting to grow wary that all this "new" in Ashley's life was going to edge out the "old" - namely Margot herself.

"So glad you're here, Ash. It's been a while since we've had time to talk like this."

"Yeah, I know. I've missed you, Margot. Talking on the phone or chatting online just isn't the same as looking right at you and being here." *And? Come on, Ash. You know I'm dying here.* "I didn't realize you were such good friends with Peter Mulvaney. Wasn't he kind of dorky in middle school? He's kind of cute now." Margot knew the look that Ashley was giving. It was one of interest. Even though she had spent hours upon hours over the last few months talking about Brad and how wonderful, charming, and stupendously fabulous he was, she was going to get her flirt on if she could only get a little scoop. Margot wasn't about to give it to her. She had to make it perfectly and blatantly clear that Peter was off-limits. Flirting wasn't even a maybe in this scenario.

"Yeah. We got to be friendly since we have a couple classes together. I guess he's cute. I haven't really noticed." Margot didn't know why she was trying to act so nonchalant about the whole thing. She liked Peter, and now that Ashley didn't think he was the dorkiest, ugliest boy in the world, why couldn't she make it known that she liked him? Then Margot realized what the problem was. She knew how clear it was. And how annoying. But it was still a problem. She was afraid of Ashley talking her out of something. She knew that as soon as Ashley knew that Margot liked Peter, she would find ways of making Margot think that getting together with him was a terrible idea. More room for her to snake her way into flirting for the little bit of time she'd be around. Margot knew that Ashley didn't mean to be this way, but she just came across as conniving like that. Margot hated to think that it was along the lines of something Carolyn or Lisa would do, but she knew it was true. Ashley was becoming a little more like them when it came to something like this. That was why telling her about being friendly with Cassie was another no-no in Margot's mind. But she knew she had to pull off the bandage and get going with telling the truth. The revelations would be good for their friendship, or so Margot hoped.

"Ashley. I was actually hoping we could talk."

"Sure. Thought that's what we were doing, but I'm all ears."

"Well, I wanted to tell you this before Peter stopped over. I mean, I didn't expect him to be here when we got back. It was a surprise. I mean, who would've thought he'd be here?" Margot knew she was stuttering a bit and going on about something that wasn't yet being made clear to Ashley.

Ashley was just staring at Margot, waiting for the punchline to her drawn-out speech. "I... well, I think it's important that you know..."

"Spit it out, Margot. I mean, you're driving me crazy. What is it?"

"I like Peter, okay?" Margot realized it had come out a little louder than she'd wanted. She didn't need her parents – especially her dad – hearing that their little girl was in *like* with a boy. She'd never hear the end of it. They knew that she was fond of Peter. If they didn't, they were completely lost. But she didn't need it broadcast to the world, and she knew she had said it quite loudly.

"Yeah, he's a great guy. So what?" For all of Ashley's confidence and desire to flirt, she could be kind of dense sometimes.

"Ashley, come on. You know what I'm saying. I *like* Peter. We went out the other night, and I..."

"You *what*? You didn't tell me that! Why were you keeping something like that a secret? I feel like such an idiot! I never would have said about his being cute and all." This is what Margot was afraid of. She was changing her mind about Peter. She wasn't going to let Margot have any sense of happiness here. It was just not in her to let them both be happy at the same time. "Margot. I mean. I never would have guessed. That's..." *A horrible idea for you to go out with him. Ridiculous – he's not even your type. Absurd – he's way too good for you.* Even though Margot knew Ashley would probably never say any of those things – especially the last one – she couldn't help but think that something irritating was about to come out of Ashley's mouth. Instead, she heard, "That's awesome. You deserve it."

While Margot metaphorically scratched her head and waited for the realization that Ashley had actually said something nice to her to sink in, she found herself smiling. "Really? You're happy?"

"Why wouldn't I be? Now we can swap stories about boyfriends!"

"Well, he's not actually my boyfriend," Margot said wistfully.

"Yet."

"What's that?"

"I said *yet*. He's not your boyfriend *yet*. By the time I go home, that's going to have changed."

"But Cassie said..." Margot caught herself, but too late. She had already said the "C" name, and Ashley was jumping all over it.

"Cassie? Cassie who? Cassie Shearer? What about her?" Ashley didn't sound upset. Just a bit dumbfounded. "What has she got to do with this?"

"We've kind of been..." Margot waited a second, as if a pause would make this already interesting news sound even more dramatic. "Friends."

"Wow. Well, I guess this is what happens when you move away and your best friend doesn't tell you things." Even though Margot knew this was a swipe at her for not having told Ashley anything and everything about this year so far, she was thrilled with the fact that Ashley was still calling her "best friend" to her face. Despite Ashley's annoying tendencies, Margot really enjoyed her company and was happy to have her there. Especially after how she had reacted to the news about Peter. It was as though a weight had been lifted off of Margot's shoulders and placed instead on the seemingly unattainable task of making Peter into the boyfriend that Margot had wanted for months.

THIRTY-EIGHT

The morning of the play's opening day arrived, and with it a whole new level of anxiety and pressure the likes of which Margot felt could never be topped. This was the day that would determine at least a portion of her fate, and the days to come wouldn't be any less intimidating. She'd have to grin and bear it. At least she had Ashley by her side, and a new friend in Cassie. But the thought of Walter being so over-the-top excited and Peter being, well, Peter, was a bit much for her to swallow.

This is why it came as no surprise when Walter called her house a mere fifteen minutes after she had gotten up to prepare for the day.

"Margot! It's here! The day is finally here! I can't believe it. Can you? Oh, I know you're going to be great. I mean, if we get on stage. I'm sure Mr. Richardson is going to give us our own chance to be in the show. I just know it. You think so, don't you?"

Despite Margot's sheer happiness that she had been cast in the play and the day had finally arrived, Walter's happy-go-lucky attitude was still just like Walter – too over-the-top. But he was right. Or at least she hoped so in this instance. Since the show was taking up four performances that weekend, one that very night, a matinee and evening performance on Saturday, and another matinee on Sunday, Margot surmised that Mr. Richardson could still change his mind and give one of the performances to the understudies. It wasn't what she desperately wanted, but at the same time it was. She was terrified of having to do love-related scenes with Walter, but terribly ready to showcase her talent for the whole school to see. The guy who had been cast as lead understudy after Walter had to give up the position had dropped out a couple days earlier, after his parents had told him off for failing three quizzes within the week before the performance. This brought Walter back to being first understudy to Max.

"Yeah, Walter. It would be nice. But I've really got to go. I've got to get ready. My make-up and my..."

"Oh, you'll look great for sure, Margot. Don't worry about it. But I'll let you go, I guess. I want to let my leading lady get ready and prepared for opening night."

It was very nice of Walter to say, but the "leading lady" bit made her twitch a bit. It was the next worst thing to being his "best girl."

The entire cast of the freshmen play had been given a reprieve from school the day of the opening show since Mr. Richardson had been kind enough to request the time off for his actors and actresses. Since it was a Friday, Margot couldn't be upset. It was always a test day in at least two of her classes, and her teachers had been nice enough to hold off on their maniacal schemes to ruin her chances at a decent GPA until the following week when the play was over. Ms. Pelham had even offered extra credit in her Honors English class if anyone came to see the play and wrote a one-page report on it. When Margot had asked if she could get extra credit just for being in it, Ms. Pelham said she'd have to write the same report, but about her experience as an actress and how it felt to get into the character she had been cast to play. It felt like an okay compromise, but Margot still felt that it wasn't quite fair that she had to do double the work (being in the performance and writing about it) as those people who only had to sit back and enjoy the show while writing up what were sure to be a dozen or more lackluster reports on *10 Things I Hate About You* rather than *The Taming of the Shrew*. She wondered if Ms. Pelham would even be able to note the differences between the two versions of Shakespeare's play in the students' writings.

While Margot was up and about getting ready, she could hear Ashley starting to move around in the bedroom, since Roxie was becoming more playful as though something interesting was happening down the hall. Ashley had been so tired that she hadn't even heard the phone ring when Walter called. Her jet lag was still wearing on her, even though she tried to hide it with her perkiness. When Margot returned to her room after finishing up with her daily morning bathroom routine, Ashley was sitting cross-legged on the bed in her pajamas, looking as though she wanted to say she knew something that Margot would have to guess.

"What's up, Ash?"

"Margot, the phone rang while you were in the bathroom."

"Okay. Who was it?"

"Oh, I think you know who it was."

"Ummmm... actually, no. Who was it?"

"You didn't tell me you have another boy liking you! Gosh, I'm gone for a few months and you have them beating down the doors for you. I don't know what we were doing wrong in middle school, but apparently you've found your knack in high school."

"What in the world are you talking about?" But just as Margot asked the question, she knew the answer. It was almost as obvious as the fact that the Pope is Catholic. Walter. It had to have been Walter.

"Walter called. He was just so excited that I was here. He had no idea. Why didn't you tell me that Walter Gribble likes you too?"

"Gosh, Ash. This year so far has been crazy, and Walter is not only the tip of that iceberg, but probably a good portion of it. Between him and his mom, I almost never have a spare moment to myself where I think I'm away from them."

"You mean to tell me that Walter Gribble isn't all you've ever hoped for and more?" The sarcasm in Ashley's voice made Margot want to laugh. At least having Ashley around wasn't so bad in that she knew the inner workings of Margot's mind, and their past experiences in middle school. Walter had always been bothersome, and the fact that he was lusting after Margot made Ashley's mockery that much more exciting for her.

"Come on, Ash. Give me a break." They started to laugh a bit over it, which actually made Margot feel better, but at the same time a little worse. Walter wasn't trying to do her any harm, but a little laughter at his expense wasn't going to hurt him either. So, she told Ashley as much as she could in the next thirty minutes before having to get downstairs for breakfast. Even though Mr. Richardson had given the cast the day off, he still expected them at a dress rehearsal by 1 pm, and there was still stuff to do at home before then. The phone had to ring, though, just at the moment they were headed downstairs.

"Ooh, ooh! Let me get it! I'll pretend to be you, Margot, and tell Walter how sweet he is for all the attention." Margot smiled at Ashley, bypassing her to reach the phone. As she answered it, Ashley made kissy faces and turned her back to Margot, hugging herself as if she was having her own little make-out session.

"Oh, hi Peter." With that, Ashley stopped everything, getting closer to the phone in hopes that she'd be able to listen in to the conversation. "What's up?"

"Hey, Margot," said Peter, with a slight crack in his voice. "I'm so sorry to have to call and tell you this, but I'm sick. I have a cold, and it's not a great idea for me to come to rehearsal and the play tonight. My little brother came home yesterday coughing and sneezing. If he'd have just stayed away from me like I told him to, this probably wouldn't have happened. I really wanted to come tonight. I definitely plan to be there tomorrow, okay?"

What could Margot say? She looked at Ashley, who looked puzzled as to how she herself would respond. They were nice girls, but they wanted what they wanted, which was Peter to come tonight, just as Peter said he wanted to come. They gave each other a knowing glance that they knew he wasn't lying – I mean, what better option could he have on a Friday night than going to see the school play that contained Margot, Cassie, and Walter, his three best friends at this point in the school year?

"Well, getting better is what's most important. Just do that and we can talk tomorrow and hopefully you'll be able to come. I'm not performing tonight anyway, so maybe by the time you're back, I'll be playing the lead."

"Yeah, but I wanted to see Cassie in her opening night too." Despite liking Cassie and wanting to be her friend oh-so-much, Margot had a feeling as though she had had a knife twisted in her back. This phone call was supposed to be about Peter missing Margot, not about his missing Cassie and her wonderfulness. Margot knew she was probably overthinking things, but it was hard for her to imagine Peter liking her at all, let alone when he mentioned Cassie in the same conversation as he brought up being sorry about not being able to see Margot herself.

"Just get better, okay? Talk to you tomorrow." Margot hung up the phone, perturbed, but trying not to look too much like she cared.

"Give me a break, Margot. You know he's really sick, right? There's no way he'd pass up the opportunity to go see you guys in the play. He's been at like every rehearsal, hasn't he? Didn't you tell me that?"

"Yeah, I guess. It's like, you know, I can't read him."

"You know why?" Margot looked at Ashley with the supreme intention of learning the ways in which a boy's mind works. It seemed that Ashley's question was leading them in that very direction. "Because he's a boy."

"Oh, that explains it. Thanks for the insight, Ash. You've really shown me the light."

"Okay, okay. I know you're upset. Don't take it out on me. I didn't do this. You know how those middle schoolers get colds and stuff all the time. They're like bees that are drawn to walls full of honey-coated sickness. Okay, not the best analogy, but you know what I mean. He's sick, and you want him to get better, don't you? At least he called. He didn't have to do that. That means something, doesn't it?"

Margot wanted to believe it did, but she honestly didn't know any more. He mentioned Cassie in the same call and didn't seem too excited about the fact that Margot might have her own moment on stage in Cassie's place at some point. It was clear to her that she just didn't know what to think anymore. Not that she ever had, or ever would. She felt completely lost.

"Are you girls coming down for breakfast? It's been sitting on the table for a while now." Surprisingly, Mr. Maples was the one calling up the stairs for the girls. Usually it was Margot's mom trying to eavesdrop and gather information on what was going on that was keeping Margot from making her way to the table on time. When they got downstairs, they realized that Mrs. Maples was so busy preparing more pancakes and cut-up fruit that she couldn't be bothered to come get them.

"Mom, what's the deal?"

"It's your big day! I thought a nice, big, tasty breakfast might be just what you needed. I can put it all away if you want, though. I'm sure I can find someone..."

"No, no," Margot said, cutting off the end of her mom's sarcastic sentence. "Looks great. Thanks so much." And Margot meant it. Her mom loved her; she knew that. But she couldn't remember a time that she had gone out of her way like she was doing right now to make Margot feel so comfortable and warm and...*ding dong!*

"Who could that be?" Margot couldn't decide if her mother had something special planned and that something special was showing up at the door right then, or if something was amiss, or if it was just a fluke that the front doorbell was ringing at such an early hour.

As Mrs. Maples made her way down the front hallway, all Margot could make out was Mrs. Maples' simple greeting to the person on the other side of the door: "Kelly?"

Margot knew instantly that the second option she had created in her mind as what could possibly be lurking at their front door was coming true. She tried to brace Ashley for the impact of the infamous Mrs. Kelly Gribble, but it was too late.

"Oh my, oh my. Walter just had a bout of nerves come on. Oh gosh. He was so prepared. I mean, I don't know what happened." As Mrs. Gribble spoke her words, she was slowly but surely inching her way down the hallway, into the kitchen, most likely smelling the wonderful apples and cinnamon that graced the tops of their pancakes.

"Oh, good morning, Margot. And... you do look familiar, don't you? Do I know you?" Sidestepping Mrs. Gribble's supreme lack of what normal people would call decorum, Margot introduced Ashley to their uninvited breakfast-time guest. "Oh yes, Burnham. Your parents are Mary and Mark, right? Nice folks. How are they?"

Before Ashley could answer, Mrs. Maples took on some authority, telling Mrs. Gribble that they were just in the middle of a family breakfast. Margot thought it was great how her mom emphasized the *family* part of it.

"Mrs. Gribble, I just talked to Walter a little bit ago. He sounded just fine."

"Well, of course he sounded great to you, Margot. You're his best girl. He wouldn't want to make you feel as though anything was wrong."

Margot hastened to avoid the fact that Mrs. Gribble had called her Walter's "best girl" in front of Ashley, but she could see Ashley's face widen with a mixture of delight and full-on astonishment that Mrs. Gribble was just as pushy as Margot had described her to be.

"Well, what happened?"

"Oh, Margot. I only came over here because I want you to call him or come over and talk to him or something. I know I could have called, but I thought my coming was the best thing, because I wasn't sure if you all would be home." It seemed as though Mrs. Gribble knew a bit about her own aggravating skills; she thought the only way to get the Maples' – especially Margot – to comply with her was to corner them in their own home so they'd have nowhere to turn.

"Fine, can I finish my breakfast first? Then I'll call Walter."

"Sure. Oh, how awful you must think I am to have interrupted your breakfast. And such a good one by the looks of it. I'll see myself out. I'll tell Walter that you'll be calling."

"Won't it be better if he just hears from me? Maybe it'll perk him up even more that way?" Margot didn't know why, other than the fact that the play had to go well for her and her alone, if no one else, that she was trying to appease not only Mrs. Gribble, but Walter. It was as though some weird force had taken her body in its clutches and was controlling her thoughts and speech.

"Yes. Yes, certainly. I see what you mean. Hearing from you will be just the shot in the arm he needs to get him ready for his big debut. I mean, *your* debut together. I'll be going now. You're just the best. Walter sure knows how to pick 'em." Even though she hadn't actually said the words "best girl" again, for which Margot was eternally grateful, she knew that was what Mrs. Gribble was thinking. The play was all she needed to cement Margot and Walter's "relationship" in the minds of the masses. Seeing them on stage together, even if just to introduce them as the understudies, would give her the perfect chance to point out how wonderful she felt her son looked with his "best girl." And with Margot's luck, Carolyn and Lisa would be nearby when Mrs. Gribble professed her undying devotion to whom she was sure would one day be her daughter-in-law. The fact that they were ninth graders who weren't even in any kind of romantic relationship didn't faze Mrs. Gribble one tiny bit.

Margot knew she ought to take it as a compliment that Walter's mom was so keen on her. Having someone's mother like you so much would certainly make for an easy way in. That is, *if* you liked the person whose mother liked you. Margot was dead set on finding a way to get Mrs. Gribble off her back. Finding out what that way was seemed bound to be the hardest part of the equation.

THIRTY-NINE

"Where's Walter?" Margot couldn't believe she was searching for the answer to the question that she had tried so hard to ignore. Knowing Walter's whereabouts was surprisingly paramount in her mind. Mr. Richardson had called the cast down for a last-minute meeting, and for some reason unbeknownst to her, she was worried that he wouldn't make it in time.

"I'm sure he'll be here soon," offered Ashley, trying to ease Margot's nerves which were beginning to get the better of her. Not knowing how soon Walter would show up was weighing on her mind. She was quite thankful that Mrs. Gribble hadn't been around to see her question Walter's whereabouts, though. It would have been just the ammunition she needed to push even harder – if that was even possible.

Then Margot realized what she needed to do. *I can't believe I didn't think of it before! I need to push Walter into the arms of another girl. Mrs. Gribble won't believe her eyes, and it will take some of the attention off of me and put it on that girl for a bit.* Eager to let Ashley in on her plan, she took her aside into one of the classrooms in the theater wing.

"I know I have the cast meeting in a few minutes, but I just thought of something. What do you think of setting Walter up with someone else and figuring a way to make Mrs. Gribble see it happen? It would get her off my back, and maybe Walter would leave me alone too."

"You mean you don't like all the attention he's paying you?" asked Ashley with sarcastic enthusiasm. "You're his best girl, after all."

Margot looked at Ashley in all seriousness. "Say that again and…"

"Lighten up, Margot. I'm just joking. Anyway, you said you don't mind Walter all that much."

"He's okay, I guess. But not like that. I like Peter, and you know it. Give me a break, okay?"

"Your idea sounds do-able. Maybe. The only problem is, who wants Walter?" Margot hadn't thought that far. The idea sounded good in its preliminary planning stages in her mind, but executing it by finding a girl who might actually like Walter seemed impossible. Especially on such short notice. Despite his being a nice guy, his nerdy status was well-known among the girls of Kipperton High. But Margot didn't want to wait on this plan. Mrs. Gribble was getting pushier each and every day. Showing up this morning at her house during breakfast was really the last straw.

"I'll figure it out. Just let me think a little," said Margot, hastily forgetting that deception was far from her strong suit.

"Margot! Margot!" Walter was rushing down the hallway like a chicken with its head cut off, unsure where to go. "I know I'm late. Where is everyone?" Margot couldn't believe that he hadn't asked her how she was or told her how nice she looked, or said anything at all complimentary. Then, Walter ended his nervous rant with, "Thanks so much for calling, by the way. It was so nice to hear from you. It definitely calmed my nerves. Your voice makes me feel better." Despite the sweetness he was trying to exude, Margot couldn't help but feel bothered.

Before she knew it, and before a plan was even in place, Margot found herself blurting out, "Well, Ashley was worried about you too." Ashley shot Margot a look that could have made her burst into flames. She had hardly expected that Margot would throw her into the middle of this ridiculously juvenile situation, especially since Ashley considered herself more "worldly" now, having a boyfriend like Brad and all, Margot guessed.

"Uh, yeah, I was, uh, wondering when you'd get here, Walter. Mr. Richardson called the cast meeting a while ago, and you weren't anywhere around. Margot told me that you're Max's understudy."

"Wow, thanks, Ashley. So glad you're here! Maybe we'll have a chance to hang out later. Margot has such good friends." Ashley smirked, all the while watching Walter as he was unable to steer his gaze completely away from Margot. Little did Margot know that deterring Walter from her was going to be much harder than she'd thought. He had barely glanced at Ashley to say thanks.

They headed in to the cast meeting, and Max, as could have only been expected when they arrived anywhere where he was also in attendance, sneered at them. One would think this was just for being late, but Margot knew better. Max was a jerk in every sense of the word, but despite her best efforts, she truly couldn't understand what he so hated about her and Walter. Was it just that they weren't "cool" – whatever that meant?

Margot thought about all the times she had wished she was cool, but her definition certainly didn't match Max's. If she had had to define the word a few months back, she would have thought that it meant being a nice person, yet knowing all the great spots to hang out and how to talk with people without having to feel inadequate about herself. It wasn't that much, she realized now, as compared to Max's version of the term – being a world-class idiot who doesn't know how to treat anyone with any form of respect. It had only been over the last couple months that Margot realized that Cassie truly personified what it meant to be cool. She had been nice to Margot from the moment they had that little one-sided talk in the bathroom at Benino's. She had helped her feel more confident about liking Peter – not that the confidence had really stuck, but it was a start, if nothing else. And she had stuck by Margot, Peter, and Walter at the dance when Max was being that nuisance Margot always had known him to be. What Cassie had ever seen in him was truly beyond Margot's comprehension. He was nothing more than a...

"Margot? Ms. Maples? Ms. Maples?!" Mr. Richardson had gotten progressively louder, in attempts to pull Margot's attention away from what he considered her daydream, but what she considered a lackluster attempt to understand Max Poler's motivations.

"Uh, oh, yeah, hi Mr. Richardson." The other students giggled a bit under their breath while Max continued to look on in pure annoyance.

"Ms. Maples, thank you for joining us," Mr. Richardson said in a mocking tone. "I'm hesitant now to say this again, but since you didn't hear me the first time, Ms. Shearer called, and she is losing her voice. She wants to try to save it for tomorrow night's performance, so you're on tonight. Do you think you can handle this?" The whole idea of this was throwing Margot for a loop. And Mr. Richardson's last statement, no matter how much he really wanted to know the answer, bugged her. He obviously thought she was incapable of even being the understudy he had chosen her to be.

"Uh, yeah." Then, realizing how she sounded hesitant, she changed her tune with a resounding, "Yes! I mean, definitely. I'll take over and Cassie can take it over again tomorrow hopefully." Mr. Richardson seemed semi-soothed. He had not made any secret to the cast that he wanted the play to go off without a hitch. His reputation, or at least his ego, depended on it.

The next instant was when Margot actually was able to process what just happened. And it hit her like a ton of bricks that even though she was going to be living her dream of being the star of the play, her co-lead would be none other than the diabolically aggravating Max. Then, she looked at Walter, who looked half-pleased for Margot and half-depressed that he wasn't getting the chance to break a leg. When Margot went back into the hallway after the meeting was over, her face showed a mixture of excitement and uncertainty.

"What's up?" Ashley looked terribly interested, and Margot was truly in need of some inspired guidance as to how to handle this situation so as not to let anybody be hurt. She feared that Max was likely to say something to cause her not to keep her cool, and then she would be forced to slap him or some other juvenile reaction would occur, and then, with her luck, she'd be out of the play, and Max would be the hero who saved the day in some way or other, despite having no female lead to play opposite. That would probably be the thing to please him most, though. To have the whole show to himself. Mr. Richardson would have a conniption fit, but Max would be in seventh heaven. Walter, though, knew all the lines to the play and would probably offer to play Margot's part just so the show could go on. Margot thought about the last scenario. If Mr. Richardson were to ever agree to Walter taking on Cassie and Margot's part, the look on Max's face would be priceless. There was no way he would ever give up his role, so playing against Walter would be his only option. The ridiculousness of the situation made Margot smile.

"Margot, I said 'what's up?' Didn't you hear me?" Margot realized she had been trailing off too much, thinking about Max and the play and other such stupidity. How often could she think about Max? He was weighing on her mind way too much.

"Yeah. I heard you. I'm the lead."

"What do you mean?"

"I'm the lead. Cassie's sick. She lost her voice, I guess. She's trying to save it for tomorrow's performance. I'm on tonight."

"That's awesome, Margot!" Ashley looked truly thrilled, which made Margot feel better. Ashley was always the one to find ways to cheer Margot up, and apparently that hadn't changed, despite their distance over the last several months.

"But, Cassie's sick? And Peter's sick? Don't you think it's weird that..." Ashley cut herself off. "Never mind."

"What's weird? They're both sick. There's been a bug going around."

"Okay, yeah, I guess," said Ashley.

"You mean, you think that maybe they... no. That's not what you're saying." Margot stared at Ashley, trying to get her to say what she had been planning to say. "You think they got each other sick. Like they were doing stuff *together*."

"I didn't say anything," said Ashley. But that didn't do anything to quell Margot's fluttering butterflies. Now she wasn't only nervous about the play, but about the fact that her supposed friend, and her allegedly soon-to-be boyfriend, were possibly in the middle of some torrid love affair.

FORTY

"We can't tell her." Peter sounded worried.

"Why not? She's going to find out eventually."

"That's not necessarily true. Can't we just wait? I mean, her response will be the same whether we tell her today or three weeks from now."

"Maybe she'll have a different response than you think. We might as well get it over with." Cassie just couldn't get her point across. It was like trying to push a rock through a brick wall. There was no budging. "Come on. You really don't get how she's going to react to this? It's a conversation you're going to have to have at some point. I don't want to have to lie to Margot until you finally get up the courage to just do it." Cassie was doing her best to be adamant. Margot's feelings were foremost in her mind.

"All right. I suppose she deserves the truth. I'll tell her tomorrow, okay?"

"Why not tonight?"

"You've got to be kidding. It's opening night. I can't throw this on her now."

"Fine. Give her her moment in the spotlight. I'm glad she's getting it. She really does deserve it. Plus, I am *kind of* losing my voice, so sparing it for tomorrow night wasn't the worst idea. It wasn't really a lie. Mr. Richardson didn't seem like he was going to do the understudy thing anyway, giving them a night to be the stars. This will give her a chance. It's too bad about Walter, though. Max will never give up anything to him."

"What did you ever see in him anyway? You would have been much better off with, well..."

"With who? You?" Cassie looked at Peter as he sported a shy, bordering on humiliated face.

"I was going to say with somebody who actually gives a care about other people, but now that you mention it..."

"Peter, stop being silly. Let's get going. The show starts in an hour and a half, and we better get a move on if we're going to see her before the show."

"She'll be too nervous," Peter claimed.

"There's no backing out now. You agreed, and we're doing it. It'll be over before you know it," Cassie countered.

FORTY-ONE

Doing her best to cover her nervousness, Margot called Ashley, hoping she'd pick up and come to Margot's rescue. Mr. Richardson had made anyone who wasn't in the cast disperse to the lobby so the actors could get in the "mindset" of their characters, as he had so purposefully put it. Margot didn't care, though. She needed Ashley. She always seemed to know what to say to calm Margot's nerves.

"On my way, Mar. Oh, your parents just showed up. I told them you're starring in the show tonight. They're so excited!"

Margot could just picture her dad roaming the auditorium, sharing with everyone who would listen how his little girl was making her stage debut. *She's growing up so fast. It seems like just yesterday that I was putting her in diapers.* She tried to shake off the sounds of her dad's voice in her head, but it was all she could think of now. Then, as soon as Ashley appeared, she remembered the drama that was holding her life hostage. Peter and Cassie. It couldn't be true, could it? Had these last few months of growth in her relationships with Cassie and Peter all been a lie? Maybe they really had been sneaking around behind her back, trying to make her think that they liked her when they were just laughing at her. That time when Cassie left the house and she and Peter smiled at each other – it must have been their inside joke about how stupid Margot was.

"What's wrong? You have this weird look on your face," Ashley questioned, summoning Margot out of her nightmare of a daydream.

"Oh, uh..." Margot considered how to answer this. "It's nothing. Just nerves, I guess. I'll be okay." Ashley looked skeptical, but she let it go, knowing that Margot was more often than not honest with her, and if she wasn't saying something, either nothing was wrong or she really didn't want to talk about it. As they turned the corner to head to the auditorium, that's when Ashley realized that maybe everything wasn't perfectly fine. Her first clue? Peter and Cassie, turning the bend at the other end of the hallway – *together*.

Margot began to walk a little slower, her mind racing with thoughts about whether or not she could handle a confrontation right now. And even if she could, would she confront them? She and Peter didn't really have a relationship after all, and all she had to go on was the fact that they had both said they were sick. Yet they were both standing right in front of her. Shouldn't Cassie be home, in bed? Was she also trying to show Margot up just before she went out on stage? Was there no end to Cassie's selfishness?

Margot, realizing that she wasn't going to be able to handle seeing the two of them after all, or hearing the doomed words of how she was such a good friend to the both of them (*what a load of bull, anyway*, was her thinking), turned to Ashley to say that she'd forgotten something in the bathroom and hastened away in the other direction just before Cassie and Peter got close enough to talk to them.

"Hey Ashley. Good to see you!"

"Sure, whatever," said Ashley. "What are you doing here, anyway? Thought you were sick in bed losing your voice."

"Oh, yeah, well, I wanted to see the show, so Peter picked me up. I'll just sit in the audience and enjoy Margot's performance."

"Just like you're enjoying everything else she wanted," muttered Ashley under her breath.

"What?"

"Oh, nothing. It's just that you clearly know how to outshine Margot at every turn. She thought you were her friend, you know. How selfish can you be?" Ashley, not bothering to wait for Cassie's response, set her sights on Peter.

"And you, you, well, I don't even know what the word is. How could you do this to her?"

"Do what?"

"Don't play stupid. You know she likes you. You'd have to be blind to not see it. I admit I didn't see it at first, but I haven't been around her for the last few months day in and day out. You two have." She looked between

Peter and Cassie when she said this. "Leading her on is just mean. I'm not going to let you hurt her anymore. Just stay away, okay?" Even though her last words were said as a question, they were meant as a statement of fact. She looked between them again and turned to follow Margot.

"What in the world was that about? She makes it sound like we've deliberately hurt Margot. Why would she even think that?"

"Peter, sometimes you really are naïve. Margot likes you, you idiot! I've told you so, but you can't seem to get it through your head. She must think something is going on between us. I don't know why in the world she'd think so, but..."

"You make it sound like the biggest impossibility ever. I'm not that awful, am I?"

"Peter, come on. You know what I mean. And obviously you're not awful. Margot thinks you're great."

"But Walter thinks *she's* great."

"Seriously? Walter? I like him. He's a nice guy. But you've got to be kidding me, Peter. You're the one she wants. She's told me so. How many times do I have to tell you? You've got to just go tell her and get it over with. Ashley's probably with her right now filling her head with more about how we're no good and have been plotting against her this whole time."

"Why don't you go in there and fix it then?"

"She's not going to believe me. We've been friends for the last couple months, sure, but I'm still another girl who, at least in Margot's opinion, has always had the upper hand when it comes to guys. I don't know why she thinks that, though, given my track record with Max of all people. I see the way she looks at me. She can't understand why I hang out with her. But I can't understand why she hangs out with me. I was friends with Carolyn and Lisa, two of the whiniest, brattiest girls in school, and they were nothing but mean to her. How she ever trusted me in the first place is beyond me, and now she thinks I've been with you, the guy she likes? Don't you see how I'm the worst possible person to go in there right now? You have to wait for her and talk to her."

"I can't do it. The show's about to start."

"That's why you have to do it." Before Cassie could say any more, Max turned the corner, headed for the cast entrance to stage left. Cassie pulled

Peter to the side quickly, not wanting to make eye contact, or any other kind of contact for that matter, with her ex.

"Isn't it better for her to have some conflict and tension going on in her life to make her performance more realistic?" Peter whispered, noting Cassie's tension.

"Not when she can get totally flustered and forget her lines as a result of her nervousness over seeing and talking to you. Take my advice and just do it. You'll be much better off. And so will Margot."

FORTY-TWO

The curtain was set to go up in only twenty minutes. The dress rehearsal had passed by in a flash, which Margot didn't know whether to be happy or even more nervous about. Max, always the professional, had tried to trip her up at every turn, both literally and figuratively. When she walked by him, not once, but twice, he stuck his foot out a bit, and one time she even stumbled. Yet, she saved the scene with a chuckle, laughing off her own klutziness, and making Max feel even more stupid when the other actors laughed, obviously enjoying her quick wit.

Margot considered how the play was truly like a parody of her life. It was as if it was mocking her own meager existence. Max was playing Petruchio, a gentleman of Verona, who was trying to woo Katherina, a stubborn, headstrong woman. She couldn't help but think that she and Max should switch roles – they would certainly be better suited to play the opposite lead. However, she also was keenly aware that Katherina was going to fall prey to Petruchio's courtship, something she could never imagine herself doing in real life with Max, but something she knew her character would just have to deal with. She realized that maybe her own unwillingness to deal with Max on a regular basis would give her character more depth, since Katherina was never eager to deal with Petruchio, either.

Then, Margot thought about Bianca, Katherina's more desirable sister. *Why didn't Cassie get that role? She's messing around with Peter already. She's perfect for it.* Despite Margot's best attempts to delete the picture of Peter and Cassie together from her mind, it wouldn't disappear.

As Margot finished in the make-up room and was headed for the costume closet, it all came to a head.

"Margot! Hey!" Peter was a few feet away from her.

"P...Peter? What are you doing here?" Margot asked in truthful astonishment. She couldn't imagine why he would step away from Cassie for one moment to spend any time with her.

"I wouldn't miss seeing this performance. My mom said I could come as long as I sat in the back and promised not to get too close to anyone. She doesn't want me getting anyone else sick, but she knows how much I wanted to see the show. She told me to tell you to break a leg."

"How did she even know I was performing tonight?"

"Well, Cassie wanted to come too, even though she wasn't feeling well, and my mom dropped us both off. She knew that if Cassie wasn't going on, that you must be."

"It always comes back to Cassie, doesn't it?" Ashley chimed in, appearing out of nowhere to come to Margot's aid. "What are *you* doing here? I thought I made myself clear."

"You did. I decided to come anyway," said Peter, trying to sidestep Ashley's bothered tone.

"Where's Cassie? I mean, since you came with her and all," continued Ashley, not at all subtly.

"She's down the hall. She's actually the one who's been pushing me to do this already. She thinks it's time you and I talked, Margot."

"I bet she does," Ashley continued, not giving Margot a chance to speak her own mind. "Isn't it enough that you got the girl? Now you have to bother the one who's spent the better part of this school year liking you *and* being friends with your new girlfriend? You really are an idiot. Margot's better off without you. You and Cassie deserve each other." Margot looked frazzled, unsure of whether to stop Ashley's Peter-centric gibes.

Then, realizing the terror that she knew accompanied Peter's "I want to talk" tone, Margot rushed from the cast room, alternately furious with Ashley and hoping for a miracle. The likelihood that she would hear something other than the "you're such a good friend," or the "you're like a sister to me" speeches that had run through her mind countless times the past few months was slim to none.

How could Ashley have said that? What was she thinking? Just because I like Peter doesn't mean she has to blurt it out to him like that. Can't I live in some sort of fantasy a little longer? At least there, my heart is aching, but not broken. Finding out the truth will hurt too much.

Just then, Peter rounded the corner, apparently having dodged Ashley's certain attempt to block him from following her. Margot found herself with her back against the wall, both literally and figuratively, uncertain where to go, what to do, or what to say.

"Margot – hey, wait." Margot had turned her back, looking for the nearest exit. There was a set of double doors about twenty feet down the hall, but she knew Peter had already seen her and it would be more awkward to just ignore him. So, she turned her left side profile toward him and said, "What is it?" in as non-annoyed and non-tear-filled a tone as she could.

"I want to talk to you."

Obviously. Margot knew her inner-self sounded sarcastic, and she hated herself for directing that inner tone toward Peter, of all people. She still liked him, despite everything that was going on. She was just in such a jam that she didn't know how else to react.

"Do we have to? I mean, I'd really rather not have this conversation."

"Well, yeah. I mean, is that really how you feel?"

"Yeah, I'd really rather not have this conversation."

"No. I mean, is that how you feel about me? Is what Ashley said true?"

He's playing with me now. He knows it's true. He's taking advantage of the situation. Just prolonging the inevitable. Margot looked down at her feet and leaned the small of her back against the wall. She wondered why in this instance nothing was interrupting her. Nothing was getting in the way. It seemed that every time something bad happened to her, someone or something was there to watch it all play out. She found herself even hoping that someone would come and call her away. It scared her that even Mrs. Gribble or Max would be a welcome distraction to get her out of this situation. Despite their obviously aggravating personalities, at least their presence would take her away from having to deal with Peter. Finally, she said, "Yeah, okay. It's true." She knew it had come out sounding a bit meaner than she meant it to. Her words certainly weren't mean, but she had said it in such a way that it sounded like Peter had forced her into feeling that way.

"It is? Really?"

Building her courage, Margot continued, "Come on, Peter. I mean, you couldn't tell all this time? It seems like everyone else knows. I mean, Ashley's my best friend. She wouldn't tell a lie about something like that."

"I wish I had known sooner. It's just..."

"You know what? Don't even say anything. I'd rather not know for sure that my bubble is burst. We can just stay friends, and that's that. No big deal."

"No. I don't want to be friends." Margot had already started walking away as Peter said this. She couldn't believe how much the words stung. She turned around suddenly, an angry expression on her face.

"You don't want to be friends? Just because I like you as more than that? Maybe Ashley's right and I'm better off not liking you then. Being friends would have been too hard anyway, so you've made the decision easy. Why would I want to be friends with such a... such a..."

"Don't say something you're going to regret. Just hear me out, okay?"

"No!" Margot couldn't believe her own tone of voice. She was really angry. He had played with her emotions. She had been under the impression that he was a decent guy, but he couldn't get past his own ego, not wanting to be friends with her after Ashley had poured out her own heart for her. She turned around again, her steps getting faster as she made her way back down the hall, far away from him.

"I like you too, okay!" Peter yelled it louder than he expected to, and Margot turned around again, unsure if she had heard him correctly. She half-expected Walter or Mrs. Gribble to pop out of a hidden door in the brick wall, ready to squash this moment. And what a moment it was.

"What do you mean, you like me? You just said you didn't want to be friends."

"That's right. I want to ask you out. If you'd listen to me long enough, you'd find out that I'm not such a bad guy. I like you like you like me. I'm glad Ashley said what she did."

"She shouldn't have said anything." Margot knew that she was thankful to Ashley, even though she felt the need to still be angry at her for doing something that Margot hadn't approved of at the time.

Even though this was the best moment of what Margot had deemed a ridiculously bad freshman fall semester, she couldn't bring herself to look at

Peter. Her eyes were locked on the perpendicular lines that made up the floor of the theater wing. Peter was also having trouble looking straight at Margot. Their truthful revelations to each other seemed to have made both of them tongue-tied.

Peter was the first to break the silence. "So, what do we do now?"

"Well, um, I think that we should save this conversation for later."

"Why?" Peter asked with a note of unhappiness clearly etched in his voice.

"Well, I have to go on in like ten minutes."

"Oh, yeah, that."

"Will you be here after the show?"

"Sure. Sure, I will," Peter said hesitantly, yet with all the certainty in the world. "That's why I came. Well, *part* of why I came." With this, he smiled with the first true sense of certainty at Margot, and she smiled back, locking eyes for a brief moment. And then the bubble burst.

"Margot! Oh, Margot, you really look great. Mr. Richardson sent me to find you. You're on in just a few, and I came to..." Walter stopped mid-sentence, noticing Peter for the first time. "Hey, Peter," he said as kindly as he could, trying to seem as cool as Walter Gribble could seem about what he considered an infringement on his hopefully soon-to-be requited relationship with Margot.

Without thinking twice, Margot inched her way out of this precarious situation by heading toward the door and telling Walter she was on her way. Like a lovesick puppy, he tore his gaze away from Peter more than willingly, following his "best girl," otherwise known as his "leading lady" for this play-filled weekend. Even though Margot had been bothered by this term before, she had a newfound sense of respect for Walter's attempts at loving-kindness. She figured that maybe there was more "like" going around than she had been willing to admit, no doubt thanks to some of the revelations that were making their rounds today.

FORTY-THREE

A standing ovation. Roses being flung on stage to mark a superb performance. Bows and curtseys and hand-holding as they showed how humble and modest they were at the audience's approval. Hand-holding with Max. Max – the other star of the show who had pulled off the wondrous feat of being good at something other than ridiculing and shaming Margot on a regular basis.

It seemed like a dream, yet it wasn't. Granted, the roses were being flung only by Margot's dad, and Mrs. Gribble was the one who stood up first, leading the applause in as dedicated and impressive a manner as possible, but Margot couldn't deny the overwhelming feeling of awesome that was enveloping her.

Students, teachers, and parents alike were genuinely smiling. Mr. Richardson was even clapping backstage.

Looking around, Margot scanned the crowd for any sign of Peter. She saw Ashley, who was seated next to Margot's parents, and Cassie, who smiled brightly in Margot's direction. Any ill will that Margot had thought she had toward Cassie disappeared even before the play, and in that moment, Cassie was a welcome presence. Carolyn and Lisa were already making their way off the stage to visit with their parents and other friends, as was the rest of the cast. She couldn't deny that they had all done a fabulous job – even the dippy Carolyn and aggravating Lisa.

Margot looked backstage, hoping Peter was waiting for her there, but she only saw a very excited Walter, waving almost furiously for her to step in his direction. For someone who would seemingly be bad with, or at least uncomfortable around girls, Walter was quite unaware of Margot's evasive strategies that she had been employing so far this school year. He was quite aware of his own ability to stay on top of her until she would eventually, in his estimation, give in to what he surely had concluded were his "charms." She did have to admit that he was not nearly as bothersome as when the school year began.

"You were great out there. Too bad Cassie was sick, but wow. So great. I mean, really."

"Thanks, Walter." She really wanted to ask if he had seen Peter, but even though he was notorious for bursting her bubbles, she wouldn't burst his in this moment of happiness for her. She felt she was being too nice, but it made her happy to know he really thought she had been great. She even believed he'd think so if he wasn't crazy about her. She didn't have to ask about Peter anyway, though. He showed up just then, as though he'd heard her thoughts.

"Walter, I've..."

"Gotta go, right?" He didn't seem at all rattled. It was as though he expected her to have to leave. She figured that this was because she was always trying to find an "out" with him.

"Well, uh, yeah."

"Will you be at the cast party to celebrate opening night later on?"

"Yeah, see you there, okay?"

"I thought you'd be busy with your parents," said Walter, not even noticing Peter yet.

"Yeah, we're going to Benino's and then I'll head over to the party. Save me a seat, okay?" At that, Walter perked up, becoming his over-eager self once more. She didn't know why she'd said it. But she knew that she meant it. Hanging out with Walter wasn't the albatross around her neck that it had been all those months ago when eighth grade had ended. Truthfully, she kind of looked forward to seeing him there. As Walter walked away, he must have seen Peter, but he ignored him, keeping to himself and surely counting his blessings that Margot would throw such a bone in his direction.

Then, Margot saw him trying to keep his mom from coming nearer. Somehow, he succeeded, likely telling her that she had told him to save her a seat. She figured this, because Mrs. Gribble smiled at Margot in what seemed to be a knowing way, and waved happily in her direction. Then, as Walter pulled her away little by little, Margot saw that Mrs. Gribble looked disgruntled, likely because she couldn't talk to Margot herself. And even though she tapped Walter on the shoulder several times, he seemed unfazed by her, and kept walking. Margot didn't know whether he had finally gotten the point that he should just let things go as they may without Mrs. Gribble's incessant nagging, or if he was scheming in one way or another to get things to go more his way than he felt they already were.

"You were really great up there, Margot," said Peter.

"I didn't see you in the audience. Where were you?"

"I sat way far back like my mom told me to. As soon as it ended, I came around back to find you. Walter got here first, I guess."

"Well, I mean, he was Max's understudy."

"Sure, sure."

The silence was awkward, and the miniscule amount of words they were coming up with seemed forced. It had never seemed so hard to talk before. Their revelations to each other had somehow made them ill at ease.

"I think I should get going. My parents are probably waiting up front."

"Oh, sure, yeah."

"Do you want to go to dinner with us?"

Before Peter could answer with a resounding yes, yet another interruption came into play. It was as if Margot was magnetized to attract them.

"What a show. Little Miss 'Never-Will-Be-Best' gets her chance to shine for one night and winds up with Mulvaney."

"What's wrong, Max? Too tired to come up with a better nickname for me?"

"Whatever. First, you get Cassie – a consolation prize if you ask me, and then you opt for her *understudy*." The word sounded so demeaning when Max said it.

"Take it back, Max," Peter muttered. Margot, who normally would have had a tear in her eye at a remark like that, found herself oddly fine, and not even angry – just apathetic.

"It's not worth it, Peter," she said softly.

"Listen to her, Mulvaney. You don't want to end up in Dr. Perkins' office again, do you? What a jerk you are to even think you can mess with me."

"Like you've messed with me all these years? I used to think we were friends, but I see now that you were just..."

"Just what? Just better than you?"

"Come on, Max. I know you better than this. Or at least I thought I did. You were the first friend I had when I got switched to Ms. Dessler's class in third grade. We started out as partners on that book report, remember? So, *what* happened to you? You weren't always this mean and spiteful."

"Don't try to psychoanalyze me. Can't two people just grow apart?"

"Yeah. Yeah, they can. But that's not what happened with us. You just turned against me."

"I never did like geeks, anyway."

"It's stuff like that. Why do you have to say these things? What did I ever do to you?"

With that question, Peter did not know what he had gotten into. It seemed to have opened the floodgates for Max to practice his acting chops some more, except this time, everything in his monologue was the truth.

"What did you ever do to me? You know what, I'll tell you! This has been a long time coming, Mulvaney. Hope you can take it without bursting into tears or anything. I remember that book report. I actually liked having you as my partner. Ms. Dessler always picked me first for everything, so it was good to have someone else who she thought enough of to pair me with. Before you got placed in that class, I had taken that GEC test. Remember that? I passed and was so excited to get started." Margot and Peter looked at each other, befuddled. They knew what it was alright. It was the test to get into the Gifted and Exceptional Children program. Margot had been in it herself for the end of elementary school. She hadn't known that Max had taken it. Peter hadn't taken it because his parents wanted to let him be more well-rounded. They knew he was smart, but putting him in a program with more of a strenuous workload, on top of having him take music lessons and be on the PeeWee baseball league seemed too much. So they didn't push it, and Peter never took the test.

After Max waited a few seconds to see the fact that he had taken the test register on his adversaries' faces, he continued. "Then I kept hearing everyone calling those kids the "geeks," because of the spelling of that stupid acronym for the program. Afterward, I knew I didn't want to end up getting called that, so I told my mom and dad I didn't want to be in the program because I didn't want to leave my friends. I mean, I would have had to switch schools and everything. So, luckily, they went along with it. Little did I know, one of my best friends, Sam, moved away over the summer, and the other one, Cameron, joined the rest of the geeks in that GEC program without even telling me he'd been accepted. By the time I found that out and told my parents I'd changed my mind, the deadline to sign up had passed, and I couldn't get in anymore. Well, that was the last time I let myself be sad about a friend dropping me. If anyone was going to be the one who got dumped in a friendship, it was going to be the other guy. I was done being stepped over."

"Come on, Max. You were in the third grade. You were still my friend after that. Obviously you were okay with me for a while. What changed between us? If you were so smart, why didn't you join the honors classes in seventh and eighth grade like I did? Why did you keep your intelligence a secret? It's nothing to be ashamed of."

"Wow, Mulvaney. So deep. It's easy for you to say. If I show my smarts, I've got something to prove all over again. And then I get hurt – all over again. It's easier to be the clever leader of a group of dummies than a semi-smart guy in a sea of super-smart geeks. Who wants to be called a geek, anyway?"

"No one. So why do you make fun of me and Margot?"

"Easy. She was in that program. I would see her walking home after school with Cam sometimes, and the fact that he was so happy without me made me so damn jealous and frustrated that I hadn't joined him and just been a geek too. He also seemed to have an easier time talking to girls than I did. Maples here seemed like she was becoming his best friend or something, and I couldn't stand that. Not only had he left me for a bunch of smart crap, but he had a quasi-girlfriend too?"

"That's no reason to hate Margot," interjected Peter.

"Yeah, I mean, Cameron moved away after fifth grade anyway. Why did I still have to be your verbal punching bag?" questioned Margot.

"Who better to be mad at than you? When we got to Perry Middle School, I thought I'd get to maybe be friends with Cam again, but he left too, and you were the perfect person to take my frustrations out on. Plus, you started hanging out with that Ashley. I wasn't good with girls, and I wanted to ask her out. But the fact that she was friends with you made it impossible. I knew I wouldn't be able to turn her against you. You two were as tight as anything. Just like me, Sam, and Cameron had been. If I had wanted to get in good with her, I would have had to be nice to you. And that wasn't happening. You were the enemy."

"You said 'were' – so I'm not anymore?"

"Well, yeah. I mean, you are, but..."

"But this still doesn't explain why you stopped being my friend," said Peter.

"I shut you out, okay? I didn't want you to know what had happened before, so I bottled up all this anger I had over what had happened back in elementary school, and I threw all the crap I felt right at you. I hated myself for not wanting to be smart with you, but I was afraid of what that might do to me. It might lead me right back to being as envious as I'd been way back then."

Margot wondered if she had heard Max correctly. He had actually said he was afraid of something. Was she hearing him right?

"I decided that it was easier to let you go and be angry at you just like I'd been at Cameron than to just tell you the truth. Plus, I missed the mark in the English and math placement tests for the honors classes in middle school. I didn't get in anyway, so what was the point of trying to stay friends with you when you were switching classes?"

Peter didn't know what to say. Max may as well have poured out his heart in a confessional for all the feelings that were now out in the open. Instead of having to come up with something, he was saved when Cassie, out of nowhere, blurted out, "And what about me?"

"How long have you been standing there?" asked Max. "Why the need to scare me half to death?"

"You deserve it, and you know it. What a creep you've been. Just because you might have Peter and Margot thinking you're not so bad doesn't mean I'm cutting you any slack. We started dating last year in eighth grade. I wouldn't have dated a jerk. What made you change your tone with me? I was a good friend – and a good girlfriend – to you. What was the point in shutting me out? And that too-smart-for-you excuse won't work. You know I'm not in all the honors classes."

"You started hanging out with these two. What choice did I have?"

"Seriously? That's the whole reason you started being a world-class jerk? There's got to be more to it. Did you ever really like me, or were you just trying to be popular since you could see that some of the other guys liked me?"

"Whatever. I don't have to take this."

"Don't cop out on me. You're going to answer me. And soon. I deserve something. After the way you treated all of us, we deserve answers. You're not leaving till you give us some."

Margot knew her parents were waiting for her. They were probably going to start heading back any time now to see what was going on. In some ways, she wanted them to hear Max's revelations. They probably thought he was a good guy. She'd never told them otherwise, she supposed. The only time they'd really seen him up close and personal was in Dr. Perkins' office, and even then, he'd come across as the innocent one – he'd had no alcohol bottle in his pocket, after all. For all her shortcomings, she knew that giving someone else, like Max, the upper hand by talking about him outside of the confines of school grounds, would be terribly stupid on her part. It would make her no better than him, someone who probably stayed at home at night coming up with ways to make her life – and the lives of her friends – a living hell.

"I didn't want to be with you anymore. Why's that so hard to believe? I just turned 15, and being with one girl isn't at the top of my list of things to do right now. Give me a break for being a teen guy."

"So, this is about you and how your teenage years will be wasted if you spend them with me? Well, at least I can walk away from this knowing that your being a jerk is truly the reality here. Are you already seeing someone else?"

"Well, no, but..."

"So, you dumped me for the *off-chance* that you'll meet someone who likes you for you? You're not the greatest of catches, Max. I hate to break it to you." Cassie's last line was said with as much disdain as she could muster. The past year seemed like such a wash to her, and she knew she couldn't get it back, no matter how hard she tried. Life with Max had treated her to sorrow, the likes of which she had hoped she'd never experience. She realized that it may have seemed super over-the-top for someone who was only almost 15 years old, but a year of your life at that point in time seems like forever, plus some.

It was at this point that Walter came sprinting down the hall. He might as well have been shot out of a cannon, he was moving so quickly. A look that mixed sheer determination and utter panic streaked across his face as he bolted nearer and nearer.

"You...know...what? I just...can't wait...anymore." Walter's breathing was rushed, his voice hesitant.

"Wait for what?" asked Margot, trying to sound unsuspecting, but overly fearsome at what might just come out of Walter's mouth.

"To tell you that I... I like you." Walter looked shocked at his own words. All eyes trained on Margot. "I know it may come as a surprise," Walter continued, "but it's true." Margot was aghast. She had no idea how to respond. It was only then that she became dreadfully aware of the innumerable people who had become privy to the outpouring of Walter's heart.

"I...uh...I..." It was all Margot could do to utter those few syllables. Ashley, who had come into the room shortly after Cassie, had her mouth wide open, and Peter stood there, looking as perplexed about how to handle the situation as he could while Margot's insides felt like they were going through the loops of a rollercoaster.

Then, just as quickly as he'd appeared, Walter blurted out, "Okay. See you at the party," and walked quickly in the opposite direction from which he'd come, turning around a couple of times to wave goodbye in what he most surely considered a sweet way, but which came across as extreme anxiety.

Making eye contact was not something at the top of Margot's to-do list. For every annoying quality that Walter embodied, he was also a bold, tenacious guy. She had to give him credit, though she would never openly admit it, she promised herself. He had done something she would never in a million years have had the guts to do with Peter. It was only after Peter approached her that she had been able to get the words out – and even then she'd had trouble stringing them together.

The craziest part of this whole encounter was that Walter had said it may come as a surprise. For all her naïveté about the teenage boy's mind, she was not so blind as to have realized how much he liked her. That kiss at the beginning of the year alone was one she would never forget – and not for lack of trying. It had been one of those insurmountable odds she had been tasked to face as she embarked on freshmen year. And it hadn't even been the tiniest sliver of the molehill she was meant to face for the rest of her first semester of high school – and it was still only November.

FORTY-FOUR

"I did it, Mom. I told her."

"Oh, Walter, honey. What'd she say? She must have been thrilled. Oh, I know it. How'd it go? Come on, now."

"I didn't wait to find out."

"What? You didn't wait? You're kidding. You have to go back, then."

"I can't believe I did what I did, and now you want me to go back? Mom, I love you and all, but that's the last thing I'll do because you told me to. Your advice was good and all, to get my feelings out there, but now I'm too afraid to hear what she'll say."

"Walter." Mrs. Gribble spoke in as calm a tone as she could. "She's your best girl. How could she say no to you? I'm as sure of her being happy with you as I am that you are the best son a mother could ask for."

"Mom! How many times have I told you not to call her that. She's not my girlfriend yet!" He said the last word with all the hope he possessed packed into it. "Please let me deal with this in my own way. I'll see her at the cast party tonight. Maybe she'll tell me what she thinks then."

"But Walter..."

"I said I'll wait. If I can wait, then you definitely can. Give me a break, okay? I just did something I never thought I'd have the strength to do. Can't you just tell me you're proud of me and leave it at that? I'll let you know what happens, okay?"

Mrs. Gribble looked at Walter with a mixture of pride and aggravation. Living vicariously through her son was her way of life. His hesitancy was mucking up her plans. She wasn't used to waiting for what she wanted. That's why she even binge-watched all her TV shows, because she just couldn't bear having to wait a week, or heaven forbid, the entire summer, to see what would happen in the very next episode.

"Fine, dear," she said through somewhat clenched teeth, albeit nicely. "But be sure you let me know. You know how I feel about Margot. Such a sweet girl. Ever since that night at Benino's, I knew you were perfect for each other. Actually, I knew beforehand, but being together that night was like sealing your relationship with a kiss." Mrs. Gribble laughed, and continued, "Literally and figuratively."

Walter blushed. This talk in the car was the first time he had had the chance to see his mother as the helicopter parent that she was. Sure, she meant well, but she was too involved in his life. He had grown up thinking that it was great that she was around so much, happy to help him take on any obstacles that surfaced in his path, but he realized now that it had only hindered him from becoming more well-rounded, more social, and more certain of himself around girls – and everyone else for that matter. Tonight was the first time he'd ever had the strength to go up to anyone – not just a girl – and tell them what he thought of them. It had taken away his feelings of inadequacy and ineptitude and replaced them with purpose and instinct.

***

"Margot, it's time to leave." Mrs. Maples was standing outside, her voice muffled by the door.

"Where's Dad?"

"Right out here. We're both so proud of you, honey. You did a great job."

Margot knew this was true. She had felt so good about herself when the curtain went down, and then when it rose again and the applause seemed to infect the entire crowd.

"I'll be right out." Margot looked at herself in the mirror. After Walter had burst into the room and let his feelings explode for everyone to see and hear, Margot had done her own sprinting, out of the cast room and into the single-stall bathroom at the end of the theater hallway. Ashley had tried to follow her, but Margot had insisted that she wanted to be alone. Peter, at a loss for how to respond, followed Ashley's lead and waited outside the bathroom with her. Max and Cassie had stayed in the cast room, deciding how to act around one another now that there were no buffers in the room to keep them from demeaning each other further.

What in the world is happening? I guess when you do enough complaining about never getting what you want, someone has to hear it and decide to do something about it eventually. I just never thought it would all end up like this. I mean, it's flattering that Walter likes me. I guess. I mean, I never considered the now very-real possibility that he would fess up his feelings for me – and in front of all my friends no less. And my enemy. What great material this is going to make for Max. And Peter. Oh my gosh. Peter. He probably thinks I ran off because I was embarrassed. I mean, that's true. But Walter had already left. Why the need to run off? I have two boys who like me. Two boys. It sounds weird to say it. Two boys. Margot, you're repeating yourself. Get a grip. Maybe my dad was right all those times he told me how pretty I am, and I scoffed and told him he's got to be kidding. No one would ever think I was good enough – not when girls like Cassie were around to catch their attention. But Peter noticed me. I'll even cut him some slack for liking Cassie first. If she's good enough to be in Peter's line of vision, I certainly am. What harm would it do for the nice guys to actually finish first for a change and the nice girls to finish there right along with them? Why do the bad girls and jerky guys always get the breaks? It sure would be nice to buck that trend and distort reality to make it a little more honest, don't you think?

Margot got a fix on her thoughts, took a deep breath, and turned the lock. No sooner had she stepped out the door then she saw Peter. Ashley was a little bit down the hallway. She looked ready to descend on the two of them at any moment if Margot gave her the go-ahead.

"Hey."

"Hey," repeated Margot.

"You okay?" Peter looked genuinely interested in her answer.

"Yeah. It's just..."

"I know. A lot went down tonight, didn't it?"

"Yeah. And there's still the cast party tonight."

"You're still going to that?" The nervousness in Peter's voice transferred some jitters to Margot. The whole situation was unreal to her.

"Yeah. I mean, I owe it to Walter to..." Margot caught herself before continuing. *I owe it to Walter? What do I owe to Walter?*

"I guess you're right," Peter interjected before she had a chance to continue. "You'll have to let him down easy. Nice guy. Some guts."

"Yeah." The repetition finally got to Margot, and she thought that throwing another few words into the mix couldn't hurt anything. "Gotta let him know how I feel."

"So, I'll call you later?"

"You're not coming? I mean, the props committee counts as kind of the extended cast, you know."

"Nah. You'll already have Cassie and Ashley there. I'll just go home. My mom won't want me out since I'm sick and all."

"Oh yeah. Forgot about that. We'll talk later."

"Sure thing. Bye, Margot."

"Bye, Peter." The words sounded different than when she had said them before. Saying goodbye now was not a nervous indicator of wondering about what the future held in terms of Peter's feelings for her. Rather, it was a nervous indicator of how their next conversation would go.

***

Max and Cassie looked at each other again. Their exchange of words had certainly hurt. Max would never be mature enough to show it, though. He was putting up a front that was not easily torn down.

"I guess we can't be friends, then." Cassie said the words as though she genuinely hoped it could have worked, even though she knew it was never even a possibility. Max was cleverly frustrating, as though he knew each and every way to possibly drive a wedge between him and anyone who tried to get remotely close to being his friend.

"I guess not." Max was matter-of-fact as he ended the conversation. "I have plenty of other friends."

"Sure you do. Have fun with them." Cassie's sarcastic tone bothered Max. But he let it go. He knew how she felt about Carolyn, Lisa, and the rest of his so-called friends. Despite her thinking he was just a heartless jerk, he knew deep inside that he was capable of change. But he also knew that it was not something that he was willing to do. At least not yet. He was popular and that was all that mattered. If the second half of ninth grade shaped up to be as positive for him as he felt the first half of the year had been, he was certain that high school would be full of memories that he'd never forget. The problem, as Cassie most certainly knew, was that those memories were bound to be full of regret for the time he could have had if he had chosen his friends better and considered his own common sense over his fear of a geeky reputation.

***

After Cassie left the cast room, she met up with Margot and Ashley in the hallway, and they made up with each other. Now that Ashley knew that Cassie wasn't trying to make a play for Peter, she became much easier to be around, and she and Cassie found common ground in discussing their boyfriends – or lack thereof. Ashley came clean and said that she and Brad had actually only lasted till a few weeks ago, and during those couple months they had dated, he was always playing sports or going out with his friends. They only actually went out together a handful of times. Ashley was uber-apologetic to Margot, saying that she didn't want to seem like the ultra-sensitive girl who's broken up over her break-up, so she continued the charade of dating Brad, based on vicarious discussions with a new girlfriend she'd made at her new school. Lila, the new friend, had a boyfriend she'd been dating since the beginning of the school year, but he was apparently the exact opposite of Brad, buying Lila flowers and surprising her with tickets to the movies and concerts. Ashley had actually been with Lila and her boyfriend at the movies when she had told Margot she had to get off the phone because of the no-cell policy. She just left out the part about not actually going with Brad.

She filled Margot and Cassie in about her break-up, citing that she'd found out he was flunking three of his classes and didn't care about trying to catch up. Despite never having been the most exemplary student, Ashley couldn't stick it out with a guy who wasn't concerned at all about his education. He didn't even realize that his ridiculously low grades were going to get him kicked off the sports teams he was so proud to be on. Ashley conceded that he reminded her a lot of Max. Margot kept her mouth shut about Max kind of liking Ashley but never making a move because of Margot.

Ashley also said that her parents were thinking of moving back. Or at least nearby. There was a job her dad was considering taking a few towns over. And despite Margot thinking that Ashley was always trying to one-up her in terms of stealing the spotlight, this made her happy. Having her best friend around again was not something she would take for granted, of course, and boy, would it be nice.

She wondered what it would have been like if all that stuff about Max and Cameron hadn't happened, and if she and Cameron hadn't become friends and been in the GEC program together. Would Max have still turned out to be an ever-present nuisance? She tried to convince herself that the answer was yes, but she knew that something good must be inside of Max for Cassie to have ever even considered being with him.

***

Walking into the cast party was kind of exciting. Even though it was only the first night of the show, celebrating her success since Cassie was going to be front and center for the other shows was quite intoxicating. Margot's parents had dropped the three girls off, and Margot made sure to even kiss her dad on the cheek before exiting the car. Letting him know on her own terms that she was still his little girl, at least a little bit, meant something to her. Cassie was close with her parents, and Ashley knew Margot well enough to not make fun of her. After all, Mr. Maples was kind of like Ashley's second dad.

As they were walking into the party, Mrs. Shearer called Cassie on her cell.

"Yeah, Mom. I know. I won't be out too late. Just give Dad his medicine, okay? Yeah. *I know.* Just a couple hours. Back by 11:30. Yeah, yeah. See ya then." With a click, the call ended. "My mom is *so* annoying," Cassie complained. Even though Margot knew it was wrong of her, she kind of felt good about that. It made Cassie so much more real, and more like an equal. She supposed that's what Cassie had been trying to convince her of

231

during the entire time they had been semi-friends and then full-fledged buddies, but she had just realized it on her own, which felt good.

***

The first person Margot saw at the party was Walter. *Of course. Who else?* That's just how her luck seemed to go. But the weird thing was that she didn't seem to mind anymore. His earlier outburst had somehow dredged up feelings within her – feelings that she didn't even know she had. They scared her, and they were beginning to torment her as she tried to push them aside. She kind of thought he was kind of, sort of, maybe a little bit... cool. Of course not in Max's or Carolyn's or Lisa's sense of the word, but in the I-like-to-hang-out-with-you-because-you-are-a-good-and-fun-to-be-with-person kind of way. And he was even slightly... *cute*. She couldn't believe she thought so, not even a little bit, but she attributed it to the fact that he had done away with his glasses the previous week in an attempt to be prepared for the play so he would look like a cooler, more sophisticated guy. Even though most people would think that glasses would add to the sophistication factor, opting for contacts instead had given Margot a better view of his face, without the taped-up glasses and such obscuring her view of it.

Being aloof was not Walter's strong suit. Even though he hadn't approached Margot right away, she could tell that he was eyeing her, which made her feel only slightly uncomfortable, because she wondered if he noticed how she'd been kind of eyeing him. He, like her, was obviously trying to find as unobtrusive an opening as possible to approach her. He looked pretty comfortable talking to Nathan Fromidge, almost as if he wasn't his normal, hesitant self. He had his wits about him. This didn't mean he had become a social butterfly overnight or even over the course of the day – transformations like that didn't happen so quickly. At least Margot didn't think so. She often wished they did. It would certainly help her social standing if something like that was possible. But Walter seemed as though he had been in a cocoon of dorkiness and had emerged from it stronger and more sure of himself than ever before. It could have been overwhelmingly disconcerting, but instead, it was a welcome change, and a far cry from the Walter who had invited her to his party on the last day of eighth grade.

232

To think – a couple months ago being seen with Walter seemed like a fate she'd only have to muster the strength to handle if her mother forced her, and now she found herself curious what he was doing, and when she could talk to him next. *What's going on?* she asked herself. *I can't believe what I'm thinking. Walter is not cute. Peter is cute. Peter is sweet. But so is Walter. I mean, no one can claim that he isn't a romantic at heart.*

Margot was thrown out of her thoughts when Walter finally approached her, with Nathan in tow. Cassie and Ashley were already milling around the room, mingling with other students and snacking on chips and trail mix. Before Walter could say anything, Margot burst out with, "Hey, Walter? Can we talk?"

"Oh! Yeah, yeah. Do you mind, Nate*?" Nate? When did Walter become on a nickname-first basis with him? When had he even had the chance to hang out with him long enough to feel comfortable using a nickname?* Margot realized that there were obviously things about Walter that she didn't know. This made her feel slightly strange, as she considered the fact that she felt as though Walter was always hanging around her. This obviously wasn't the case, based on his discussion with Nathan.

Nate nodded and headed over to the snack table. He began chatting with other members of the publicity committee, of which he was a member. Somebody bumped into him, causing the bowls on the table to shake a bit and some drinks to spill. Margot couldn't help but think that maybe it wasn't her who was prone to accidents, but Nathan Fromidge. Klutziness seemed to follow him around. Margot thought about how quickly Walter rid himself of Nathan to talk to her. An overzealous Walter – not too much of a change there. Confidence in himself and an unobscured face hadn't diminished how he really felt about her, obviously.

"Sorry I didn't come over sooner. Nate and I were chatting about the chess meet coming up in a couple weeks."

"Oh. He's on the chess team with you. That's right." Margot realized that she had known that little bit of information. Back when Walter had found her an unwanted spot as secretary for the chess club, she had been appalled at how he had ingratiated himself into her life. She hadn't gone to even one meeting. She always found an excuse for having to be somewhere or take care of something. Despite wanting to rid herself of Walter for all those months, she could never find the words to tell him to bug off. She realized in this moment that maybe this was because she hadn't ever really wanted to – at least not completely.

"I know the team would love it if you showed up for practice to help us out at the meet. There's a lot of prestige in winning, you know. We'll be the talk of the school if we pull it off." *Yeah. The sarcastic, this-is-too-good-to-not-make-fun-of talk.* Margot bit her tongue rather than say what had just popped into her head. Instead, she responded, "Sure. When's the next meeting?"

As Margot and Walter chatted, the minutes ticked by, with Margot unaware of just how easy it had become to talk to Walter without needing to find a reprieve. She hadn't even looked for Ashley or Cassie to save her. Instead, they were looking her way, in awe of how comfortable she looked with Walter.

And just as this ease began to settle in, instead of Walter or Mrs. Gribble, or even Max ruining the moment, the new sense of normalcy was tainted by a last-minute arrival. Peter. He strode over to them, just like a boyfriend would, looking unhappy that Margot wasn't spending her time with her girlfriends, but rather with another guy. No matter that it was Walter. It was another guy, and Peter had locked horns with jealousy in that instant. Of course Max made his way over, surely eager to see just what would come to pass between whom he considered to be his two main nemeses. The guys whose lives he had taken careful attempts to throw into disarray over the last several months, and even years. Apparently, without his friendship, no one was supposed to be capable of living a happy life.

"Peter. What's up?" Margot tried to act nonchalant, but she knew that this was not going to go well. Peter and Walter obviously were going to have some hostility toward each other. They had both declared their feelings for her this evening, one in private, and the other very publicly.

"Margot. Walter." Peter spoke in short, clipped sentences, clearly bothered by the scene unfolding in front of him.

"Hey, Pete." Margot had to hand it to Walter. He was very calm in this situation. Unlike Peter, who was very clearly distracted by his aggravation.

"It's Peter. Not Pete. Not even my friends call me Pete. And you're not my friend anyway."

"What are you talking about?" Walter looked semi-astonished by this pronouncement. It was only then that Margot realized that Walter had no idea that Peter had professed his interest in Margot earlier that night. Peter was aware of Walter's admission, but not Walter of Peter's. Margot wondered if once Walter found out, his confidence would diminish.

"A friend wouldn't make a move on the girl his friend likes."

"What?"

"You heard me. I said I like her."

"Who?"

"Don't play dumb. This isn't a bit we're doing here. Margot. I like Margot."

"You do? I...uh...didn't know."

"That's all you have to say?"

"Well, yeah. I didn't know. I like her too. I mean, I told her tonight. In front of you and everyone else. I think it was pretty obvious at that point." Walter looked down at the ground for a moment, reminding Margot that he wasn't the confident, debonair person he surely wished he could be.

Peter's voice was getting louder, and despite Walter's not-to-be-expected calmness, the rest of the cast and crew at the party were beginning to gather. Pushing their way to be front and center were none other than Carolyn and Lisa. Max was off to the side a bit, and Cassie and Ashley were right behind Margot. Carolyn and Lisa looked genuinely interested in the drama, but every once in a while, their gazes focused on Margot, wondering just how she had fallen into the middle of this girl tug-of-war.

"Just stop!" Margot couldn't believe her ears. Her voice had overpowered her two potential suitors. All eyes were on her. Then, just like Walter had done earlier, she quickly turned around and ran outside.

Cassie and Ashley were first to follow her, then Walter and Peter went. The rest of the party was quiet for another few seconds, and then started milling around again, questioning what had just happened and what the result might end up being. Carolyn, Lisa, and Max went back to chatting as well, most likely plotting how they would use all this new information and Margot's outburst against her, Walter, and Peter come the next school day.

"I've had enough, okay?" Cassie and Ashley nodded their understanding as Walter and Peter appeared. "I don't know what I want.

Yesterday I had nothing, and now I have two guys who like me. Two guys who I actually kind of like." Walter's ears noticeably perked up at this comment. He obviously had been under the impression – and until the day before, rightly so – that Margot was only interested in him as a friend, and he had really only just broken that barrier. Peter, on the other hand, looked flabbergasted. He had been under the impression – also rightly so – that Margot liked him. It was Cassie who had told him. Unless she'd been giving him false information to build him up. It would have to be too-good-to-be-true. But Margot had seemed to really like him when he'd told her he liked her. Yet, their conversation had become harder. This was unlike Margot's conversation with Walter, which had weirdly become easier.

"You've got to make a decision, Margot. I thought you liked me." Margot did like Peter. He was right. But her feelings weren't as clear as they had been just a couple hours earlier. Walter's revelation had thrown everything on its head, and she was amazed at this. How someone else's feelings could somehow change hers seemed strange to her. But they had. Walter was like a different person in her eyes all of a sudden.

"Are you forcing me to choose? I don't know if I can."

"You've got to." Even though Peter was pushing the issue, Walter was standing quietly, looking at her with puppy-dog eyes that she used to find irritating, but now found weirdly kind.

"Okay, Peter. Walter. I want to be friends with both of you. I really like you both. You're great guys and great friends and..." She realized she was rambling and not making a decision. Peter looked worried, Walter looked thoughtful, and Cassie and Ashley looked intrigued. This was more action than any of them had thought they'd see. The play had seemed like enough to fill the excitement quotient for the evening.

"We're both great friends, and...? Which of us do you like more? You've got to know." Peter was getting anxious.

"But I don't. I just don't. And if you're going to force me to choose, I'm going to have to say... Walter."

"What?!" The question rang out from all four friends at the same time. Even Margot heard it inside of her own thoughts. Walter looked supremely surprised, Peter astonished, Cassie astounded, and Ashley oddly happy. But not for herself. For Margot. She looked happy for Margot, like she had just witnessed her best friend make one of the most important decisions of her young adult life. Like she had finally come to terms with who she wanted to be and how she wanted to get there.

"Well, I can't say I'm surprised." *Max. Of course. Because not one moment of my freshman year can happen without something going wrong.*

"What's that supposed to mean, Poler?" Peter had reverted to using last names. This was not a good sign. He looked like he wanted to get angry at someone, and Max was getting ready to fill that void.

"Honestly? It means I wouldn't have been surprised either way. You're both not bad guys. Even though you're dorks and all, it doesn't mean that some girl can't find you interesting and kind of cool, in your own weird way. She was bound to choose one of you sooner or later. And Dribble – I mean, Gribble – here has been trying to woo her from day one. It's just the fact of the matter, Peter. Give her a break for finally seeing him as more than the geek down the street."

For all of Max's dubious charm, his words rang true. Walter had been doing his best to be with Margot all along, and Peter had only just realized what he was missing. Margot couldn't believe it, but she had to hand it to Max. He had found the heart of the matter. And he had even said it with a little bit of grace.

"I guess I was a little late to the game," Peter conceded.

"I do like you, Peter. But if you're forcing me to choose, I have to see what's there with Walter." The words sounded strange. But she meant them. And the fact that she meant them made her feel even stranger. Who would have ever thought that Walter Gribble was going to be the first boy she really dated? That is, for more than one date. Then, she found herself answering that question in her head: *Mrs. Gribble.* It was so ludicrous that it made her want to laugh. *She knew all along. She knew that I would eventually give in to him. Geez. I hate to give her credit, but she was right.*

"You don't have to choose, Margot." Walter said it quietly, almost as if he didn't want to be heard.

"What?"

"I said you don't have to choose. I don't want all of us to stop being friends. Why don't we just go back to how we were?"

"But Walter... I thought..."

"I know what you said. And I really can't believe you said it, or that Max backed you up." He looked at Max with newfound respect. "I really appreciate it."

"I meant it." Margot looked him straight in the eye.

"I know, and that's why I thank you. For seeing me for me." Walter looked at the group of misfits in front of him. They all had their own issues, but they were all a part of this situation, and he realized then and there that he was saying what he really wanted. "We'll go back to how we were. And if something happens between you and me later on, we'll know it's for the right reasons. Same thing with you and Peter. We'll just see what happens. How does that sound?"

"I think it sounds pretty awesome of you." Ashley – always throwing in her two cents. In this case, though, it was right on. Margot knew it, Peter knew it, Cassie and Walter knew it.

So, without even heading back into the cast party, they all decided to head down to the coffee shop to grab hot chocolates and danishes for a nighttime snack. Because, come what may, being friends trumped any hateful feelings they were going to have toward one another. Max even tagged along. He fought it tooth and nail, but Margot knew he wanted to come. It was like he had had a breakthrough. He had finally realized that the friends you have make you the person you are. And with friends like Carolyn and Lisa, he was only bound to be a jerky, flaky, cool-for-the-wrong-reasons kind of guy. It had only taken a few months of seeing this group of friends make the right decisions while he had made the wrong ones to come to terms with this fact. Margot even thought she saw him glance shyly at Ashley. Maybe it was just because Cassie was around and he didn't want to draw attention to looking at her, but Margot thought there might be more to it. Maybe seeing Ashley again was the catalyst Max needed to make amends for his past and become the at least semi-nice guy that Margot thought he just might have inside him. *Why else would Peter have spent any time being his friend otherwise?* Margot thought.

"Hey, you guys?" Everyone turned to look at Margot. "Thanks for making these last few months pretty okay. Even though they've sucked in more ways than I can say, they brought me here with all of you – even *you*, Max. Sorry, had to throw that one in. I mean, you did make my life pretty messed up." Max nodded knowingly. "But all the rest of you, you made it all easier. And I'm looking forward to everything that's still to come."

ABOUT THE AUTHOR

Beth Rodgers is an author, editor, and college English instructor. She started writing as a little girl and never gave up on her dream of one day being a full-fledged author. Besides her love of writing, she is an avid TV and movie watcher, and she loves to hunker down with a great young adult novel any chance she gets. She lives with her husband and son in Michigan.